D0458984

WITHDRAWN
FROM THE RECORDS OF THE
MID-CONTINENT PUBLIC LIBRARY

F
Jackson, Jeremy.
In summer

N3
b-04

MID-CONTINENT PUBLIC LIBRARY
South Independence Branch
13700 E. 35th Street
Independence, MO 64055   SI

in Summer

ALSO BY JEREMY JACKSON

Life at These Speeds

JEREMY JACKSON

in
Summer

THOMAS DUNNE BOOKS
ST. MARTIN'S PRESS 🦎 NEW YORK

MID-CONTINENT PUBLIC LIBRARY
South Independence Branch
13700 E. 35th Street
Independence, MO 64055
SI

MID-CONTINENT PUBLIC LIBRARY

3 0001 01112549 1

THOMAS DUNNE BOOKS.
An imprint of St. Martin's Press.

IN SUMMER. Copyright © 2004 by Jeremy Jackson. All rights reserved. Printed in
the United States of America. No part of this book may be used or reproduced in
any manner whatsoever without written permission except in the case of brief
quotations embodied in critical articles or reviews. For information, address St.
Martin's Press, 175 Fifth Avenue, New York, N.Y. 10010.

www.stmartins.com

Book design by Jonathan Bennett

ISBN 0-312-32642-4
EAN 978-0312-32642-5

First Edition: May 2004

10 9 8 7 6 5 4 3 2 1

June

One

I WOKE UP AT ELEVEN AND WENT DOWNSTAIRS AND ATE MY bowl of cereal standing at the counter. Clearly, this was a summery thing to do. I drank the milk at the bottom of my bowl and put the bowl and spoon in the dishwasher. I headed toward the stairs and then there was a spark of activity in my brain and I went back to the dishwasher and looked inside and discovered of course that all the dishes in there were clean. I removed my dirty bowl and spoon and unloaded the dishwasher and enjoyed how dry and clean the dishes were. I put my dirty bowl and spoon back in the dishwasher and looked out the window.

On the patio I stood in the sun. You couldn't really say it was morning anymore, though technically it was. The flagstones were warm beneath my bare feet and I felt satisfied by the fact that I was wearing only shorts. I touched my hair and my hair was hot from being in the sun for just a minute. I smelled coconut oil on the breeze and looked around. It was as if the trumpets of summer were announcing themselves all around me. It has been less than twenty-four hours since graduation, and here we were, already in the realm of summer.

I walked through the soft grass to the front of the house and stood there with my hands on my hips. The cat was situated in the grass like she had been placed there for a photo shoot. She was a black cat and she loved sunlight more than anything and she looked up at me with happiness and she kneaded the grass with her front paws and started purring. I couldn't remember why I was out here. Then I smelled the coconut oil again and looked around. The neighborhood was green and heavy and completely devoid of human activity. There wasn't even the sound of a lawn mower. The mail truck was parked at the bottom of the hill, but the mail carrier was nowhere to be seen. The shadows below the trees were dark and the air was dry and I didn't need a full view of the sky to know that it was completely cloudless, completely clear, absolutely open.

My bike was hanging upside down, dangling by its wheels high in our garage, as if it were a bat in hibernation. How long had it been since I'd ridden it? I couldn't recall. October maybe? But as I lifted it from its hooks and felt its astonishing lightness, I experienced a rush of love for it, followed closely by an immense sense of guilt for having neglected it. After all, I had built it myself. I had ordered the custom frame and carefully selected the components and assembled it all. I had brought the bike into this world, and therefore I was responsible for its well-being. Also, I knew how much it cost.

I pumped up the tires and looked at the chain and of course the chain needed to be cleaned but I would do it another time. I went inside and got my cycling shoes and then returned to the bike and mounted it and pedaled up the hill, circled the cul-de-sac twice while I watched my derailleurs, and then tucked down and came down the hill, rolled past the house, and went into the neighborhood.

It wasn't as if I actually expected to find anything, but when one smells coconut oil, one is obligated to look for a sunbathing girl. Or *girls*, plural. Especially on the first day of summer vacation. Also, as a lifeguard there was some strange sense of duty at work in me: I was expected to make sure that all sunbathers were safe and that they hadn't brought soda onto the deck or left small children unattended in the pool. So I trolled the neighborhood, scanning the backyards, or what I could see of them. I didn't see anyone, much less any sunbathers, and I didn't smell the coconut oil anymore and by the time I reached the stop sign at Bergall Road, I didn't really care.

I put myself into the ride. I loved the bike and the bike loved me and the bike was smooth and responsive and it gave freely and fully of itself. It held no grudges and harbored no resentments and I began writing an advertisement for it in my head, but that quickly ended because it was foolish and because it came between me and the day. My legs and lungs were working marvelously and there was no thinking involved and as we moved through the noon sunlight, my bike and I, I felt as if this would last forever, as if this *were* forever. Even the hills were welcome. The air around me was expressive and charged, and I was not sweating.

The pleasure was simple and easy to accept.

This was summer.

This was June.

This was me, here, now.

I came off the highway at Borswick Lane and cruised past the berry farm and the country club. There were some great curvy roads out here, out where all the rich Republicans had their mini-estates. I put on some more speed and then started the turn onto Carrol Road. I was pedaling hard through the turn, and I saw the patch of sand before I hit it, but at that point there was nothing I could do and my bike slipped gracefully out from beneath me and I met the asphalt and kept sliding until I rolled into the ditch. I heard my bike bang into the signpost.

I hopped up from the grass. I literally jumped up. I hadn't hit my head. I looked around. There was no traffic. There were no people. There were dusty smudges all along my right side where I'd slid across the road. I didn't feel anything, though. I didn't feel a thing. I touched my face. Everything was adrenaline. My body felt big and also without boundaries. I didn't really know where to look. I had to breathe slowly. So I breathed slowly. I made sure I wasn't standing in the street. I looked at my watch, but the numbers didn't mean anything to me. I looked down at myself again, and this time it was blood, blood, blood. Where moments ago there had been smudges, now there was blood—my right ankle, right shin, right knee. The right side of my back was raw, as were my right elbow, forearm, and palm. Also, the knuckles of my right hand were bleeding. I sat down in the grass, then I got right back up. I leaned against the signpost. There was sweat in my eyes. Now that I wasn't riding anymore, I was hot. I was sweating. The nearest house was a stone's throw away. I could hear birds in the forest, and I could hear a golf cart behind the forest, but that was all. I looked at myself again. I was thirty minutes from home. There still wasn't a cloud to be seen. I didn't have my wallet. I didn't even have a shirt. I had to stop and think about where I was. I had to think for a second. I mean, I knew where I was, but I had to kind of rebuild the whole city around me, rebuild the context of it all. The adrenaline had wiped everything away and I had to rebuild the world.

I was fine. I was mostly fine. It didn't seem to hurt that much. Who lived nearby? Did I know anyone who lived nearby? Should I flag down a car if one came by? What would I say? Would I have them page Mom at work, or what?

The rear wheel of the bike was still spinning, but as soon as I picked up the bike I could see that all was not well. I tried not to look too closely at the bike. I didn't really want to look at it. I didn't want to know what was wrong. Whereas I was mostly all right, I knew that my bike was not. It was an amazing machine but it was also fragile and its injuries were my fault, all my fault.

Who did I know who lived near here?

I tried to mount the bike but the seat was crooked so I had to get off and readjust it. Then as I tried to pedal away my right foot slipped off the pedal. I looked down. The pedal was bent. And my blood was running down my leg and filling my shoe. I could feel it in there.

Who did I know who lived near here?

I was rolling again. Wobbling.

Finally I figured it out. Finally it came to me. One minute my mind was a fog and the next minute clarity returned and there, right in front of me, was the answer: Jenny. I knew Jenny. Jenny lived about a mile away. She would help me.

Wouldn't she?

Or did she truly hate me? Would she leave me to bleed on her lawn? Would she turn on the lawn sprinklers?

I didn't see a single car on my way to her house. I rode slowly. The bike made horrible scraping noises. I carefully laid my bike on the lawn and hobbled toward the house. I wasn't sure why I was hobbling. I hadn't sprained my ankle or anything, but I was hobbling nonetheless. Where was everyone today? The world seemed abandoned. The whole world seemed empty and still. There was too much air in the atmosphere, too much *space*. It all made me feel small, and Jenny's huge house loomed larger than ever, like some kind of retreat center. On a hunch, I peered over the fence into the backyard, and there she was, reading by the pool in her bikini. I whistled a greeting, which was usually the way she greeted me, not vice versa. She looked up immediately.

"Leo," she said.

Suddenly the only thing I felt was the stinging. All the places

I was skinned were stinging, and all the places that weren't skinned were throbbing, and I had to sit down right then, right there, and I had to close my eyes.

And moments later, when I heard the gate open, I smelled coconut oil. I looked up at Jenny, and her skin was glistening.

Two

THREE DAYS LATER, A HUNDRED MILES AWAY, AS I WAITED ON THE front steps of my aunt and uncle's house, I heard Paer start up the jeep five blocks away at the grain elevator. That's how loud the jeep was. I knew all the streets of Charbourg, even though it wasn't my town, and I named the cross streets to myself as the jeep came closer, and I heard Paer pause at the stop sign at Dean Street and then start back up again. Finally he pulled into the dirt drive. I loaded our fishing gear and lunches into the backseat and got in. I told Paer that we should take the jeep to the garage and look at it.

"What?" he yelled over the noise of the engine.

I repeated myself.

We drove down Dean Street and then toward the school on Park Street. The windows of the school reflected the sunlight and there wasn't a single car or bus parked out front. The flag was up, however, flapping in the sky. We passed the convenience store and Paer waved to a girl who was gassing up her pickup.

"Who's that?" I asked, craning around.

"Freeda Sweeney."

We came onto Main Street and pulled into the garage and

talked to Jerry and three minutes later we had the jeep up on the lift. I could see right away that there was a hole in the manifold. It was too big to patch.

"That's okay," I said. "We can replace it ourselves."

"I don't want to hear this," Paer said.

Paer's jeep dated back to the Korean War, and he had bought it for $75 two years ago and we had fixed it up with another $300, plus a free paint job from a friend. Frankly, the paint was the nicest thing about it. It was satiny black paint. The jeep glowed like a black pearl.

"I don't want to hear it at all," Paer said. "I've been working since 6:00 A.M. and now we're supposed to be fishing, not fretting about the jeep."

"We'll just have Jerry keep an eye out for the part."

"Fishing," Paer said, and I admired my cousin's focus.

It was a hot day and Paer was covered with dust from the elevator. The jeep didn't have a top, and the windshield could be folded forward onto the hood, combat style, which was how we rode today. My favorite part of the ride out to the creek was the point at which Peterland Road went from blacktop to gravel. There was a drop-off there, and the jeep bottomed out on its springs and bounced a couple times, and then there was an agreeable whooshing sound as we sped over the gravel and a billowy plume of dust rose behind us.

The creek was clear and inviting and Paer changed into his shorts and we waded across. The water stung my scabs just a little bit. We started stalking upstream along the bank, dropping our spinners into the holes alongside the fallen trees that lay in the channel. We were after the big bass that we knew were in these holes. Paer fished in front of me, hitting only the best holes. He changed his lure, putting on a small crankbait. I fished less discriminately than Paer, which yielded me two sunfish and two baby bass—the tiny kind we called fish sticks. As I watched one of those little guys streak away after I released him, I heard an engine behind me and looked back and saw Brent Barlow's four-by-four driving out onto the gravel bar where the jeep was parked. I could see some girls in the cab of the truck. I thought I recognized Kathy Baker sitting by Brent, and another girl had her arm out the window. Brent stopped the truck and got out.

"Hey, Timmy!" he yelled at Paer.

Paer stopped reeling in his lure and looked over his shoulder at Brent. He didn't turn, but just looked over his shoulder.

Brent reached into the cab of the jeep and released the parking brake. The jeep was nosed right up against the water, parked on a slight incline. After he released the brake, Brent jumped back, expecting the jeep to roll into the water. But it didn't move. He pretended not to care.

"Have fun fishing, Timmy!" he yelled, and then got back into his truck and rumbled away in low gear. Back up on the bridge, he opened the throttle and put down some rubber on the concrete and then was gone.

That was another thing about the jeep: the parking brake was just for show. It didn't do a thing.

I put on my sunglasses.

"Crap," I heard Paer say, and I looked and saw his rod was bent nearly double. He had a big fish on. A big, big fish. But the fish was running with the lure, heading for the roots of one of the submerged trees, where it would surely snag the lure and escape. Paer's drag was droning as the fish ran, and Paer was fumbling with the drag knob, and finally the fish was stopped and Paer stepped down from the bank into the water to get a better angle on the fish. I reeled in and watched.

The fish cut across the current. A school of minnows jumped from the water all at once when confronted with the big fish. Paer staggered in the water, nearly falling; this was a strong fish

11

and our little ultralight rods weren't built for such action. Then suddenly the fish was charging straight at Paer, and Paer was reeling in furiously, trying to keep the line taut. But when the fish changed directions and swung away from Paer in a quick motion, Paer's rod suddenly whipped back, hitting his face, and there was a whizzing sound as the lure came through the air toward me and hit the left lens of my sunglasses with a crack. There was an explosive light and for a second I thought I had been blinded. But all that had happened was that the lens of the sunglasses had popped out of the frame.

I took off my sunglasses and picked up the lure. Paer was rubbing his face.

"You okay?" I asked.

He nodded.

"You've got to see this," I said. Two of the hooks on the lure's rear were bent straight. The fish had bent the hooks. I'd never seen such a thing.

Paer looked around at me and I could see that a big welt was going to form where the rod had snapped into his face. He started to wade toward shore and the tip of his rod suddenly dropped into the water.

The fish had broken it.

"Why'd he call you Timmy?" I asked when we got back to the jeep.

"It's his idea of an annoying nickname."

"But your name is *Paer*. You don't *need* an annoying nickname."

Paer was a family name. Our great-grandfather's name.

"Thanks," Paer said. "I guess."

He started the jeep and the noise of the engine ended our conversation.

"We forgot to eat our lunches!" I yelled, but clearly Paer didn't hear me.

He reached for the gearshift.

"Bologna and mustard!" I yelled.

Paer yanked the gearshift and the whole thing came loose, right out of the gearbox, like pulling a tulip out of the ground. We both looked at it for several seconds. I took it from Paer and examined it carefully. There didn't seem to be any trauma. Some connecting mechanism must have failed. Paer was staring straight ahead, expressionless. I looked down into the gearbox. There certainly wasn't anything we could do without tools or at least a flashlight.

Paer got out of the jeep. I reached over and cut the engine. The world was quiet again.

"Hey," I said to Paer.

He was walking right into the river.

"Paer," I said.

When he got in waist deep he ducked below water. He resurfaced and swam twenty feet downstream, doing a flailing freestyle. Then he ducked underwater again. He resurfaced and treaded water briefly and then and came back upstream and walked out of the water.

I knew that we were both blaming Brent Barlow, even though he had nothing to do with it. But Brent Barlow had tried to drown the jeep, after all.

And Brent Barlow had basically stolen Kathy Baker from Paer back in April, right before prom. Paer told me about this as we walked toward town, eating our sandwiches. It was a decent day for a walk, but it was three miles back into town, and after walking fifteen minutes we were relieved when we saw Freeda Sweeney coming along in her pickup.

"What are two nice boys like you doing out on a lonely road like this? One wet boy and one dry boy."

"I object to the characterization 'nice,'" I said.

The last I remembered seeing Freeda Sweeney she was a gangly eighth-grader. Now she was seventeen and just a couple inches shorter than me.

"The jeep's thing came off," Paer said, and he held up the gearshift to show her. I don't know why he had felt compelled to carry the gearshift with him instead of leaving it with the jeep.

Freeda was happy to help and she was dressed in jeans despite the heat of the day and of course she had some strong rope in the back of her pickup and moments after she picked us up we were back down at the creek and Freeda was locking the hubs of her truck's wheels so that it could go into four-wheel drive. I watched her work and remembered that she rode horses. Or she *used* to ride horses at least. I didn't know if she did anymore.

While Paer tied the rope to the jeep, me and Freeda stood by the open door of the pickup. Not only was she wearing jeans, but also cowboy boots and a short-sleeve Western shirt.

"I'm a big fan of those boots," I said, which was a half-assed compliment. She leveled a sardonic look at me.

She pointed at my scabs. "What's all this about?" she asked.

I told her how I'd wrecked my bike a few days ago. "I killed my own bike," I said.

"You're saying you're a bike murderer?"

"Well . . . ," I said. "It was more like bikeslaughter than murder."

Before our conversation went further Paer yelled at us and Freeda swung up into the cab of her truck and started the engine. But the reason the jeep hadn't rolled into the creek in the first place was that Paer had left it in gear, of course, and that was the same reason the darn thing wouldn't roll backwards now, despite the power of Freeda's big Chevy. She *dragged* it several feet, but that obviously wasn't going to do, so the jeep stayed put and

Freeda drove us back to town and Paer got out first and I dawdled and thanked her for helping and then asked her what she was doing this summer.

"No," she said, "what are *you* doing this summer?"

"That's a fair question," I said, but I was scared by her directness and I jumped out of the truck and slammed the door and went inside and Aunt Corene was home and she said, "Lee-o?"

And I said, "Yee-up?"

"Do you boys want burritos for dinner?" she asked. Paer had crashed on the couch and his eyes were already closed. I found Corene in the kitchen.

"Burritos would be brilliant," I said. "I'll help."

So I spent the next twenty minutes chopping, shredding, putting things in bowls, and setting the picnic table. At one point I looked into the living room and saw that Paer was asleep. I pointed him out to Corene.

"Poor kid," she said. "He has to get up so early for his job."

"He's had a hard day," I said.

We ate and ate and ate, and Paer didn't talk much, and Gracie, Paer's little sister, talked about her dancing lessons and Corene talked mostly about the upcoming crafts fair, and Uncle Cort laughed with Aunt Corene and after we were done eating Uncle Cort looked around at the evening and then he looked each of us in the eyes, and then he said, "Look at those starlings there nesting in the gutter."

I told the story of the fish that got away from Paer. Cort liked the story and he asked Paer several technical questions about the lure and the drag and so forth.

"There are some big fish in that creek," Cort said.

"Oh, we almost could have been eating fish right now!" Corene said.

"Fish after burritos?" I joked, and we all laughed except Paer.

Paer said, "I've had that rod since I was six. I've had that rod for two-thirds of my life."

After dinner, Corene tried to push some melon sorbet on us.

"Now," I began, "you know that I love you, Aunt Corene. And you know I love my visits out here with you and Cort and Paer and Gracie. But it's just that melon sorbet isn't my thing, and it isn't Paer's thing."

"It's not my thing either!" Gracie said.

"And it's not Gracie's thing," I added.

Gracie settled for some cookies. But Paer and I headed off toward the convenience store. On foot, of course.

"She won the barrel race last year at the fair," Paer said, as we walked. It was the only thing he'd said since we left the house.

"Who?"

"Freeda Sweeney."

So she did still ride horses.

We had our soft serve right there on the curb in front of the store, with the gasoline fumes wafting over us, and we watched the cars and trucks roll down the hill.

"Yee ha," Paer said after he'd finished his cone. I still had some eating to do.

"We could go work on the jeep right now," I said.

Paer shook his head. "I don't want to think about it," he said.

"It's up to you," I said.

He shook his head again.

Suddenly there was a distant metallic clamoring, which I soon enough recognized as amplified music.

"What the blazes is that?" I asked.

"You're telling me you don't recognize the national anthem?" Paer said.

"I can tell what it is, but why's it being played?"

"Must be a ball game over at the school. Which would explain why there's so much traffic tonight."

Maybe there had been twenty cars pass while we sat there.

We wandered up toward the school, then walked through the dusty parking lot and came to the T-ball game. It was Charbourg's six-year-olds versus Richland's six-year-olds. Richland had some very fine bright red polyester uniforms, but as far as I could tell, Charbourg had no uniforms. Except that they wore team hats. The dinky wooden stands were full of mothers and aunts and older sisters and grandpas. Many of the dads were behind the dugouts coaching their kids. I looked around and everyone seemed extremely tan for the first week of June. These were farmer tans.

"Say now," the announcer said over the PA, "it's verifiable: the concession stand is *open.*"

The skill level of the kids was such that in almost all instances it was more advantageous to *run* the ball all the way to first base in order to make an out instead of trying to throw the ball there. It had been a long time since I'd been to a T-ball game, but it was fun enough, and laughter was slightly more common than applause. In that sense, it was kind of like viewing a musical comedy. Paer and I sat way at the top of the home stand, up there where if you leaned back—*whoop*—there was nothing behind you but air.

"*No batter, no batter, no batter . . . ,*" Paer droned, taunting the opposing team.

The poor tyke being taunted swung with Herculean might, but hit more of the T-ball stand than the ball itself. The ball, though, toppled forward and dribbled a few feet into the infield, which in this game amounted to a hit.

"Run, Desmond!" the kid's father yelled from across the way. "Run to the base! Go on, now!"

Almost everyone was pleading for the kid to run, even those

among us who were aligned with the home team. The kid in question seemed confused by his options, or perhaps he wasn't sure which way to run, and his batting helmet was huge on his head. Our smart home team "catcher" (who of course didn't catch pitches because there *were* no pitches) finally figured out that it was his responsibility to fetch the ball that was only six feet away, and as he grabbed it, the runner at long last started to run, but it was too late and the catcher tagged him.

"*Eeeezout!!!*" the umpire yelled with excessive enthusiasm. Paer and I looked at each other and laughed.

I felt something tap my back.

"Boy!" someone yelled behind me. I looked down and saw Freeda Sweeney back there. She threw another pebble and hit my forehead.

"Ow," I said.

Me and Freeda went down the slope to the track and walked its circuit. From here, we couldn't see the ball field, and the game's sounds weren't so much comical anymore as they were comfortable.

"I'm just glad I'm not playing," I told Freeda.

"Because you'd feel awkward being the only player over four feet tall?"

"That and because I'd probably miss the ball and smack the stand. Or worse yet, I'd just miss altogether and swing through empty air. I actually remember that feeling, that feeling of swinging with all your might through empty air. I'm getting nauseous just thinking about it."

"Then let's not think about it," she said. "And for the record, I don't think you would miss the ball at all. You'd hit it dead-on."

Down here, on the north side of the track, red-winged black-birds were trilling in the fencerow. The day's breeze was easing off. Somehow, quite magically, afternoon had become late after-noon, and late afternoon had become evening. And the evening was resplendent. We went back to the ball game because Freeda's little brother was playing and she wanted to cheer for him. "Watch this," she told me, as her brother walked to home plate. And I watched, cringing, as the little guy swung three times at empty air and therefore struck out. He swung so hard on the third attempt that the weight of the bat twisted his body around and he fell down. It was the first such strikeout of the game and it drew a great deal of supportive cheering from the home crowd.

Anyhow, we won. Somebody had to.

Freeda's brother went home with Freeda's parents, and so Freeda and Paer and I were left in the parking lot after the game. We were talking and Freeda and Paer were sitting on the tailgate of her truck and I was shuffling in the gravel and mostly I was feeling self-conscious because Freeda kept smiling at me.

"Who's that?" Paer said, looking back at the ball diamond. There was a kid slinking in the home dugout, watching us. Everyone else was gone.

"That's Brent Barlow's brother," Freeda said.

We went over. Freeda asked the kid if Brent was supposed to drive him home.

The kid nodded. Then he said, "Yeah, my brother . . ."

We hadn't seen Brent all evening.

So we sat in the dugout with the kid and waited for Brent. But Brent did not appear. The sun was getting close to setting and inexplicably the field lights came on. Paer got up and went over to the switch box behind home plate and turned the lights off.

"They're on a timer," he explained when he got back. "And someone forgot to turn the timer off when the game was over."

I wasn't sure what the point of a timer was if you had to turn it on and off.

We drove Brent's brother home. He sat between Freeda and me, and he was suddenly very talkative and he talked a lot about basketball because he recognized Paer from the varsity team and of course Brent had also started on that team. Brent's family lived out at the intersection of Route CC and Latham Road and when we got there Freeda went inside with the kid and she came back out and was smiling and she got back into the cab of the truck and started the engine and shrugged.

"They're a great family except for Brent," she said.

Freeda took us back to town and dropped off Paer, and then she drove me out to her farm. We crossed the creek and I looked for the jeep but it was too dark already. I could feel the thrumming of the truck's engine through the soles of my feet and I liked it and I extended my arm out the window and let it ride in the night air.

Freeda's farm was just past the creek, and we pulled up in front of the new barn. There were lights on in the house, but we went straight into the barn and were greeted in the darkness by the low chuckle of a horse saying hello. Freeda flicked the lights on and we walked down the clean central aisle of the barn to one of the back stalls.

"Hiya, boy," Freeda said as we neared the horse.

The horse said another rumbly hello and put his head over the side of the stall and rubbed against Freeda. She held his head and stroked it and looked him in the eyes and smiled and then introduced me.

"This is Leo," she told the horse. She turned to me. "And this is Harrison."

I put out my palms and the horse sniffed them for several seconds with his great horsy breath and then he put his head back against Freeda. He was a big bay stallion with a slender white flame on his forehead.

"I've never ridden," I said. "I mean . . . I've never ridden."

"Oh, boyo," Freeda said, "me and you are going to have a great summer."

She was talking to me, not the horse.

She was talking to me.

Freeda and I kissed and the horse walked away from us and we kept kissing and the horse came back over and wedged his nose into the action.

There was some new noise above us.

"What's that?" I asked, looking up.

It was like the barn's roof was sighing.

Freeda said, "It's raining."

It rained all night and it rained all the next day, too. Toward dark Uncle Cort drove me and Paer out to the creek and we stopped on the bridge because there was nowhere else to go. The road on the far side of the bridge was well underwater, and the gravel bar was long gone, too. We got out of the car and looked down at the water, which had risen to within a few feet of the bridge, and then we looked upstream and downstream and then up at the clouds. And in the short time it took us to absorb the scene, we were all completely drenched. We got back into the car and Cort took out his handkerchief and wiped his face and then looked at the floodwaters through the windshield.

"Well," he said, "that jeep may have survived Korea, but I figure it won't survive this flood."

Three

THE SOUTH BRANCH OF THE CREEK WAS MUCH CLOSER TO town, and we walked there early one morning with our fishing poles. Paer's pole was now shorter than it had been before the fish broke it. He had clipped the pole at the highest line guide and was determined to keep fishing with it.

We went down this narrow gravel lane and arrived at the creek and saw that Cort was right—the water on the south branch was pretty clear and at an almost normal level only two days after the flood, whereas the north branch was still murky and very high.

I'd never fished the south branch. I looked at it. It was small and shallow and full of golden gravel.

"This is gorgeous," I told Paer, who was already tying on a spinner.

"The holes are few and far between. Smallmouth territory."

"Smallmouth territory," I said. "That's great."

"Neutral lure colors," Paer said.

"Neutral colors," I said.

We were standing on a one-lane concrete-slab bridge that was only three feet above the water. On the floor of the bridge someone had written "Katie Kane" with a piece of limestone.

"Who's Katie Kane?" I asked Paer.

"Dunno."

"I like her name," I said. "I like her name and I like her bridge and I like her creek, I do."

Paer walked over to the edge of the bridge and made his first cast.

I repeated myself while I selected a lure: "I like her name and I like her bridge and I like her creek, I do."

Paer cursed and started fiddling with his spool—he had some kind of line tangle already.

"Neutral colors," I said to myself. "Smallmouth territory. Katie Kane."

After dinner Corene gave me the keys to her car and I went and jingled them in front of Paer. He was watching TV.

"Come with?" I said.

"Are you really going out there?" he asked.

I jingled the keys some more.

"I told you," Paer said, "you still won't be able to get there, even from the north."

"Where ya goin'?" Gracie asked. She had just come in from the kitchen and she had a Popsicle. "I'll come."

"I'm just going for a drive."

"I'll come," she said again.

"Hm . . . ," I said.

"Let me get my purse," she said.

Gracie was eight.

"Hm . . . ," I said again, but she'd already left the room.

We pulled out of the drive and I rolled down my window and we headed down the street, and Gracie said, "Okay, turn left at the hardware store."

I went straight.

"I'll be your guide!" Gracie protested.

"But we're going up north. Out on Peterland Road."

"Oh," Gracie said. "I thought we were rambling."

"Sorry," I said.

"It's okay," Gracie said. "It's not your fault."

"Thank you," I said.

"You're absolutely welcome," Gracie said.

Gracie worked on her Popsicle and I drove and it was a calm evening and the last part of Gracie's Popsicle fell off the stick and into her lap.

"Oh, great" Gracie said, and she scooped up the Popsicle fragment. "I'm not sure I should eat this now. I'm not entirely sure."

"I think it'd be fine."

"Just to be on the safe side," she said, and she threw it out the window. "When in doubt, throw it out! As Mom says."

I asked her what flavor the Popsicle had been.

"Red," she said.

We had reached the edge of town already. I accelerated. Corene's sedan was huge, and it drove like a boat, but it was pleasing.

"You know," I said, "the day after tomorrow I'm going home."

Gracie was looking out the window though, concerned.

"Where are you taking me?" she asked.

"Up Peterland Road," I said. I explained that we had to take a roundabout loop on account of the road still being flooded out.

"You're taking me *roundabout?*" she exclaimed in mock alarm.

"I am."

"You are?"

"I am."

"Is that even proper *at all?*"

"I have no idea," I said.

"Mostly you're my favorite cousin," she said.

"No," I said, "you're *my* favorite cousin."

"Then we cancel each other out."

"That's a shame," I said.

We rode for a while.

"Well," she said, "it was nice to get some rain but I'm afraid that it came too much and too fast to do the crops any good."

"Good point," I said. She was repeating something she'd heard.

"Now remind me," she said, "how long a drive it is from our house to your house."

"Well, if I'm driving it's like two hours. If your dad is driving, it's like two and a half hours."

"What are you saying?"

"Nothing."

"You're saying you're a fast driver and Dad's a slow driver?"

"That's about right."

"Well . . ."

"I'm saying your dad is a conscientious driver."

"Conscientious . . . ," she echoed.

"So when're you going to come visit me and Mom?" I asked.

"I'll have to get back to you on that one," Gracie said.

"You should see this swimming pool I work at," I said. "I can get you in free."

"I'm listening," she said.

"We have two slides."

"Uh-huh."

"And we have one of those big mushroom things that has water raining down from it."

She didn't respond to that.

"And," I continued, "you can get two taffies for a nickel at the concession stand. Two for a nickel! That's a steal. How can you beat that?"

"You can't beat that," she said.

"There's no way you can beat that."

"Wait just a second," she said. "I just remembered I've been to your pool. It's not all that special. It's fine. I've been there though, last summer."

"Well, I can still get you in free."

"That's hardly worth a two-hour drive. We have a swimming pool here in town."

"I've seen the swimming pool here. It's more like a flooded basement than a swimming pool."

"Flooded basement! There's no house on top of it!"

"I'm just saying it's small."

"I'll give you that," she said. She rummaged in her purse for a moment and then pulled her legs up and sat cross-legged on the seat. "What're you going to be when you grow up?" she asked.

"A ninja," I answered.

"That's not even an actual job. You're just saying that."

"Okay, so what do you want to be when you grow up?"

"I just finished third grade and you're asking me about my career plans?"

"I'm just trying to make chitchat here, Gracie."

"Maybe a parachutist," she said. "Or a butcher."

"A butcher!"

"Like Mr. Franks," she said. "Have you met our butcher, Mr. Franks?"

"I'm not sure I have."

"I think you'd remember him if you had. He's just a nice human person."

"The world needs good butchers."

"He's the butcher for our whole town. Basically."

"My hat goes off to him," I said.

"What does *that* mean?"

"It's just an expression. It means I acknowledge his integrity and hard work."

26

"Well . . . ," she said, "I *guess* so."

"Look at this light," I said. "Our skin is glowing."

The sunset was reflecting off some clouds just overhead and the orangy-peachy light was absolutely effusive. Partly it had to do with the fact that we had just come into a stretch of land that was very open and rolling—as opposed to the wooded ridge we'd been traveling along so far. The hills were contour-plowed and planted with corn alternated with strips of grass. And this new landscape felt like a new country altogether, or at least a new state, and there was simply a lot more sky here than where we'd been, and also a sense of freshness.

"I'm glad I'm out driving around with you," Gracie said.

I smiled at her.

"And you're right about the light," she said. "What can I say about it? I feel like a *sponge*," she said. "I feel like I'm a sponge and this light is going inside of me. I'm *absorbing* the light."

"Well said."

"I'm *full* of the light."

"That sounds nice."

"If you *squeezed* me, light would come out."

"Is that a request?" I asked.

She laughed.

"The light is never like this at home," I said.

"Well, the smog and everything," Gracie said.

"Hey, it's not a big city or anything. We don't have smog. It's just that there are so many trees and buildings and you can never really see the horizon. And the sunsets just aren't as good."

"The *ozone* pollution," Gracie said.

"I don't think we have ozone pollution."

"*Everybody* has ozone pollution."

"I suppose," I said.

"When's your birthday and what do you want?" she asked.

"Oh, heck, my birthday isn't until winter."

"What do you want?"

"I haven't quite worked up a list yet."

"Maybe you should get started."

"My birthday list always gets lumped together with my Christmas list anyway."

"That sounds like trouble," Gracie said.

"It is, believe me. So what's on your birthday list?"

"I'll give you a copy when we get home. I printed it out."

"I like an organized girl."

"Well, I just wanted it to be there in black and white."

"I understand what you're saying."

"Do you know when my birthday is?"

"I do."

"Okay then, when?"

"Let's see, it's the fourteenth, which is, what, next week I guess?"

"That's right."

"I remember when you were born. I was about your age."

"That's weird."

"Not really."

"Will you come to my party?"

"You know, I would love to come to your party but I probably have to work that day."

"What time do you have to work?"

"Probably noon till seven.

"Hm. You'll miss my party."

"I'm sorry."

"There will be a lot of girls there."

"I like the sound of that."

"In fact, you're the only boy I've invited."

"It sounds really good."

"Most boys are dull."

28

"I agree. Sometimes I think I'm dull."

"I wouldn't have invited you if I thought you were dull. Or ugly."

"Stop it with all this flattery. I'm going to blush."

"I think you are blushing."

"I think that's just my sunburn from fishing every day."

She reached across the car and touched the pad of her index finger against my cheek and then withdrew it.

"You're right," she said. "That's a burn."

It took us thirty-five minutes to do the roundabout route on what was normally a ten-minute drive from town. We came around the last bend and we were in the lowlands and we came out of a patch of woods and I could see Freeda's farm just another quarter mile down the road. But between us and the farm was a stretch of floodwater, reflecting the darkening sky, and I could tell by the fence posts that the water was at least four feet deep and it was moving.

Gracie and I got out of the car and walked to the edge of the water. Gracie bent down.

"I'll draw a line here and we'll see if the water goes higher or lower," she said.

There were no lights on in the house and I could see no one. Even if I were prepared to swim, the water was too dangerous. And even if I had had a boat it would have been basically impossible to keep it on the narrow road, and if it got pushed off the road into the fence or the trees, that would be trouble. So their farm was an island, cut off from both directions, and their phone hadn't worked since the flood came.

"Do you want me to yell for Freeda?" Gracie asked.

"Probably not," I said.

"Or I could yell for her brother or for her parents."

"No," I said.

Gracie slapped her shoulder. "Wow—these mosquitoes," she said.

We were being swarmed by them.

"You're right," I said. "Let's head home."

Four

PAER WAS TRYING TO HOLD THE CALF STILL.

"We don't have time for this," Paer said.

"We're okay," I said.

It wasn't that the day-old calf was strong, but that it jerked and bucked in unexpected ways, and it was impossible to control completely. It had been born "knuckle-ankled"—its front hooves were bent backwards, so that it walked on its ankles.

The calf thrashed sideways and its head hit my ear and my ear rang.

"Jeez," I said.

"Come on," Paer said. "Let's give up."

But we persisted and in a few minutes I had successfully straightened the calf's front legs by taping each of them tightly between two small boards—makeshift splints.

The calf ran away from us when we released it and it fell down and got up and fell down again and lay there. It was weak from not getting enough milk. It called for its mother, who we'd shut in the barn. We were out at the old farm place, where Grandpa was letting Paer run nine cows and their calves. Grandpa didn't live here anymore. No one did.

A couple minutes later, one of the calf's splints had fallen off, and the other one was slipping.

"We have to do this right," I said. "Or not do it at all."

"I don't know," Paer said. He was upset. His face seemed just slightly swollen, and he kept watching the calf. If we had been ten years old, he would have been crying. But we were eighteen.

"We don't have time," Paer said.

I looked at my watch.

"We need to get down to the river soon," Paer said.

"The river can wait," I said. "Let's do this. We can save this calf. Come on."

Paer was watching the calf, whose legs were shaking.

"We have to go back into town anyway to pick up the canoe," I pointed out.

I drove Cort's pickup. This was Saturday, and Uncle Cort had still been asleep when we left the house.

"I wish Grandpa had never given me those cows," Paer said.

"All I got for graduation was a *watch*," I said. It wasn't true.

"But he gave me the rejects. Of the nine cows, only three have had healthy babies. Three out of nine."

"Wait—you mean they were *all* pregnant when he gave them to you?"

"That was the whole point. I would double my herd instantly. But the first calf was stillborn. Two died of blackleg. Then that one momma fell into the gully and broke her back and we had to shoot her and pull her calf, which didn't survive. And then there's the one that was born stupid, didn't know how to nurse. And now this one with the funky legs. So I have three healthy calves, one cripple, and an idiot."

"We'll help this calf, and then you'll have four healthy calves."

"It's like some kind of chasm," Paer said, and I thought I'd misheard him so I asked him to repeat it. "It's like a chasm," he said.

"What is?"

"This summer. This whole thing. Now that we've graduated, I mean."

"I'm not following," I said.

"Okay," Paer said, "tell me this: is this our last summer vacation or our first summer of adulthood?"

I hesitated. "Both, I guess."

"You can say that because you're going to college."

"No, I think it's both. I think it's a borderland."

"Borderland?" Paer said. "Like how?"

"It's awkward. A transition. It's a borderland. Between worlds."

"It's more than awkward. And it's more than a borderland. It's some kind of chasm, like I said. It *is* adulthood. It's a chasm and it's unavoidable and my jeep was a victim, and my fishing rod was a victim, and my cattle are victims, and my girlfriend was a victim. And this is just the beginning. Where does it go from here? Where *can* it go? Nowhere good."

It took us fifty minutes in Cort's shop to weld the two simple steel frames. Where the metal would touch the calf's leg we wrapped it thickly with adhesive gauze. Then we pulled the canoe from behind the garage and dragged it across the lawn to the truck. There were some wasp nests that we cleaned out and Paer got into the canoe and stomped three spiders. We lifted the canoe into the truck and each took a bit of rope and tied the canoe to both sides of the truck bed.

Gracie came out of the house, eating a bowl of cereal.

"I *think*," she said, "that if you guys *think* you're going to find that jeep then I think you're crazy and then what would you do with it anyway? It'll be junked. It'll have mud in the crankshaft or blowhole or something."

I tightened the knot I had just tied.

"Miss Fancy Pants," I said.

"I am *not* Miss Fancy Pants," she protested. "I'm wearing *shorts*."

We got in the truck and rolled away and drove out to the farm and this time the calf was lying down and she didn't even put up a struggle at all and the metal braces fit pretty well and I put on a little bit of extra padding by wrapping some more gauze around them and then they fit pretty much perfectly. When we left her, teetering on her front hooves, she called after us, and then she followed us all the way to the gate and watched us go out. Paer went in the barn and let the calf's mother out and then we stood at the fence and waited, but for some reason mother and calf were in no particular hurry to reunite themselves and so we left and drove the truck down past the machine shed and old corn crib and then down through the pasture along the fence. The grass brushed against the underside of the truck. I looked back up the slope at the farm and it made a pleasing impression from here and the white farmhouse wasn't in bad shape even though it had been empty for years.

We bumped along through the bottomland pasture and then turned down a sharp incline and came out onto a wide gravel bar. The creek was still high and murky, but it had fallen just enough that it was safe to canoe. We pulled the canoe out of the truck and slid it into the water and Paer climbed into the front seat and I pushed us off and then took the backseat and we were off.

The sky was a flat gray color and the breeze was at our backs. The high waters made the upstream work hard, but the two of us did fine because we knew what we were doing and we were strong enough and we stuck close to the bank where the current was slower. We didn't say anything and we had a long way to go before we got to the first gravel bar—about two miles. From there, the route would get trickier with more turns and more narrow spots and we didn't know what new hazards the flood might have put in our path. But we should be able to work our way upstream all the way to the bridge where the jeep had been. The trip back downstream would be easy.

As we made our way upstream, the current seemed to grow stronger, but I figured that it was just that we were getting tired. We weren't used to fighting such a persistent current—normally the creek was pretty tame. When we got to the first gravel bar, we dragged the canoe up onto the gravel and took our fishing rods and got out. I was thirsty and I wished we had brought something to drink. We walked up the shore and Paer stopped and looked out at a tangle of tree trunks midchannel.

"Big momma catfish," he said.

"We should have brought bait."

I walked a bit farther up and started casting a spinner across the current. The current was strong and fast here where the creek was narrow. The current dragged my lure downstream too quickly. And the water was murky enough that I figured the fish couldn't see my lure. It was an exercise in futility, but that never stopped a fisherman. I wasn't even sure why we'd brought our rods. But I kept fishing, walking slowly upstream, until I stood at the very tip of the gravel bar, fishing the broad apron of smooth water just above the faster section. Nothing was going to bite, nothing was going to happen. No fish were out and about, and we still had a long way to paddle, but I made another cast anyway but something was wrong and the lure didn't go anywhere and a bunch of line uncoiled from my spool and I had a big mess on my hands. The lure was hooked around the tip of my rod and I had a bird's nest tangle of fishing line to deal with. I looked back at Paer and he was still fishing the big logjam and I took out my clippers and started clipping away my line, trying to clean up the mess, and my feet were suddenly wet. I figured I was standing too close to the edge of the gravel bar and the water had seeped up into my old running shoes, so I took a step back and concentrated on my line and clipped the spinner loose and put the blade of the spinner in my mouth to hold it until I got some clean line ready. I tried to ball up the big mess of tangled line but of course it resisted all attempts at tidiness and I didn't want to just leave it here so I stuffed it into the back pocket of my cutoffs and started to string the clean line through the guides and that's when my feet were suddenly wet again and this time I stopped what I was doing and looked down and the lure dropped out of my mouth into the water and what was happening was that the water was rising so fast that the tip of the gravel bar was disappearing even as I watched. I picked up my lure and held it in my palm and stepped back and watched the water very carefully. It was rising steadily. I'd never seen such a thing.

"Paer," I said.

I looked up at the sky. It hadn't rained here overnight, but clearly it had rained upstream. I put my lure into the small tackle box in my front pocket.

"Paer," I said again, louder.

I looked back at him.

"Paer!" I yelled.

"What?"

I told him to come here and he did and by this point the water wasn't moving down the gravel bar at an insect's pace but at a snake's pace. Paer looked at it for maybe two seconds and cursed and then we both turned at the same time and walked straight down the center of the gravel bar toward the canoe. We did not run and we didn't say anything and when we got to the canoe we could tell that the water had been rising already and as soon as we were back out on the water we could feel the difference, we could feel that the river's strength was waxing, and we could see that the current was broader and faster, and we were as a leaf upon a torrent.

Without talking, we made the decision to ride the left side of the current, where it hung close up against a steep bluff. We used the current for its speed and we paddled hard and we felt the river rising higher and we felt ourselves moving faster and we tracked our progress in our heads and we thought about what was in front of us.

It started to rain.

Halfway home, there was a point where the creek split into two parts and flowed around a small island of trees. And the left bank here was thick with low-hanging tree branches that would knock us out of the canoe or capsize us. We would have to cross the current to the far side of the creek, where the channel was open. I told Paer this and he agreed and we powered out and pulled into the center of the current. We rode it for several moments, waiting as long as we could to make any last-minute judgments about our path. But as we approached the island now, I could tell that the waters had risen high enough that the current was no longer splitting itself, but was barreling straight over the island at full force. The river was trying to push us right into the island, right into the trees. The water was roaring as it coursed around the trees and I knew we were too late and that all our strength couldn't pull us entirely clear.

"Power!" I said, and Paer dug in and I was doing what steering I could but the fact is that the current was so fast we didn't have the control we needed—you can only steer if you're moving faster than the current, after all. And the tip of the island passed just ten feet away and we were just to the right of it and trying to pull ourselves farther away but we hit a sudden side current and this pushed our nose to the left and before we could react we were headed toward the dangling branches of a silver maple, whose limbs were normally well above the water, and Paer ducked and held up his oar for protection and I heard a small branch crack and something caught the oar and plucked Paer from the boat and I didn't have time to see where he'd gone before I, too, was headed into the branches and I lay backwards and held my oar down, flush against my body, and the branches scraped me and the canoe hesitated and then tipped for a moment and then righted itself and then I was out of the branches and the canoe was sideways in the stream and I put my oar in and swung the tip of the canoe around so that I was facing upstream and I looked around and then I saw Paer floating just downstream from me, among the tree trunks of the island. He was trying to grab the trees as they passed him but because he was facing upstream he couldn't see the trees until it was too late to get ahold of them.

I paddled backwards and there was not much thinking going on at all, only reacting, and piloting backwards was difficult and I was simply trying to keep myself away from the trees. Paer was still bobbing along and he hit one small tree trunk pretty hard and it slowed him enough he was able to wrap an arm around it and hold himself there and he saw me and I was about to pass him and I yelled at him.

"Stand up!"

And he did, and the water only came up to his waist, and in other circumstances this would have been funny, but the current was still strong and it was hard for him to hold on to the tree and my task now would be difficult and if I fell into the river, too, I didn't know what would happen to either of us. The canoe was our best chance. Paer was not a strong swimmer.

I fought against the current so that I wasn't moving downstream anymore, and somehow I fought harder and started inching upstream. I had to constantly flip my paddle from one side of the canoe to the other in order to control my course. I nosed the canoe into the trees, and here the current was just slightly weaker and I moved through the trees as best I could—pushing off one here with my bare hand, digging at that one with my paddle, sliding alongside one using it as a kind of support—and I don't know how long it took and I don't know everything I did to get there, but I came alongside Paer and he clambered on his stomach into the canoe, bringing water with him, and now I noticed how much water there was in the bottom of the canoe—from Paer, from the rain, from our paddling, from our near capsizing—but there was nothing to be done about it and now that Paer was in and I had stopped paddling we were moving swiftly backwards downstream through the trees and I turned around completely on my seat and faced downstream and did some improvisational steering to bring us through the trees safely and when we got back into the clear current of the creek, I turned back around, dug in, and swung the canoe back around so we were facing downstream. Paer was facing me in his seat.

"You're bleeding," he said. I looked at the gash on my arm. From the tree branches, I guessed. Or fighting my way upstream through the trees.

I asked him if he was okay and he said he was fine and he turned around on his seat in order to face downstream but he didn't have his paddle anymore and so everything remained in my hands. Without Paer's power in the front of the canoe, it would be difficult.

In fact, for several minutes, I did almost nothing. The canoe drifted right down the center of the current, well away from any danger, and I occasionally ruddered us to keep us straight. I was saving my strength.

The gravel bar where we had put in—and where the truck was still parked—was just upstream from a jumbled collection of boulders which in normal conditions served as excellent cover for fish, but which in this high water would be transformed into pure white water. We'd observed such floods from shore before, and were always amazed by the roar of the water as it churned over the rocks. You could hear it clear up at the farmhouse, three-quarters of a mile away.

When we turned the last bend and came within sight of the truck, I moved the canoe tight against the right shore and paddled hard in order to keep our speed up. We could hear the noise of the rapids now, and we knew we didn't want to go there and as we got closer I paddled harder and the gravel bar was much smaller now than it had been when we put in and I realized that the landing zone I was aiming for was only two or three feet wide and that if the current got the best of us and pulled us just a few feet to the left and caused us to miss the tip of the gravel bar, we would almost certainly have no chance to make a landing.

"Duck down," I told Paer. He was blocking the most crucial part of the view. He didn't hesitate at all, but bent forward, and I couldn't help but wonder what it was like to be in his position and not be able to see what was happening.

I gathered more speed and kept my eyes focused on the target and hugged the shore and gauged the distance. I could feel the current on my left like some kind of magnetic force.

But I kept us on course, and I brought us in as straight as an arrow, and as soon as the front of the canoe scraped against the gravel, Paer jumped out and pulled the canoe onto shore and then I got out and Paer went to the truck and I pulled the canoe completely clear of the water.

The back wheels of the parked truck were mostly underwater and Paer got in the truck and my legs were weak but somehow I remained standing and I didn't want to look at the river anymore and I kept dragging the canoe away from the water, even though there was really no reason to do it.

Paer yelled something, but it was lost in the roar of the rapids.

He yelled again, "Where're the keys?"

I jogged over to the truck. Even below the driver's door there was water.

"I don't know where the keys are," Paer said.

"I never had them."

"I know, I know, I know."

We looked at each other.

"They must have fallen out of your pocket when you were in the water," I said.

"What can we do?" Paer asked.

"The tractor?" I said.

"No gas," he said.

"We can get some rope at the farm," I said.

"That won't help."

"Maybe we can find a come-along?"

"I don't know."

"It's the only thing I can think of," I said.

"Could we hot-wire it?"

"We'd need tools."

"Wait!" Paer said, and he took the little plastic tackle box out of his front pocket and he opened it and there, alongside his hooks and spinners, were the truck keys.

I backed away from the truck and he started it and gunned it and it roared out of the water and he put it in park and gunned the engine again and then got out and I rushed over and we got the canoe and loaded it and didn't bother with tying it in and we got into the truck and drove up the slope and up to the farm and down the gravel road. That's where the truck died and we couldn't get it to run for more than a minute at a time and so we stopped and got out and I started poking around and we were still pretty close to the farm so we walked there through the rain and looked for what tools we could find but there wasn't a phone there and then we walked back to the truck and after twenty minutes I realized that there was some dirt in the carburetor and it was easy enough to flush out and that solved the problem and we were on our way.

———

When we got home, Paer got out of the truck and went inside. I wrestled with the canoe and put it back alongside the shed. I flipped it over. Back in the house, I looked for Paer. Then I heard the shower. He was in the shower. Cort and Corene and Gracie were gone. I found a note on the table.

Leo—

Going to Dalton swap meet like we said. We waited for you, sorry! Maybe see you in July? Glad you were here as usual. We had some fun! Say hi to your mom and hope the summer is a super one!

Love,
Aunt Corene

At the bottom Gracie had added this:

Will you write to me a leter. To say how you did that card trick? Which you did. And glad you were here as usual. Your Gracie Frances

I went to Paer's room and packed my things. There really wasn't much to pack. It all fit in my backpack. My toothbrush was in the bathroom, though, and Paer was still showering in there.

The phone rang and it was Jerry from the garage.

"I found that manifold you guys were wanting. I can't believe I found it."

"You didn't order it yet, did you?"

"I put down a deposit."

"I'm going to swing by sometime this afternoon," I said. "Sometime pretty soon, probably."

"You don't have to come by. I'll call when it comes in."

"Don't order it yet," I said.

"You don't want it? I thought you wanted it," Jerry said.

"I'll swing by pretty soon," I said.

And even as I hung up the doorbell rang and I went to open it and was looking forward to seeing Mom but instead of Mom there stood Ruben, Mom's boyfriend, wearing wingtips with jeans, as always.

"I'm sorry I'm late," Ruben said.

"No, no," I said, "you're not late really."

"It's that antique store in Bixby. It took this old guy a solid fifteen minutes to run my credit card. He had to follow instructions from a booklet."

Ruben came in and stood in the living room and then took off his sunglasses and looked at the furniture.

"What'd you buy?" I asked.

"Hm?"

"What'd you buy?"

"Oh. An old pocket watch. That's all."

I pointed over my shoulder to the stairs. "I've just got to get my backpack," I said.

"Sure."

I went upstairs.

"Oh," Ruben said as I climbed upstairs. "Your mom is covering for Dr. Beshears, which is why I had to come get you. She's in-house."

I got my backpack. I opened the door to the bathroom and the steam almost made me gag it was so thick.

"Paer?" I said. "I'm hitting the road."

"What?"

"I gotta go," I said. "I'll see you soon."

"Take it easy," Paer said.

In the car, Ruben asked me how my week had been and I

remembered that I was going to stop by the garage and so we had to turn around just outside of town and come back to the garage and I went in and paid Jerry for the fifty-dollar deposit and told him never to mention the deposit or the manifold to Paer and also not to ask about the jeep unless Paer brought it up. Jerry was puzzled but I didn't see what else I could do and Ruben was idling outside in his coupe and so I left.

As we headed out of Charbourg, Ruben started talking about how his car's sunroof wasn't closing properly lately, how it wasn't sealing well and rain was coming in sometimes. I slid the sunroof open and closed a few times and I could hear the whistle of air coming through it even when it was supposedly closed but there really wasn't anything I could do right now and so I promised that Ruben and I would look at it together tomorrow and I closed my eyes and fell immediately asleep and slept until we started hitting the stoplights on the outskirts of town, two hours later. I stretched and breathed deeply a few times and I was almost instantly awake and completely refreshed and I looked out the window at the familiar neighborhoods but felt somewhat discombobulated in that on account of my nap I was suffering under the illusion that no real time or distance had been put between myself and Charbourg and that if we turned the car around we would be back in Charbourg in two minutes and Paer would still be in the shower.

And I remembered I'd left my toothbrush there.

Ruben's cell phone rang and he answered it and handed it to me. It was Mom. She'd just finished a delivery and was headed into another one and she said she'd left money on the counter if I wanted to get something to eat and I reminded her that the pool's staff-only opening party was tonight and that I would eat there and she laughed and asked me if because we were life-guards we were allowed to break the rule against swimming after eating and I said of course we were allowed to break that rule and that it was a phony rule anyway and that eating before swimming actually *enhanced* your performance and enjoyment.

At home, Ruben said he'd just wait in the drive. I went inside and the house smelled like home and I rushed up the stairs to my room. I played back my answering machine as I changed into my swimming trunks.

The only message was from E. B.—Elizabeth Biddle, one of Jenny's friends. She was apparently on a cell phone, because the message was in bits and pieces: "So what . . . some . . . of crazy ploy? Some kind of . . . her house bleeding profusely? I think you . . . Florence Nightingale thing, but . . . shouldn't . . . I . . . sorta crazy. And you expect her to forget how you . . . semester, and . . . a *freshman* to prom? But . . . worked. You should call me. This changes everything, Leo. We'll . . ."

Ruben's car was in the driveway with its doors open, and it was pinging softly because the keys were in the ignition. It was the kind of European coupe that very clearly announced that its owner was an anesthesiologist. But at the moment I couldn't find Ruben. I walked around the corner of the house and he was in the backyard, looking at the plot where Mom's vegetable garden usually was. This year, the garden plot was empty, covered by black plastic.

"Garçon!" I said, and Ruben snapped around and came back to his car and we headed out of the neighborhood and toward the pool. I went through the pool house and everyone was already on the deck and the pizzas had been mostly consumed and it appeared that the diving contest on the three-meter board was already under way. Almost all the lifeguards were here, including several from last year: John, Thayler, Wanda, Keller, Pepper, and Sam, as well as Greg, the manager. There were three girls who were new, and two guys I didn't recognize.

One of the guys did a respectable backflip.

"Leo!" Thayler yelled when he saw me come onto the deck. "He walks among us!"

Greg came over and shook my hand and Wanda asked me to join the competition. "We're down to John, Greg, and Fifi," she said.

"Who's Fifi?" I asked, working on a piece of pizza.

Wanda made a vague gesture in the direction of the new girls. "They all look the same to me," Wanda said. "That's why we call them all Fifi. That's not really their name."

"I don't think there's any cause to be mean," Greg said.

"I'm not being mean," Wanda said. "Besides, you're the one that hired three gorgeous blond airheads. It's not our fault we can't tell them apart."

Greg walked back to the competition.

"*You're* a gorgeous blond airhead," I told Wanda, "and I can tell *you* apart."

"Listen, Lee," Wanda said, standing too close to me, "she's the best diver and you're the only one who can beat her and we need you do to it because this is about pride and honor and duty and also a bet between the new lifeguards and the old lifeguards about who will clean the bathrooms for the next four weeks."

"Jeez," I said. "Four weeks."

"You're our hero, Lee," she said.

"I'm just trying to eat some pizza."

"You do everything well," she said. "Even eat pizza. But I'm telling you to hurry it up, because we need to kick Fifi out of this thing."

"What's her real name?"

"I don't know. It's either Rachel or Becky."

"She looks like a Becky."

"Let's see," Wanda said. She turned to the distant group and yelled out the name and the girl in question answered and then

Wanda yelled, "Leo here says you dive like a fat man and that he's joining the competition and the whole thing is over and you're going *down.*"

Becky didn't really have anything to say to that. She kept her composure.

"That wasn't called for," I told Wanda.

"Don't be prissy."

I drank a significant quantity of soda and then joined the competition. This diving contest had been a yearly event at our pool opening party, and I'd won it three years now. Quickly, John was eliminated by a bad entry on an easy flip. I warmed up with a twisting dive with my hands held straight against my sides—a crowd pleaser. After that, Greg forfeited.

Becky did a clean and graceful gainer. Everyone clapped and hooted. They were all sitting at the side of the pool, dangling their legs in the water. I waited for Becky to walk back around to the rear of the diving board where I was standing. The low sun was shining into that little corner of the deck.

"My name's Leo," I said.

"I'm Becky," she said.

The pump house was humming behind us.

"That stuff Wanda said was Wanda's, not mine," I told her.

"I figured."

Thayler yelled from the deck: "Get a move on already!"

Greg yelled: "No fraternizing."

Wanda yelled: "He uses sex as a weapon!"

"That true?" Becky asked.

"I wouldn't even know how to do such a thing."

"It's your turn," she said.

I bested Becky's gainer by adding a twist.

She did another good dive, but I wanted the competition to end, so I decided to pull a triple forward flip. No one else could do this dive on the three-meter board. The trick was in getting a good jump—it all came down to getting a lot of spring out of the board, and being completely fearless.

I stood at the rear of the board and cleared my head. I walked down the board, calculating my approach. I returned to the rear of the board and breathed slowly three times. I closed my eyes, opened them, then started.

I had gauged my approach well, and I came down on the tip of the board just right. The board bent beneath me—all that potential energy building up below me. But at the critical point—where the board was bent as far as it would go, and my body was preparing to spring upward—something gave way. My feet slipped off the tip of the board and I continued moving down. My head snapped forward and I realized that it had hit the board and then I felt my face slap the water and I felt the water around me and it felt excessively warm but I couldn't hear anything and from behind me a globe of darkness glided in and enveloped me and a long time passed in which I seemed to be dissolving in layers into the darkness but when the light returned I saw Wanda's face right above mine and I felt her arms beneath me in the water and I realized that only a handful of seconds had passed and now sound returned and Wanda was talking to me and I was answering and that was a good thing.

"There's no way I'm going to suture that thing," Dr. Gehring said in the ER, looking at the cut on the back of my head. "You couldn't *pay* me enough to suture that thing. Let nature do its magic, that's what I say."

After glancing at the X-ray films, examining me for about sixty seconds, and asking four or five questions, he was apparently done and now he was writing on my chart. "Of course," he said, without looking up, "we're going to clean that gash with an excruciatingly painful disinfectant."

"Super," I said.

After he left, the nurse came in and told me that a young woman was asking to see me and that I had to give my consent before she could come in. I gave my consent and the nurse left and I realized I didn't know who it was I'd just consented to seeing. Then Jenny came in. It seemed that after getting no answer at my house, Thayler had tried to think who else he could call and he called Jenny. I showed her my head wound and she seemed impressed because she clenched her teeth and inhaled in a hissing way. She asked me why every time she saw me recently I seemed to be bleeding. And I told her that the summer was trying to kill me. Or at least maim me. First with the bike wreck. Then with the fishing lure that would have blinded me if I hadn't just put on my sunglasses. Then with the flash flood. And now with the diving board that attacked me.

She laughed for so long that when Mom finally came in, wearing her scrubs, Jenny was still laughing, and Mom hugged me and looked at my wound and read my chart and asked me how I was and asked me why we were both laughing and I told her how the summer was trying to kill me and I told her about today—the flood and the diving accident—and she laughed along with us, but then she started to get laughy-weepy, and she wiped her eyes and I figured she was just relieved that I was okay, and tired after being in the hospital all day, and happy to see me after my week with Paer.

"I never gave this summer any reason to dislike me," I said, trying to keep Jenny laughing. "But here it is, trying to kill me again and again."

Jenny kept laughing, but Mom's weepiness overtook her and I couldn't figure out what was wrong and I asked her and she waved me off and Dr. Gehring came and said, "Don't you worry, Julia: your boy is indestructible. He's like Tupperware, this kid."

"I'm like plastic storageware?"

"Listen," he said, "I have Tupperware from the sixties, kid. The *early* sixties. What decade are you from?"

"The eighties."

He and the nurse cleaned the cut while he and Mom talked about the hospital's ownership woes. When the wound was cleaned and bandaged, the doctor looked at Jenny for the first time.

"This your wife?" he asked me.

"Oh, heck no," I said. "We're divorced."

Jenny smiled a small smile and then she looked down at the floor and then back at me.

"Well, I'm glad to hear that," Dr. Gehring said. "And as for you, bucko," he said, pointing at me, "I don't ever want to see you in here again, got it?"

"Understood."

"Basically," the doctor said, "I mean take care of yourself."

"Will do."

"Keep out of trouble," he said, scribbling some more on my chart.

"Okay."

"Keep your feet on the ground," he said.

"Gotchya."

"Literally," he said.

"Uh-huh."

"And don't take candy from strangers."

"Candy . . . ," I said.

"Now get out of my emergency room."

He said good night to my mom and then left and Mom said she had to go back upstairs. Jenny volunteered to drive me home, and in the silence of Jenny's van I found myself without words and I was tired and somewhat stunned by the dimensions of my day, which finally seemed to be ending. I thought of the knuckle-ankled calf, and the river, and I wondered what Paer was doing.

And I looked over at Jenny and watched her steer us down the highway. She was a good driver, a steady driver, a clearheaded driver. She always had been. I felt comfortable and safe and I was glad she was with me. As we crossed town, the plummy remnants of the sunset were dissolving in the west, and after we pulled into my driveway Jenny came to the side door with me and I got the key out of my pocket and then I told her that I was glad she had come and that it all seemed very pleasing and very surprising and that if maybe it was okay that I thought I would call her tomorrow. She said that she would like that and she kissed me on the cheek and then went to her van and backed away. I tried to unlock the door but the key wouldn't go in at all and I realized it was the key to the back door, so I walked around the house and walked past mother's garden and I stopped and looked at it and for the first time it seemed odd to me. Mother loved her garden. Mother's garden was always beautiful and bountiful—a ruckus of flowers and vegetables. And when I had asked her once about her garden, she said that one of the reasons she liked it was because it was an act of faith—faith that the future would be fruitful and good. And it seemed odd to me that she had not planted her garden this year, and I didn't like it.

I unlocked the sliding patio door and as soon as I slid the door open the cat slipped past my ankles and disappeared into the night. There was nothing I could do.

Five

I TAPPED ON THE DOOR TO MOM'S BEDROOM. I WAITED, THEN I opened the door, picked up the breakfast tray, and went in. The room itself seemed to be asleep. In the dimness, I could hear the faint breath of the central air. The shades were drawn on the skylights, blocking the morning sun. And the tall plate-glass windows on both sides of the room looked out into the leaves and limbs of our oaks, which gave the impression that the room was being held aloft by the trees.

I put the tray down on the chest at the foot of the bed, then stood there for a moment. I looked at my watch and then looked at Mom. Her bed and her comforter were so big that she essentially disappeared into them. Plus those overstuffed down pillows. A spray of hair was the only evidence of her.

"*Mi madre,*" I said, singsongy.

I went back to the door and turned the dials that operated the skylight shades. Mechanically, without a sound, the shades slid open like eyelids and the sun came angling into the room, lighting up the huge western wall.

"*Mama mia,*" I said, walking back to the bed.

I heard her sigh a waking sigh.

"*Meine Mutter,*" I said. "*Ma mère.*"

In one motion, she sat up. "*Mon fils,*" she said.

We arranged ourselves cross-legged on the bed. Mom smiled at the tray of food and rubbed her hands together. She pushed up her glasses and lifted the lid off her cup of coffee. The steam bloomed from it.

"I love that part," she said. She looked at the rest of the food. "Berries?" she said. "Where'd you get strawberries?"

"I went to the farmers' market at seven."

"Busy, busy bee," she said.

We crumbled the hot biscuits into our bowls, spooned the sugared berries over them, squeezed nests of honey atop it all, then poured on the cream. We ate with spoons, and we ate without talking. When my bowl was empty, I put it down. Mom was only halfway through hers. She put it down and put a hand to her stomach.

"I think I'm a little nervous," she said. "I can't eat it all. Not that it isn't wonderful—because it *is.*" She took her coffee mug into both hands and sipped and then held the mug close to her chest.

"Tell me the sun part again," I said.

She told me how the island of Grímsey, off the north coast of Iceland, was bisected by the Arctic Circle, which meant that on the summer solstice the sun did not set, but merely dipped low against the northern horizon—just kissing the sea—and then ascended again. And in seven days, on the actual solstice, she would be there, in the midnight sun. She was leaving later today.

"When will you sleep?" I asked.

"I won't!" she said.

"When will you dream?"

"The whole *thing* will be a dream."

―――――

53

As soon as Mom left for the office—she had some charts she needed to finish up before she left for vacation—thunder started rumbling in the south and I went out onto the second-floor deck and looked at the clouds rolling in. I went back inside and turned on the television, but none of the local stations were running severe weather coverage, so there was nothing to be learned, and apparently the storms weren't to be feared. So I went back out onto the deck and sat in the fitful wind. Finally, the clouds blocked out the sun and the lightning got close and I went inside. The rain came suddenly, and it was a steady rain. The wind died down, the rain tapered off after five minutes, and then the doorbell rang.

I opened the door to find E. B. there holding our cat.

"One wet girl and one wet cat," I said.

"I'm not wet," E. B. said. "I'm moistened."

She looked very good moistened. The cat, on the other hand, looked defeated. She'd been gone two nights.

"This cat of yours was slinking in the woods back there." There was a wooded ravine behind our house. E. B. lived on the other side of the ravine.

"Bad kitty," I said.

E. B. tried to hand the cat to me but the cat suddenly revolted and jumped down and vanished into the house.

"She never lets me hold her," I said. "But she let you hold her."

"Sort of," E. B. said, and she pointed to some scratches on her inner arm.

"Ow," I said, and I reached for her arm—for a closer inspection—but she quickly withdrew it.

"I'm off," E. B. said, and she turned to go.

"Let me give you some tea or a towel or something. Or a bandage."

"Another time," she said, walking down the sidewalk.

"At least I can give you a ride home," I said.

E. B. kept walking.

"You found our lost cat! You're my new hero!" I said. She laughed and looked back at me briefly. "Marry me!" I called.

"Another time," she said.

I watched her walk up the street and then turn down the path that led into the ravine. The sun was back out, the trees were dripping, and rivulets coursed alongside the curbs. I closed the door and felt the latch click home. But then I saw E. B. coming back down the sidewalk. I opened the door.

"I want to show you a trick," she said.

"I accept," I said.

We walked around the yard until we found a big patch of clover. Then E. B. explained the way to find four-leaf clovers. From above, the four-leaf clovers made a square shape, whereas three-leaf clovers were triangles. So the trick was to look for squares in a field of triangles—variations from the pattern. "Like this," E. B. said, and pointed out a four-leaf clover. "And that," she said seconds later. "And that."

"Golly," I said.

She explained that Jenny had told her that I was having an unlucky summer and E. B. thought it would be nice if I knew how to find four-leaf clovers. I said I appreciated it and she said it was her pleasure and then she said good-bye again. She walked away across our lawn and I watched her until she was gone. Then I stood in the clover patch and looked for lucky clovers, but I didn't find any. But I did have the three that E. B. had given me. I went back inside.

The cat was nowhere to be found. I looked in all her usual hiding places, but it was clear that on this occasion she had chosen refuge in one of her top-secret hiding places that we didn't know about. So I went to my room and got my book and took it into the living room to read. And after about an hour I saw the cat come up from the basement. When she got to the top of the basement stairs she flicked her tail and looked around and saw me and then turned and walked the other way. I got up and followed her, trying not to make any noise, and I found her on the daybed in the den. The daybed was the place she went when she was accepting attention. It was her way of saying that she was receiving visitors and would not object to petting, nuzzling, cuddling, and being talked to.

She squinted her eyes at me in a contented way.

"I looked everywhere for you, miss," I said. "Miss missy." I told her how me and Mom had searched the neighborhood and the park and the ravine for her. I knelt beside the daybed and started petting her. Her purring was immediate and loud. "I put food out on the patio to lure you, but I think the raccoons ate it. You know raccoons. Mom spent an hour on the phone calling the whole neighborhood. How horrible is that? She had to talk to all the neighbors! We were about to give up and take the insurance money."

A couple minutes later Mom came in and so we both knelt there and petted kitty.

"I've never felt her fur this soft," Mom said.

"It's rain-softened. And saliva-softened. And then air-dried."

"I want to be *in* it, it's so soft," Mom said.

"Miss Cat," I said. I petted her for a moment. "Why'd we never name her?" I asked.

"What do you mean? She's got a name. We don't have a nameless cat."

"Well the only thing we ever call her is 'cat.' "

"And Kitty! Her name's Kitty."

"Her name's Kitty? I thought that when we were saying 'Kitty' it was lowercase kitty. But you're saying that it's uppercase?"

"Of course it's uppercase. I can't believe you thought Kitty didn't have a name."

"Well, it was part of her charm, part of her mystery. Part of the mystery of Kitty."

Mom looked at her watch.

"One hour," she said.

"Are you excited?" I asked.

"Oh," she said, "I'm something."

As I drove her across town, she seemed calm and somewhat distant, as if mentally she were already in Europe. She didn't give me any last-minute reminders or lectures. Not that she ever did that kind of thing. Finally, as we turned into the airport, she said, "I've been thinking about what we talked about, about getting you a car."

"Don't worry about that now. We'll talk when you get back."

"No. I want to talk about it now. I've decided to sell the Supra, and the money from it will be my contribution."

"The Supra? But that's your car. You've had it forever."

"It's a waste of space."

"It would be like selling part of your youth."

"No it wouldn't. It would be like selling something I no longer have a use for."

In my memory, she had never driven the Supra. It had sat in the garage draped in canvas, like some unremarkable artifact in the basement of a museum.

"I want you to place an ad in the paper," Mom continued, "and handle the sale yourself. You're good with things like that. Of course, you'll have to wait until I get back to do the paperwork."

"Are you sure about this?"

We had stopped in front of the terminal. Mom leaned over and kissed my cheek. "I'm sure," she said.

I carried her bags to the curbside check-in.

"Go on, get out of here," she told me.

"I'll at least wait until they take your bags."

She suddenly hugged me, nearly knocking me off-balance. I

held her and then she let go and kissed me again and I saw that she was crying. I was about to ask her what was wrong, but she said, "Go go go go go go go," and started waving me off.

I smiled. "You have a good time," I commanded.

"You too," she said.

I walked the short distance to the car. I opened the driver's door and looked back at her. She was still waiting in line.

"I love you!" I yelled.

She smiled and pointed to me and waved. I got into the car and reached for the ignition but the keys weren't there and somehow this was a surprise and a shock and I had a small rush of adrenaline and I looked for the keys and they weren't on the floor and they weren't on the seat. Did Mom have them? Finally, I checked my pocket—my pocket!—and there they were and I started the car and slid the transmission into drive and then idled away. I caught a glimpse of Mom tipping the curbside attendant and I almost honked the horn but I figured that would be unnecessary. I drove back across town, feeling somewhat dazed. I had to make myself pay close attention to stoplights and lane changes and simple things like that because I felt detached from myself and from the car and from the present and I felt like I was floating on some immense ocean of nothingness, with no land in sight. When I got home and pulled into the garage, I realized I had driven all the way home without turning the air-conditioning back on, and I was sweating and miserable. I got out of the car and walked out the open garage door and around the back of the house. I sat in the shade of the backyard. It was warm but not muggy, and I was slowly cooling down and I didn't feel like going inside yet. I sat there looking at my sandals.

Finally, I stood up and walked back into the garage and hit the garage door button and the door started lowering. I opened the door to the house but then I changed my mind and closed the door and hit the button that opened the other garage door. I walked past Mom's sedan. I could feel the heat of the engine as I passed. And the engine was ticking as it cooled.

The far garage door opened all the way and stopped. The sunlight came in. I stood looking at the canvas-covered Supra for a moment, then I knelt and started untying the rope that held the canvas tight against the car. I removed the rope and coiled it loosely. Then I peeled back the canvas slowly. The canvas was dusty and I was careful not to release the dust into the air. I lowered the canvas to the garage floor and I nudged it out of the way with my feet. Then I took a few steps back and looked at the car. It was black and shiny and sleek. It was older than me by a couple of years. And it faced the open garage door with a certain kind of eagerness. I didn't seem to have many feelings about the car. It was just a car. A sports car from another era. A piece of my mother's life. A machine whose story was not entirely known to me. I would sell it. Mom wanted me to sell it.

I closed the garage door and went back into the house and used the kitchen phone to call Jenny. I hadn't called her yesterday like I'd said I would. But I was calling her now.

Six

"LEO PEERY!" SAID BRIAN.

We shook hands and Brian was looking at my hair and I don't think he was liking what he was seeing.

"When was the last time you were here?" he asked.

"Let's say it was early April."

"Okay, that's way too long."

"It's just that I've been so busy at the office," I said. "Plus the damn wife and kids."

"I'm just giving you a hard time," he said. He was still shaking my hand enthusiastically, and I wasn't quite sure how to end that. "We'll get you fixed up. What you got, a hot date?"

"Something in that line."

Finally, the handshake ended and he introduced me to Josie, who led me back to the row of sinks.

"I don't think I've met you before," I told Josie as I slumped down in the chair and lowered my head into the basin.

"I know I haven't met you," Josie said, "because I would remember you. Besides, I'm mostly new. I've only been here five weeks. Six weeks. I shampoo. I don't cut or style or color. I shampoo."

She took some time adjusting the temperature of the water. She was standing right beside me. I was staring at the ceiling, and the ceiling above the sinks was covered with mirrors and track lights and I didn't remember the mirrors being there before and it was odd to be staring at my reflection in this particular pose. Therefore, I closed my eyes.

"Is that too hot?" Josie asked.

"It's perfect."

She wet my hair and the water pressure was intense but not uncomfortable and the water made a noise in my hair that was pleasing.

"I'm feeling your hair," Josie said, "and I'm thinking chlorine damage."

I admitted I was a lifeguard.

"Which pool?" she asked.

"Kimble."

"That's my favorite pool!" she said, as if there were dozens to choose from. "But you know, I haven't gone swimming yet this summer. And I love swimming. I don't know what's stopping me."

"It's not really swimming weather yet," I said.

"Swimming weather?"

"It's perfect weather for basically anything else. But it's just a bit cool for swimming," I said.

"That's true, that's true," she said. "It's nice weather, but it's not swimming weather."

"But I'll take it any day," I said. "I'll take this weather any day. You know what I've always said? Okay, maybe I've never said it before and I just thought of it right now. Which is, give me more Mays and Junes, but keep your stinking Julys and Augusts. They're just muggy and miserable. Give me more Mays and Junes, but you can keep your months named after Roman emperors."

"Roman emperors?"

"Well," I said, "July is named after Julius Caesar, and August is named after Augustus. Although I guess Caesar wasn't actually an emperor."

"What about September?" she asked. "I like September."

"September is lovely," I said. "It comes from the Latin *septum,* which means seven. It was the seventh month of the Roman calendar."

"Septum," she said to herself. "How do you know all of this?"

"I remember everything I've ever heard or read."

"You do?"

"I feel like I do. I think I do."

"Well, me, I don't remember anything. I forget my own phone number."

I opened my eyes and I laughed.

With her hands in my soapy hair, massaging my scalp, she leaned over me, her thigh against my thigh, her eyes scanning my face. "I recognize you now," she said. "You were a year behind me at school. You just graduated, didn't you?"

"I did."

"Tell me this," she said. "If I told you my phone number, would you remember it?"

I said I would and she told me her phone number and I smiled and closed my eyes and she rinsed my hair and then soaped me up again and gave me a scalp massage that went on longer than I'd ever remembered a massage here lasting. Then she rinsed again, put in the conditioner, rinsed a final time, gently towel-dried my hair, and passed me off to Brian.

"And here we are," Brian said, looking at me in the mirror. He lowered the chair. We had a long conversation about what kind of haircut I wanted. Throughout the conversation we spoke to each other's reflections in the mirror, which was disconcerting as usual, not because I minded talking to a person's reflection, but because it felt odd to be talking to one person in the mirror when in fact it felt like I was ignoring the other person—the real person—who was actually standing right by my shoulder and had his hands in my hair. Also, Brian was in rare form today, flinging about a lot of hairstyling terminology that to me sounded made up, and in the end I wasn't sure exactly what kind of haircut I'd agreed to at all. The final agreement we reached sounded more like an architecture project than a haircut. But I let him go to work and I slowly drifted toward sleep.

The punch line being that when I showed up at Jenny's front door a few hours later, I immediately saw that she had a fresh haircut herself, and we quickly discovered that we'd had back-to-back appointments with Brian that afternoon and had missed seeing each other only by a matter of a minute or two. We also thought very highly of our haircuts, and we admitted as we drove toward dinner that to a certain extent we felt notably unburdened, refreshed, and more mature simply on account of our new hair.

"We're very shallow," I told Jenny.

"We're not shallow," Jenny said. "We're just vain and deluded."

"And simpleminded," I added.

"Yes, that too."

But we looked good, and when we entered the restaurant it seemed as if nearly everyone in the place stopped and looked at us. And the maitre d'—if that's what they're called in a Japanese restaurant—rushed over to us and bowed and led us without hesitation to the ornate two-person table that was in the center of the dining room. This table, in fact, was elevated above the rest of the diners on a three-tiered platform, and though I'd eaten here several times, I had never seen this table occupied. But here we were, Jenny and I, enthroned above the rest of the Friday night diners, smiling at each other across the table. It was the kind of restaurant where somehow the diffuse and enchanting light seemed to come from nowhere and everywhere, thereby lending the impression that every object and person here was glowing from the inside—the tablecloth, the teacups, my hands, my Jenny.

I picked up the menu and Jenny reached across and stopped me.

"Let me order," she said, and I agreed. A long time ago, when we had dated the first time, she had consistently threatened to teach me to eat sushi and I had consistently declined. But now was the right time, the right night, and as I watched her order, I wondered why it had taken me so long to come back around to her. We drank our tea, ate our warm edamame with our fingers. Then the sushi came, plate by plate. No sooner had Jenny taught me about one kind of sushi than another arrived. It was a parade of tiny foods, and our table became crowded with dipping bowls and small square plates and relish trays. We ate and talked and laughed a great deal, and when the food finally came to an end, I thanked Jenny for it all and then suddenly I found myself apologizing—for last year, for this spring, for everything, everything.

We drove to the park and arrived in time to see the sun sink in the northwest. We sat and watched the sunset linger and fade, but soon I began to feel some presence over my shoulder and I looked back and saw the full moon hanging above the horizon. Down the hill, the lights were still on at the pool, but it was closed and the water was calm. From our vantage point, the pool looked like a postage stamp.

By moonlight, Jenny and I walked the path that spiraled down the hill. We came to the old concrete amphitheater. It was a barren place, with a backdrop of trees. I stopped in the middle of the broad stage and Jenny took a seat in the first row. Then she got up and moved several rows up. The moon was higher in the sky now, and it was like a spotlight.

I put my hands in my pockets. "I'm not much of a singer," I said.

"Then dance," Jenny suggested.

"Without a partner, I'm not much of a dancer." I thought for a moment. "I can whistle."

I whistled a little bit.

"We're not impressed. Juggle. You juggle."

"Without something to juggle, I'm not much of a juggler."

"What *are* you?" she asked.

"What am I . . ."

"Tell us who you are and who you will be."

"As for who I am, you already know. I stand before you." I spread my arms for a moment. "As for who I will be, well, you'll see. You'll be there."

"Will I?" she asked.

At her house, we walked through the rooms calling for her parents, but we knew they weren't there because both their cars were gone. Therefore, it became a game.

"Mr. and Mrs. Previer?" I called into the dark dining room. "Are you hiding in here? We require adult supervision."

We changed into our bathing suits and then met in the kitchen and made root beer floats. These we took out onto the deck and set on the lip of the pool. Then we got into the pool and swam to our drinks. The pool was heated.

"See, that's the stuff: having floats while floating," Jenny said, and I couldn't have agreed more. We had turned off all the lights in the house and turned on the underwater pool lights.

Later, we sat on the bench beside the glow of the pool. Jenny laid her head in my lap and I stroked her hair. The moon floated above us and we talked. Everything was calm and at peace and during a lull in the conversation I started counting the days in my head but that was like rubbing salt into a wound. But I couldn't stop and so I made myself look down at Jenny and simply watch her face. Her eyes were closed and her breathing was slow and it seemed that that was everything I ever could have wanted and after a long time without talking, there was a faint whirring noise and Jenny's eyes opened and then some headlights flashed on the hedge across the yard. One of her parents was home, and some twenty minutes later the other car arrived and someone turned on a few of the lights in the house and then the lights went out and then someone turned off the pool lights from inside, leaving Jenny and me in the moonlight. But not long after the pool lights went out, Jenny sat up suddenly and looked around at the dark house and then looked at me.

"Uh-oh," she said.

Seven

"WAIT," SAID E. B. "SAY THAT AGAIN."

"We stayed up until sunrise," I said.

"You got locked out of her house so you stayed up all night?"

"What were we supposed to do?"

"How'd she get back into the house?"

"The housekeeper came at, what, six-thirty?, and when she took the dog out for a walk Jenny snuck back inside and I crept down the street to my car. Barefoot, I might add, because my shoes were in Jenny's room."

"What am I supposed to say to this?"

"I'll leave that up to you."

"Well, I'm stunned," E. B. said. "And why haven't I already heard this from Jenny?"

"She's probably still asleep. I only woke up because, oh, I don't know, you called me on the phone just now."

"I'm just stunned," she said.

"It was a good night. It was a good night."

"Did you kiss?"

"No. And I don't think I should tell you that anyway."

"Of course you should tell me. You should tell me everything."

"Ah, but you're Jenny's best friend. I've learned my lessons about telling you everything."

"Blah, blah, blah," she said. "You can't blame the prom debacle on me."

"I can try."

"So did you actually watch the sunrise?"

"Yeah, from the golf course. We sat on a beach towel."

"One beach towel or two beach towels?"

"By utilizing the singular form of the noun, I meant to signify *one* beach towel."

"Was it a big beach towel?"

"I think it was your average beach towel."

"Hm."

"Not big, not little."

"How did you sit on it? Were you touching?"

"Yes. Pretty much."

"Were you holding hands?"

"No."

"Were you *spooning?*"

"No, and there wasn't any *forking* going on either."

"Don't be filthy."

"I'm just saying that I'm not really going to answer any more of those kinds of questions."

"Ah, man, don't cut me off, Lee. Let a girl live vicariously."

"Why are you calling me, anyway? I'm losing beauty sleep here."

"Hey, don't be testy."

"I'm just asking."

"I wanted to apologize for the other day."

"What other day?" I asked.

"When I returned Kitty to you."

"Other day? That was two weeks ago. My mom says thank you, by the way."

"Well, she's welcome. Besides, I owe her for delivering me."

"Oh, that," I said. "That was like seventeen years ago. I'm sure she's forgotten that by now."

"Still, I owe her."

"Hold on: how did you know our cat's name is Kitty?"

"Because I can read, you idiot. And because that's what it says on her collar, along with her phone number and address, which is why I knew she belonged to you in the first place."

"Wait, you said you were calling to apologize. For what?"

"Because I was snippy that day."

"You weren't snippy."

"I was."

"Maybe you were curt and somewhat distant, but not snippy."

"Anyhoo, I was in a bad mood and I think I wasn't nice and I should have at least let you give me a bandage."

"I'll give you a bandage anytime, baby."

She laughed.

"I may take you up on that someday," she said. "But I wanted to apologize and explain that the reason I was testy—"

"Curt."

"Whatever. The reason I was curt was that I had just broken up with Chris the night before and I was so mad at him and I still am, and mostly I was mad at myself for being so infatuated with an immature idiot like him."

"Jenny already told me. And you really don't owe me an apology, but I appreciate it. And for the record I just want to say that you deserve the best, E. B., and Chris Heaton is not the best. You deserve someone special and someone who is gaga over you, someone who is excited to be with you, thrilled to be with you."

"Thanks. And you know what, you're right. I do deserve all that. I really do, dammit."

"There you go."

"And I deserve someone who can *kiss,* dammit."

"Aim high," I said.

"A good old-fashioned kissing *virtuoso*."

"Sing it, sister."

"A kissing *genius*."

"Oh, baby."

She sighed. "So I've been in a funk," she said. "But I feel good now, with this Chris thing done. I feel like a new person. I feel like I have more than a new lease on life: I have a new *mortgage*."

I thought about that for a moment. "I'm not sure what that would mean," I said.

"Me either, but it sounds good."

"It does sound good. And I'm glad you feel liberated. You're young. You have your whole life ahead of you."

"Hey, don't patronize me, Jimbo, just because I'm a year younger than you."

We both laughed.

"Listen, Leo Peery: I know that you and I don't know each other as well as we should, and I know that for a long time Jenny filled my head with all kinds of misinformation and propaganda about you, but I've always liked you, and I want to be your friend, and I think you're great, and I'm glad we're neighbors, and I'm glad about all of it, and I like talking to you."

"I like talking to you, too."

"And this whole new Jenny thing is huge, you know. It's huge. Huge, huge, huge."

"Well, it's large," I said. "That's for sure."

"Oh, man, you don't even know. But what are you guys going to do? What does it all mean? I mean, are you guys going to finally get together when you only have, what, two months left before you both leave for college? Could you have planned worse timing?"

"I know, I know. Thanks for reminding me. And how we lost

those ten days because she was with her family, up at that resort . . ."

"Look, no, I'm sorry. I shouldn't be bringing that kind of stuff up. I don't mean to belittle your predicament. I'm just saying . . . I'm just saying . . . I don't know what I'm saying."

Mom's phone started ringing downstairs. I got out of bed and headed toward it.

"Don't worry about it," I said. "You just don't want us to get hurt."

"That's right."

"And I hear that. But my mom's phone is ringing right now and I feel like I should answer it."

"I'll let you go. I've got to call Jenny, anyway. But I'm glad we talked."

"Me too."

"I'll see you later."

"Okay, bye."

"Bye," E. B. said.

I turned off my phone and picked up the kitchen phone. A woman asked for Mom, but I explained that she wasn't due back until this evening.

"Is this Leo?" she asked.

"Yep."

"Oh, honey, this is Carla Carney, from your mom's office."

"Oh, sure, Carla. Hi."

Carla was one of the nurses. She explained that she had planned to leave for vacation Tuesday but that her plans had changed on account of a sick aunt and that therefore she was leaving first thing tomorrow morning and she hadn't been able to pick up her paycheck yesterday and today of course the office was closed and Brenda the office manager was out of town for the weekend and Dr. Beshears was in the OR and she needed to deposit the check today or tonight and she wondered if I had the keys to the office and whether I could help her if it wasn't too much of a bother. I said sure I could help her, and we agreed to meet at Mom's office after my shift at the pool.

From the seat of the second tower, I glanced up briefly at the sun, blazing above. It hardly seemed related to the heatless, orange globe that Jenny and I had watched rise some nine hours ago. But it had delivered to us the first truly hot day of the summer. Below me, the pool was busy. Across the pool, Pepper was slumped in the first tower. To my left, Greg was in the third tower.

I looked at my arms in the sunlight. I felt the sun's heat on my skin. And it was going deeper than my skin. It was going through me. I touched my forearm with my fingers, felt the heat there. Somehow this heat was part of me, but also separate from me. I twisted around and opened up the parasol that was attached to the back of the tower. I swung the parasol around so that it blocked the sun. The parasol was red and now I was living within a small domain of red shade, which accentuated the comfortable separateness I felt whenever I was on duty above the pool. The pool itself, even seen through my dark sunglasses, was a shocking blue color, which every day surprised and pleased me.

It was difficult if not impossible to keep my eyes off the pool. Granted, it was my job to watch the water, to watch the people in the water. But even when I and my fellow lifeguards were not on duty, what did we do? We looked at the pool. We lounged in the pool house, leaning over the counter, facing the pool. We took our breaks in the concession area and drank our sodas and ate our snacks and what did we look at as we ate? The water. It is true that the sky was almost always beautiful, and sometimes it did keep my attention for a while—the sheets of feathery cirrus clouds in June and the slowly expanding popcorn clouds of July. But the pool was constant, and sunlight and shadow played off of it in a thousand different ways. It is true that the long, rising lawn beside the pool was gorgeous, and that the breeze-turned leaves of the maples and elms in the distance were mesmerizing. But the pool was more alive, somehow, than even those things.

Our shifts on the towers were thirty minutes. On a long day, you might sit in the tower as many as six times. In other circumstances, sitting alone for thirty minutes with no direct entertainment would be tedious. But in three summers I had never had a tower shift that bored or drained me. The seats were not designed for comfort, and there were only two sitting positions: slumped back or leaning forward, elbows on knees. But I'd never been uncomfortable. Sometimes you got up into the tower and you looked at your watch and then you looked at the pool briefly and inhaled the warm and summery air and then you felt a tap on your shoulder and the next lifeguard had come along to relieve you—the thirty minutes passed that fast. Other times, a shift felt luxuriously long, like a relaxing meditation or a scenic drive—but never slow or tedious.

What did you do? You watched the pool and you watched the people. There were rules to be enforced, yes. No running on the deck. Diving only in designated areas. No dunking. And so forth. But nothing ever went wrong, nothing serious. Someone got a small cut from one of the ladders. How? Easily enough treated. Someone lost a ring. We'd let them know if we found it. Some excited and/or scared little kid accidentally bit his tongue. Not to worry—the mouth is one of the fastest healing parts of the body.

But in the event something bad happened, we knew how to handle it, we had trained for it, had the tools for it, and we would do it right. We knew the procedures and techniques to confront any emergency that would occur here. Everything was well-defined and manageable and we would handle it. We knew what to do, and that was a comfort.

Someone touched my arm. It was Becky, hanging off the side of the tower. My shift was over.

"Relinquish thy throne," she said.

And now that the summer solstice had come and gone and it was suddenly hot and it was officially summer I did not feel guilty about applying the word summertime as an adjective to anything and everything. As I left the pool, I began to do this.

The summertime parking lot, at the swimming pool. The heat, the glare. And woe to the kid without shoes who tries to cross the hot asphalt.

The summertime parked car, so hot.

The summertime steering wheel, baked by the sun, too hot to touch so you steer by holding the bottom part.

The summertime kid-on-a-bike, with a beach towel draped around his neck, with a hat turned sideways, the spokes of his wheels winking in the sun.

The summertime bugs-on-the-windshield.

The summertime arm-out-the-car-window. In the breeze. Happy.

Your summertime skin, smooth from the heat, arm hairs bleached to blonde.

Your summertime stomach, empty but somehow not important. Growling. Growling. Growling some more.

"Settle down in there," I told my stomach. "Summertime stomach!" I added for emphasis.

It growled a response.

"Don't make me come down there!" I said.

It gurgled.

"I'll stop this summertime car right now!" I said. But I didn't, and my stomach continued to growl, and within a few minutes I pulled into the medical park and cruised through the empty upper lot and went around the corner of the building to the lower level and pulled up right in front of the door to Mom's office. Carla wasn't here yet but I got out of the car and went to the door because I wasn't sure which key opened the front door and there were nine keys to try.

Carla pulled up in a little pickup and I waved and tried another key on the door and she got out of the truck and she was in shorts and flip-flops and a tank top and in this outfit she didn't look like a nurse and she called out to me. "Look at you!" she said.

"Hi, Carla."

"Look at you!" she repeated, nearing. "I don't see you for a year and look at you, you've gone off and turned into a tall drink of water."

"It's true that I'm mostly water," I said, fumbling with another key.

She knew which key opened the door and soon we were in the office and Carla turned the hallway lights on and they buzzed and we went down the hall to the nurses' area and Carla looked around, thinking her check might be there, but it wasn't, so we went into the business office and looked there but we couldn't find it and so we unlocked my mother's personal office—where the payroll files were kept—and I sat down behind Mom's desk and rotated back and forth in her swivel chair and Carla found her check sitting right on top of the payroll file cabinet.

"Pay dirt," she said, and she opened the envelope and looked at the check. "I don't suppose you have any more of these lying around for me?"

I played along and looked under Mom's stapler and under her desk pad. "Well, I don't *see* any," I said.

We laughed and walked out of the office, turning off lights as we went, and Carla thanked me maybe six different times and told me to say hello to my mom when she got back and she locked the front door for me, since it was kind of a tricky door to lock, and then she said good-bye and told me to come around the office more often and chat and I said I'd try to fit it into my schedule and she got in her truck and I got in Mom's car and Carla drove away and I waited maybe a minute after she was out of sight and then I got out of the car and went back to the office door.

I unlocked the door and went into the office without turning on the lights, which was a mistake because by the time I got all the way down the hall and near Mom's office I couldn't see well and it took me a few moments to find the doorknob to her door and then I couldn't see which key was which and so I walked back down the hallway, heading toward the glow of the front door, and turned on the hallway lights and then returned to Mom's office door and unlocked it and went in. I turned on the lights and looked around at the office for a moment and then I sat down at her desk and I lifted up the desk pad and removed the sheet of paper that was hidden beneath it. This was the reason I'd come back, this paper that I'd accidentally caught a glimpse of a couple of minutes ago, and I knew I shouldn't be looking at it and I knew it was private but it was too late and what was it doing here? Why was it hidden?

It was the lab results for one of Mom's patients. The thing being measured was something called CA 125, and the normal range was given in one column and the lab results were listed in another column. The result was much higher than the normal range. I had no idea what this meant, of course, and I was feeling guilty enough about my breach of medical privacy and I started to put the paper back but then it struck me how odd it was that this lab report was hidden under Mom's desk pad and so I puzzled over the lab report and looked for the name of the patient. At the top of the page was my mother's name, "Julia C. Peery," which I assumed was listed there because she was the patient's doctor, but as I stared at the report and read it again and again it was pretty easy to see that there was no other name listed on the report and it finally registered that my mother wasn't listed here as the doctor, but as the *patient*.

Suddenly a garbly, chirpy noise filled the room and in shock I dropped the lab report—I kind of *threw* it, actually—and looked up, thinking I had tripped some kind of intruder alarm or something. But it was only my cell phone—which until a few weeks ago had been Mom's cell phone—and I wasn't used to the sound of its ringer. I pulled the phone from the pocket of my shorts.

"Hello?" I said.

"I'm calling about the car," a man said.

I was discombobulated. "The car?" I said. Had something happened to Mom's car in the few minutes I'd been inside the office?

"The ad for the Supra in the newspaper."

"Oh, sure. Sorry." I picked up the lab report and put it back under Mom's desk pad.

"I'm in town for just this afternoon and I was wondering if I could come by and have a look-see."

"Sure, sure," I said.

I gave him directions and then hung up. I locked up Mom's office and turned off the lights and closed the front door and tried to lock it. But I couldn't get the thing locked. When Carla had done it five minutes ago, I hadn't watched her. I knew there was some trick to it, some kind of simultaneous pushing and twisting—or pulling and lifting?—but try as I might, I couldn't get the key to budge. I was sure it was the correct key, and it fit the keyhole perfectly, but for whatever reason it wasn't working. Was it my fault? Well, clearly it wasn't the *key's* fault, and it wasn't the *lock's* fault. I withdrew the key and tried all the other keys on the key ring—just to be sure—but none of them worked and I fumbled for the original key again and dropped the whole key chain and I bent and picked it up and looked at the door and looked at my reflection in the glass and I tried the key one more time and then I left. The man who wanted to see the Supra would be at our house any moment.

And as I drove home, I tried to calm down and think clearly, but I knew that the ad for the Supra wasn't due to run in the paper until tomorrow and therefore how had this guy found out about it and gotten my number?

The man wasn't at our house yet, so I went inside and I went upstairs and booted up my laptop and I sat there looking at it and its hard disk was making muffled cricket noises and the operating system was loading and it was taking forever and I knew it had quite a ways to go yet and so I got up and changed out of my lifeguard garb and into some civilian garb and I looked at the computer and it was still gathering its resources. I growled at the computer and then went into my bathroom and washed my face and when I came back the computer was ready and the cable modem was already online and so I brought up a search engine and I paused, thinking, and I entered "CA 125" and the search engine immediately told me that there were some twelve thousand Web page matches and the first Web page listed was titled, "OVARIAN CANCER: Diagnosis, CA 125 measurements."

The doorbell rang.

I vaulted down the stairs and opened the front door but there was no one there, so I walked to the right, around the house, around the garage, and there, at the side door, stood Ruben, freshly showered, holding a huge bouquet.

"For me?" I asked.

I had startled him by coming from behind but he smiled at me and then he said, "Er," and he pointed to one of the tiny flowers in the arrangement, "this one's for you, but the rest are for Julia."

I told her that she'd like the flowers, and something in the way I said it made it clear that she wasn't home yet and this confused Ruben because he said that he thought she had arrived home this morning.

"She comes in tonight," I said. I looked at my watch. "Pretty soon, actually."

"Oh. I got it wrong," he said. "I wonder why I got it wrong?"

I asked him if he wanted to come with me to the airport to pick her up, but he hemmed and hawed and clearly he was uncomfortable and unsure for some reason and so before he actually answered the question, I said, "Let's get those flowers in a vase," and I reached for the side door but it was locked—and it's always a shock when the door you think is unlocked is not—and so we walked around to the front of the house and went in and Ruben lingered in the foyer and he was looking dejected. I put the flowers in water and then asked Ruben to help me push the Supra out of the garage. The two of us combined were actually too strong, because we rolled the Supra a bit too fast and I had to lunge in the passenger's window and pull the hand brake to stop the car from rolling into the retaining wall.

"Ow," I said, extracting myself from the car, and I knew I'd hurt myself somewhere, but I wasn't quite sure where.

We stepped back and looked at the Supra and it looked good in the driveway, reflecting the evening sky, and I wondered how long it had been since the car had been outside.

"That's a pretty thing," Ruben said.

I nodded.

Ruben said good-bye and walked to his car. He started the car and then he leaned out the window.

"The sunroof is still leaking, you know," he said.

I walked over, observed the sunroof from the outside.

"I took it to the dealership," he said, "and they said it needed a whole new motor assembly. Or mount assembly?"

"Mount assembly?" I said. "Sounds made-up."

"Some kind of assembly."

"I bet the gasket is just pinched," I said, and I promised again that he and I would look at it together—he just had to swing by anytime I was here. That seemed to make him happy, and he said that after we fixed the sunroof maybe we could play a little one-on-one, and I said that that was just fine by me and that beating him at basketball was always good for my ego. "Ha!" he said. He backed out of the drive and waved and drove away. I waved, belatedly, and then looked back at the Supra. I looked at my watch and it was after seven and the sun was still far from the horizon and I inhaled and looked around, trying to absorb the luxuriousness of the long summer evening, but it was something I couldn't force.

Inside, after a few minutes on the Internet, I couldn't take any more. I shut the computer off and headed downstairs. I started opening cabinet doors, looking for food. I walked into the pantry and I picked up a can of stewed tomatoes and then I put it back on the shelf and I picked up a box of pasta but boiling a pot of water seemed to be a tedious thing to have to do at the moment and so I was about to decide against pasta when the doorbell rang. I left the pantry and I was still carrying the pasta and I set it on the counter and went to the side door but there was no one there. I walked back through the house and the cat, in a playful mood, ambushed me from the cover of the den. She streaked toward me, but when she hit the tiles of the entry hall, she realized she couldn't stop and she slid flailing into my ankle and then got up and retreated immediately back into the den, embarrassed. "No hard feelings," I called after her, and I opened the front door and there was a man in a bomber jacket—a jacket in late June?—which somehow didn't go with his aviator sunglasses at all. And he was chewing gum and he introduced himself as Chuck Somethingorother. It was either Shaybing or Shellbing.

When we approached the Supra, he stopped some twenty feet from it. He took off his sunglasses and put them in his jacket pocket. He was just slightly cross-eyed. And I noticed that he had stopped chewing his gum, too.

"Your ad wasn't too specific," he said.

"Well, you know there's that price break point where if you limit your ad to ten words or less it costs basically nothing."

"It wasn't too specific," he said, and I didn't know what to say to this fact a second time.

He exhaled through his nose, eyes scanning the car. After a while, he started nodding, satisfied. "The 1984 Toyota 'MKII' Celica Supra P-Type," he said. "Two-point-eight-liter double-overhead camshaft, EFI, in-line 5M-GE six-cylinder; 225/60 performance radials. Vented disc brakes. Independent rear suspension, limited-slip differential. Alloy wheels, leather, AC, stereo, sunroof."

"Where'd you see the ad?" I asked.

He was walking toward the car now, slowly. "Huh?" he finally said.

"Because I thought the ad wasn't going to come out until tomorrow. I was pretty sure it was coming out in the Sunday paper first."

He was sighting along the body panels, looking for dings.

"I have a contact at the newspaper," he said. "She knows what kind of cars I'm looking for, and she lets me know when one comes on the market. Preferably *before* it comes on the market."

He was a professional, then. I walked to the front of the car and sat on the retaining wall and let him do his business. One of the things the ad had neglected to list was a price, and I was suddenly trying to decide what kind of offer would be acceptable.

He took his time. He poked and prodded and assessed the car methodically. He made use of a little flashlight. He looked for rust, checking inside the rear fenders, under the front spoiler attachment, on the inside seams of the doors, on the rear shock towers, and all the other usual places. He got down on his back and looked under the car in a couple of different places. Then he popped the hood. And he began asking me questions about the storage of the car—whether the garage was climate-controlled, how the fluids were maintained, and so forth.

"Of course, since it hasn't been started in years," he said, "I need to take it into the shop and have a quick peek inside before I could complete any purchase. A little internal investigation."

"Of course," I said.

"It looks like it's in great shape. Not a ding, not a dent, not a flake of rust. And it sounds like you've done all the right things with it, but long-term storage can be tricky. One time I picked up a '77 911 from an auction yard and I got it home and tore it open and there was rust everywhere—cylinders, valves, manifold. So I took it back to the auctioneers, and of course they weren't really responsible for any such surprises, but I'd done a lot of business with them and they wanted to keep on my good side, so they—"

And suddenly he stopped talking. He was in the driver's seat, and he was looking at the instrument panel. He squinted and leaned closer. Clearly he was distracted by something. He got out of the car and came around to the engine compartment again and leaned over it. His mood had changed. Why? I stood up and casually walked around the entire car. Then I sat in the driver's seat, my feet still planted in the driveway, and I looked at the instrument panel. What had he seen? Speedometer, tachometer, odometer . . .

The odometer.

Frankly I'd never even noticed it myself. I hadn't put the mileage in the paper.

The odometer read 4,201. I could hardly believe it. So low.

Suddenly, he let the hood drop closed. We looked at each other through the windshield, and we knew the stakes of this sale were greater than we'd thought. I got out of the car and closed the door. He put his palms against the car's hood like he was touching a living creature. He started walking down the passenger side of the car, running one hand along the roofline. At the back of the car he paused and stepped back for a moment and then stepped forward and I heard him sigh through his nose and he was looking down at the hatchback and I wondered if he was looking at his reflection in the glass. He put a hand on the glass.

I had moved to the front of the car and I was leaning on the retaining wall. After a long moment, he looked at me. The car was between us.

"Three thousand dollars," he said. "Contingent upon inspection."

"No," I said. "That won't work."

"Four thousand. I'll have it towed across town and inspected right now and you'll have your money by midnight."

"No," I said. "There are only four thousand miles on this thing," I said, as much to myself as to him. "This is a museum piece."

"Work with me here," he said. "I can get this car into factory-floor condition."

"I could do it myself," I said.

He looked at me intently, but I didn't care. I was looking at the car, Mom's car.

"Six thousand," he said.

Not thirty minutes later, I walked through the airport and in the distance I saw Mom coming toward me. I stopped at the security gate and she got closer and she didn't see me yet and she was somewhat alone—not surrounded by a throng of people from her flight. I watched her and saw her exhaustion and when she came through the gate she finally saw me and we hugged and she felt insubstantial in my arms. I looked down at her face and her eyes were tired and her lips were dry and she dropped her carry-on bag.

I saw through the fatigue and the jet lag and the rumpled clothes: she was sick, deep inside, and she had known for weeks.

"I'm beat," she said.

We waited at the luggage carousel and she sat down and slumped sideways in her seat, leaning on her carry-on bag. When we'd collected her luggage, we trudged to the car. We paid and left the parking lot and drove down the long airport access road and there were three jets sitting on the runway, their lights blinking in the day's final sunlight, and I was pretty sure that Mom was already asleep. But when I turned onto the highway and accelerated, she stirred in her seat and looked out the front and side windows and then looked at me for a moment. Then she settled back into her seat—she was kind of curled there.

"There were a lot of birds," she said.

I thought maybe she was talking in her sleep—or at least on the edge of sleep—so I didn't respond.

"I said there were a lot of birds," she said.

"Where?"

"Grímsey." Her voice was groggy. "Grímsey. And when you look into the eye of a bird, you don't see the individual bird. You see the collective bird."

"What kind of birds?" I asked.

"Plus there are those eyelids of theirs that close from bottom to top. You look at birds and their . . . *busy-ness* and their songs and all their bug-collecting and hopping and you think *hey, settle down. Pick a place and be there.*"

She was loopy.

"But they don't," she said. "They do not."

She went on.

"I walked the perimeter of the island. So small. And the cliffs. And there are only three things there: wind, sky, and water. And birds. Which are a combination of the three. Birds. And I don't remember any smells there and the ocean that surrounded it felt like a large lake, even though I knew it wasn't, and some of the other tourists said that it felt like the island was *moving,* but I didn't feel that."

She made a small laugh noise in her throat. *"Europeans,"* she said derisively.

She stopped talking. We were cruising along the highway still. I looked at the clock.

"I think," she said, "that birds want to exist in more than one place at a time."

"I might agree with that," I said.

"I think," she said, "that each bird is a multitude, and each multitude of birds is an individual."

This was getting out of hand.

"Tell me about the solstice," I said.

"Oh," she said. "Clouds."

"Clouds?"

"Clouds. We couldn't see the sun. They came about noon, these clouds. We were eating sausages and drinking wine and here came the clouds. Covering the whole sky, flat clouds, no breaks, dull color. They reached all the way to every horizon. Or I guess it's just one big horizon—you could see the whole thing at once. And you couldn't *see* beyond the horizon, but you could *feel* beyond the horizon, and beyond the horizon were clouds, too.

"And pretty soon the clouds began to feel like a ceiling. I began to feel like I was in a room, a huge room. The light was unchanging and the day was long and I had been up since four and I was not tired and no one around me seemed tired and that's exactly what I'd read in the guidebooks and it was a strange day and not entirely liberating. And the bonfires . . .

"So finally . . . ," she said, and then she sighed and paused. "So finally I knew they weren't going anywhere. It was getting late, it was getting to be after ten o'clock. And it was still light, of course, and I was talking to some girl who was a professor in Reykjavík—and I say girl but she was probably thirty-five. And she was traveling alone, too, and she spoke some passable English but really it wasn't very good but we liked each other and so she and I started going around to all the people and talking to them. She knew Icelandic and Swedish and some German, English, and French, and I knew English and French and finally we were talking to a man from Denmark and he was saying that he had an airplane and he'd flown to Grímsey and we were talking to him in German, which he didn't know very well and my professor friend didn't know very well, and then she was passing it on to me in French and English, and so it was hard to really pinpoint our communications precisely, but information was being passed and ideas were being born, and we three went for a short walk and then there we were, at the airport, which was really just a gravel runway, and this man's little airplane was there and it was shining and yellow, even though there was no sunlight, just clouds. And I can't remember the name of the girl, the Icelandic girl, the professor. Freya, Freeya, Theia? That's not right at all. She taught accounting or statistics? I think she actually said she taught 'numbers.' So maybe that means math. And, and . . . So the Dane—*the Dane,* isn't that great?—he points to his yellow plane, and there's a name painted on the plane and he tells the girl what the name means in German she tells me what it means in French and what she said was *soleil luire.* Sun glimmer? And in the plane—So we're in the plane, and this Danish man . . ."

She stopped talking. We had turned off the highway and were nearing our neighborhood. I was stopped at a stoplight and there weren't any other cars nearby and the car's turn signal was blinking. Mom was sitting up straight, looking around like she'd never been here before.

"So you're in the plane . . . ," I prompted.

"And up we go. Like that. Just like that. You couldn't hear much, I mean the engine was so loud, and we were shouting in our three or four languages and I'm not sure how much real communicating was going on. And the clouds were high, let me tell you. We went up, and the island kind of withered away below us and then we circled the island and there were all the bonfires down there, there they were. Like the siege of Troy. And we turned north and then we were in the clouds for what seemed like a long time. You couldn't see anything, but they made everything very bright inside the cabin of the plane. The cabin which was so small and I was right next to the Dane and the professor was sitting sideways behind us and there wasn't even really a seat back there. I think there was a toolbox, she was sitting on a toolbox, or a . . . a . . . box, metal box. . . . So, what was I talking about? I, oh, I . . ."

"You were in the clouds."

"And then we were through them—*whoosh*—although it didn't make a noise. One second it was clouds and the next second it was no clouds, and the sun was right in front of us, smack dab in the north, right above the horizon, and I looked at my watch and it was pretty close to midnight and suddenly we had a bottle of peppermint schnapps there with us and I think we were toasting the sun, the midnight sun, and the Dane was happy and the professor was happy and I was happy and underneath us was the layer of clouds, the huge sheet of clouds— nothing else. So we flew. We flew around, and midnight came and the sun dipped into the clouds, but not all the way, and then it came out and floated free and we cheered and the Dane said to me in English 'I say good morning! I say good morning!' So that was basically it. That was the solstice. A week ago now."

"That's a great story," I said. "I like that story."

"And as we came back down, the Dane kept thanking us for thinking of the idea, although I'm not quite sure who truly thought of it. I think all three of us thought of it. Each of us thought of a little part of it and without the others it wouldn't have been fully conceived. And I think if we had spoken a common language we would not have come up with the idea, not have made the assumptions and leaps of imagination that were necessary. I think. That's what I think."

We were driving into our neighborhood, nearing our house. All the talking had animated Mom, and she was watching the houses pass.

"Anyway," she said, "I told you the whole thing would be a dream."

Kitty was sitting in the middle of the den, facing the door to the garage as if she were welcoming Mom home.

"Kitty!" Mom said, and she went to the cat and I carried Mom's bags to the bottom of the stairs and then I went back to the car and got the rest and when I returned to the house Mom was lying on the carpet with Kitty and Kitty wasn't sure how to handle this and so she walked away. As I headed upstairs with Mom's bags, I heard her say, "It's so big!" I stopped on the stairs.

"What's so big?" I called.

"The house!" she said. "It's so big!"

"I had it enlarged," I said. "While you were gone," I said, and I waited. "Do you like it?" I called. But there was no response. I put the bags in Mom's room and went back downstairs and Mom was there at the counter looking at the box of pasta, reading it, and I asked her if she wanted a glass of water or juice and she said she was parched and could I get her some water and so I got her some water and put it down on the counter near her and she looked at it and then went back to reading the pasta box and then said, "When was Ruben here?"

She must have already read the card on the flowers, which were on the table in the dining room.

"Over an hour ago. Two hours ago."

Now she was sorting her pile of mail into new piles. I asked her if she was hungry and if she wanted to eat and she said no in a distracted way and she took some of her mail and walked toward the daybed but as she got near it she glanced out the window and saw the Supra, which was still sitting in the driveway and which she hadn't commented on at all when we had arrived.

"Well, I'm hungry," I said, "and I'm going to make pasta."

Now Mom sat on the daybed and started opening her mail.

"We broke up, you know," she said.

"What?" I asked.

"I broke up with Ruben before I left for Europe."

"Mom! I didn't know that. You didn't tell me that!"

"I almost didn't tell *him.*"

"But why'd you break up with him?"

"Oh, so few reasons," she said.

I had put a pot of water on the range. I turned on the burner and then leaned on the counter, looking toward Mom.

"He seemed really down when I saw him today," I said.

She shrugged.

"He seemed *lost,*" I said. "So this explains that."

"We can talk about it tomorrow," Mom said, "but there's really not much to talk about. It's just that he and I weren't heading in the same direction anymore."

"What does that mean?" I asked.

But she was absorbed in some letter she was reading.

"Mom . . . ," I prompted.

I walked over.

"Mom," I said.

She was still reading. It looked like a business letter.

"What's that?" I asked.

"The hospital," she said.

"What about?" I asked.

"All that management stuff. Looks like they're going to make those cuts they talked about."

"Jeez," I said.

She dropped the letter and looked to the side, out the window.

"It doesn't affect me, but it does affect my patients," she said.

"I'm sorry," I said. "I'm sorry."

I knelt in front of her.

"It's okay," she said. "It's not entirely your fault that the administration is morally bankrupt."

"Not about that," I said. I took her hand. My hand was shaking.

She smiled at me and touched my chin.

"What is it?" she asked.

"The car," I said, and my voice was trembling. "I didn't sell the car."

"I'm sure it will sell soon."

"No, it's not . . . Someone already offered a lot of money. But I—"

I was crying now.

"Leo?" she said, and she slid down onto the floor beside me. "What is it?"

"I want to keep the car. I don't want to sell it. I can't sell it. It isn't right. It's ours. I don't want a new car, I want the Supra. I want it to be my car."

"That's fine, Leo. That's fine."

"I'll fix it up, it won't take much money."

"We'll work something out. You can have it. You can have the car."

I sighed and then smiled.

"What's this about?" she asked. "This isn't about the car."

I shrugged. "I don't know. I'm just glad you're back, that's all. This is my last summer here, and I don't want to go."

"I know."

"I don't want to leave you." I kissed her cheek.

"I know," she said.

"I guess I'm just weak," I said, wiping my eyes.

"You're not weak," she said. "Not in the least."

She kissed my cheek, put her hand on my head.

"And I hurt my ribs today when I pushed the Supra out of the garage. I think I bruised my ribs," I said, massaging my rib cage.

"I'm sorry," she said.

"And I guess I'm just really hungry. I didn't have lunch. I didn't have supper."

"Leo! You can't live on air."

"I think maybe it's too late, though. I've missed my chances to eat and now I just have to wait until tomorrow."

"We've both had a long day, I think," Mom said.

I nodded.

"Today," Mom said, "since I woke up, I had a breakfast, a lunch, some wine and cheese, another lunch, a snack, a dinner, and some peanuts. And some gum. If gum counts."

"Gum doesn't count," I said, smiling. "Gum never counts."

She mussed my hair. "I'm liking this new haircut of yours," she said.

She told me to finish making my pasta while she went and got the present she had brought me. I sat there while she walked away and I listened to her climb the stairs and then the house was quiet and I noticed that the sun had finally and fully set and I felt drained. I got up and went to the kitchen and my pot of water wasn't boiling yet so I went and sat in the window seat and waited for Mom to come back. The backyard, viewed from these windows, had an appearance of unreality. The twilight lent it a sense of stillness and definition.

She was sick. She was dying, and that's why she cried a few weeks ago when I said the summer was trying to kill me, and that's why she didn't plant her garden this year, and that's why she broke up with Ruben. What could I do to help her? If she didn't even tell me, what could I do?

I stood up and went upstairs. I stopped just outside her room. "Mom?" I called. There was no answer. "Mom?" The door was open and the lights were on, so I went in. And for a second I couldn't see her, figured she must be in the bathroom, but then I saw her on the bed. She'd fallen asleep. How many hours had she been awake? Thirty? Thirty-five? I turned off the lights and closed her door. I stood there at the door, looking at the grain in the wood. I put my hand back on the doorknob for a moment, then let go.

In my room I paced. I opened my windows—the air-conditioning felt oppressive for some reason. I changed out of my shorts and into jeans. I picked up the CDs and clothes that were on the floor. I looked at my bookshelf and sat down in front of it and took the books off the shelves and started to rearrange them based on how much I liked them, but soon I realized that it was impossible to rank them precisely and that at the moment I didn't really like any of them. They were simply objects. They were things.

I went into the bathroom and let warm water run over my hands. I started to draw a warm bath and I sat on the rim of the tub and waited for the tub to fill. I got out of my clothes and got in the water and I was shivering and I wanted bubbles in the tub and so I poured some bubble bath in but I didn't like the smell of the bubble bath and the bubbles didn't want to froth and foam like usual. I should have added the bubble bath while I was drawing the bath.

I leaned back, relaxing into the water, but I was not comfortable in any respect. My heart seemed to hesitate for a moment and then it beat one huge beat that I could feel throughout my limbs and in my fingertips and also around the perimeter of my skull. I sat bolt upright and felt a surge of adrenaline. I looked at my fingernails and they were slightly blue and I wasn't sure this was the color they were supposed to be. The bathroom was too bright and the tile floor was gleaming. I started shivering again. I got out of the tub.

In my room, I called Jenny.

"Can I come over?" I asked.

"Can you come *over* . . . ," she said. "Can *you* come over . . . Can you—dot, dot, dot—come over . . ." Then she clicked her tongue and made fake thinking noises like "Hm," and "Er . . ."

"Jenny Previer," I said. "I'm waiting."

"Okay," she said.

After I dressed, I checked to make sure Mom's lights were still out, then I went downstairs. A lot of lights were on down here, so I turned some of them off. My pot of water was boiling away on the range and so I turned the burner off. Mom's untouched glass of water was on the counter. Kitty was on the dining room table, sitting by the vase of flowers.

At Jenny's house, I prowled around to the back. I called Jenny on my cell phone.

"Where are you?" I asked.

"I'm in the reading room. The back door is open."

"Where are your parents?"

"Out. Come up and find me."

She hung up and I looked up at the house and there were lights in different rooms. I called Jenny back.

"Which one is the reading room?" I asked.

"Behind the study," she said.

"The library?"

"No, the study. The second floor."

"Got it."

I slipped through the back door. The lights in the Previer house were controlled by a computer, and at the moment they were on a very dim nighttime setting. I had to stand for a moment in the solarium and let my eyes adjust, but it became clear that no amount of adjusting would alter the otherworldly mood of the lights. My skin looked particularly tan in this light.

I made my way into the kitchen and drew myself a glass of water. I drank the entire glass and then I put the glass in the sink. I went up the back stairs and walked to the other end of the house, went into the study and then into the reading room that was off the study. There was Jenny, summertime Jenny, wearing a floppy sweatshirt and shorts. She was all legs, reclining on the long couch with a book and her phone. She smiled and I went to her. I slipped off my sandals and knelt there in front of the couch. The room was small—or small relative to most of the rooms in the house—and it was quiet and secluded and dim. The carpeting was soft. Through the windows I could see the lingering stain of the sunset in the northwest, even though it was after ten.

"Hi," Jenny said.

I took her hand and put the back of it against my cheek for a moment.

"I found you," I said.

"Congratulations," she said.

"I came all the way across town," I said. "In the dark."

I took her hand, which I was still holding, and I turned it over and kissed the heel of her thumb and she tensed up briefly and then I kissed the base of each of her fingers and she reached out and lifted my face and looked at me.

"I wonder sometimes," I said, "what you are like."

I ran the tip of my finger lightly across her palm, tracing loops.

"I wonder . . . ," I said.

"Leo . . ."

I pushed up the sleeve of her sweatshirt and let my fingers slide up and then back down the inside of her arm. At her wrist there was the flicking of her pulse. I watched it and then I touched it and then I moved up and put my head against her breastbone and listened to the beating of her heart. I closed my eyes and she put one hand in my hair and I lost the sense of time passing. After a while, I turned my face toward her chest and my nose rubbed her sweatshirt and I inhaled so that I could smell the sweatshirt. I turned my ear to her chest again and listened.

I spoke and my voice was muffled and I knew that she could feel my voice against her: "I'm listening," I said. And suddenly she inhaled quickly and deeply and my head moved as her chest expanded and she took my face and turned it toward her own. We looked at each other and then she moved forward to kiss me but I turned away.

"Leo!" she said.

I put my nose against the base of her neck and inhaled. Then I smelled her hair. She reached back and released her hair from her ponytail and it fell down on my face and it was a surprise and I had never felt a thing like it in my life. I nosed through her hair for a moment, happily lost, then pulled back. I was still kneeling on the floor and she was still reclining on the couch.

"Kiss me," she said.

I leaned and kissed her just above both her knees. Then I kissed up her thigh. She was stillness then. I kissed against her shorts and then I begin moving up and kissing against the sweatshirt. I came to the breastbone again, then the base of her neck. I kissed the base of her neck, then I pressed the width of my hand against her breastbone and looked at it. My hand covered her breastbone and there was heat between my hand and Jenny.

Looking at my hand I said, "This is where I want to be."

"You can," she said.

"I could exist between here," I said, pressing my palm against her, "and here," I said, running my other hand up her back, inside her sweatshirt, until it was between her shoulder blades. Her skin was smooth and dry and she wore nothing beneath the sweatshirt. She was between my hands and I could feel the energy inside her.

She tried to kiss me again and I dodged and began kissing her neck instead.

"Leo . . ."

She was inhaling and exhaling, her heart was beating, her voice was sounding, her body was warm—I could feel all of this between my palms. The small amount of sweat between my palms and Jenny was not hers or mine but ours. I kissed behind her ears and then I kissed in front of her ears and then I kissed across her cheekbones and she closed her eyes and I could feel her eyelashes. She lifted her mouth toward me and tried to kiss me again but I turned my face and she kissed the side of my neck instead and I moved my other hand so that it was under her sweatshirt too and both my hands were against her back—one high, one low—and I rested my forehead against her chest for a moment and she ran her hands through my hair.

She started tugging on me, trying to pull me onto the couch. "Come up here," she said. "Come up here with me."

"I wonder what you are like," I said, my ear against her chest again. "I wonder what you are like and I wait and I don't do anything and you can blame that on me."

"Come up here, Leo."

"I don't want to think," I said.

"If you won't come up here," she said, "I'm coming down there." And with my hands still on her back, she rolled toward me and suddenly she was falling off the couch and onto me and we both let out a little yelp as she fell and then she landed on me and started laughing, but I was wincing and for a moment I couldn't seem to breathe.

"What's wrong?" she asked.

"I bruised my ribs or something," I said. "You landed on them."

I was clenching my teeth and trying to put the pain away, but it couldn't be ignored. Jenny gently removed herself from me and knelt beside me.

"Oh, I'm sorry, I'm sorry," she said. "I didn't know." She kissed my forehead.

"It's okay," I said, "I just did it this afternoon."

"You're crying," she said.

"Because it hurts," I said. "It really hurts."

"What can I do?" she asked.

"It's going away," I said. "But no more falling off couches onto me," I said. "No matter how much I want you to."

"You come to me wounded," she said. "It's our thing."

"It doesn't make any sense," I said.

"I know."

"All I ask for is for things to make a little bit of sense. Just a little bit."

"I know."

The pain had retreated and I wiped my face.

"Let me see your leg," Jenny said. And she pulled up the left leg of my jeans. I propped myself up on my elbows. Jenny looked at the pale remnants of the place where I'd been skinned in my bike wreck. Then she took both her hands and she put them on the scar.

"Now sit up," she said. I sat up and she moved behind me and she searched through the hair at the back of my head for the diving accident wound. She couldn't find it. It was healed.

"Now hold still," she said, and she lifted my shirt. "Raise your arms." She removed my shirt completely. "Show me where it hurts," she said.

I very gently traced the tender area on the left side of my rib cage. She nodded and then she pushed me backwards so that I was lying down again. She straddled me and then rubbed her palms together to generate heat and then applied her palms to my bruise. The sensation was so soft that I wasn't sure if she was touching me at all. All I could feel was heat and her presence. We looked at each other.

After a time, she removed her hands and leaned forward and kissed the perimeter of the bruised area. This time I knew she was touching me, I could feel it for sure and I must have gasped because she asked if it hurt and I had to tell her no, it didn't hurt. She continued kissing me, and it felt as if it was drawing me upward, a kind of gentle tugging, like I was being pulled toward a new and wondrous world. I could feel it across all my skin—not just on my chest. And I could feel it within my spine and around the back of my head. And there was a growing heat within my chest, a billowing sensation of warmth and connection and peace. When it expanded to a point where it had filled me completely, I shuddered. I opened my eyes.

Jenny paused. She sat up and we looked at each other. I was conscious of the weight of her, the beautiful line of her lips, the rhythm of her breathing, and the innumerable curves of her hair. But mostly I was aware of *her,* of the whole Jenny, her physicality, her emotions, all her experiences and memories, her disappointments, her potential, her mortality, her faults, her frailty, her youth. We were in the full presence of each other, and the warmth and connection and peace that had bloomed within me moments ago was now shared between us.

I put my hands on her hips. This was a gesture of connection. We were still looking at each other. She put her palms against the back of my hands, pressing firmly. Then she stirred and lifted her sweatshirt over her head and put it on the couch. She leaned over me, her hands planted beside my head, her hair coursing down toward my face, and she began to slowly, very slowly, lower herself toward me. When finally her hair touched my face, she paused. Then she lowered herself more. Her breasts came against me, then her stomach. Our faces were nearly together. Her hair was all around me, shutting out light. We were excluding the world. Our torsos were smooth against each other and I could feel the breath coming from her and moving across my face. Finally, I could not wait any longer, and I lifted my chin ever so slightly and went to kiss her. But she dodged me.

"We can both play that game," she said, and she began kissing my neck and then my chest.

"Wait wait wait wait wait wait wait," she said, hurriedly, in the midst of pleasure, but it was a voice from far away, whereas the taste and moisture of her was close to me and powerful and I could not turn away, could not slow. My mouth could have dwelt there forever, but she moved off of me.

"What?" I asked, taking her hand.

"I want you inside," she said.

It happened easily, and the heat of her charged me and she was still for a split second, as if in slight pain, and then she exhaled evenly and opened her eyes.

Then, and finally, we kissed.

Eight

AFTERWARD, IN HER ROOM, WE LAY ON HER BED. SHE TRIED TO talk, tried to stay with me, but her eyelids were heavy, and I told her to let go. I held her and watched her. Slowly, very slowly, she fell asleep. Her breaths became long and regular. Her face relaxed. The weight of her settled. Her arms and legs twitched a few times. And when she was finally and fully asleep, I held her still and I did not want to go and I did not want to sleep. This was stasis, and I would accept it.

But I did fall asleep. I sank deep into a profound stillness until from some distant quarter there came an ominous alert. What was it? There was a numbness and a sense of panic and a feeling of helplessness and a startling fear of loss.

I jerked awake. The shadows and space of Jenny's room were puzzling for a moment. There was an unexplained anxiousness within me and I tried to sit up but I couldn't. Jenny was lying on my entire left arm. I was wedged between her and the wall. I tried to gently wriggle my arm free, but to no avail. My arm was numb and seemingly paralyzed. And then I heard voices. I stopped moving and listened. There were voices in the house, and movements. Jenny's parents were home, and here I was, lying half-naked on Jenny's bed, with the door to her bedroom wide-open, with the lights on.

I listened carefully. Her parents were far away, perhaps downstairs.

I pulled my arm carefully from beneath Jenny. She didn't wake. I sat up and looked around. I was wearing my jeans, but my shirt was not in sight. It was still in the reading room, along with my sandals. At least my wallet and car keys were with me in my jeans.

I turned off the light in Jenny's room and stood at her doorway, looking down the hallway. Her parents' suite was between her room and the reading room. There were lights on in her parents' suite, but I couldn't tell if someone was up here or not. There hadn't been any voices in a while. Then there was the faint sound of water running. A shower?

My left arm hung limply and I moved it but I still could not feel it.

As I stood waiting, the lights coming from Jenny's parents' suite suddenly winked out—the door had been closed. I was pretty sure there was still water running somewhere, but I hadn't heard any noises from downstairs.

I slid through the house silently. The downstairs was dark—almost too dark. I reached one of the side doors, the one that opened onto the north side of the courtyard, and I already felt a sense of relief and release and escape. The door was locked, so I turned the dead bolt and pulled the door open and immediately I knew I had made a mistake. There was a chirping noise behind me and it was not my cell phone. I knew what this noise was because I'd heard it before, over a year ago.

I'd tripped the security alarm.

What was I to do? I slipped out, closed the door, skirted the pool, hurried through the shadows at the edge of the front lawn, then jogged barefoot to the car.

July

Nine

I STOOD IN THE ATTIC OF THE FARMHOUSE, LOOKING UP AT the sheathing. There were two windows in the gables up here, but the light was weak. I went down the attic stairs and then down to the first floor. I knew there was a flashlight here because Paer and I had used it last night when we were changing the air filter in his truck. The kitchen counters were littered with tools and the faucet was dripping and I looked around and couldn't figure out where the flashlight would be. Maybe Paer had it with him in the truck. I went to the faucet and tightened the handle but the drip continued.

"Compression faucet," I said to myself, still looking at the faucet. "Worn stem washer." This was my way of adding it to the list of things to fix.

I found the flashlight on the back porch and took it to the attic. I was inspecting the sheathing in the south gable when my toe hit something and I nearly stumbled. I looked down and there were a couple of cardboard boxes. I hadn't seen them before—the rest of the attic was empty. I opened one of the boxes—it seemed to be a boot box—and the only thing inside was a well-worn straw cowboy hat. Its sides were rolled up and the front bill was bent down rakishly and it wasn't dusty or cobwebby or mouse-nibbled at all. I walked over to one of the windows to look at it in the light. But the window was so dirty that I wasn't satisfied, so I lifted the bottom sash and the morning light came in and immediately there was a thunking sound within the wall and the window rattled in its frame. I looked at the window. "Broken sash cord," I said, putting it on the list. "Or not," I said, since it wasn't a particularly important thing to repair.

I knelt on the floor and leaned out the open window, my elbows resting on the sill. Surprisingly the outside air was basically the same temperature as the attic air. I looked again at the cowboy hat. Someone had obviously loved this hat. Someone had worn it for years. I put it on, just out of curiosity.

It fit perfectly.

Paer was coming down the gravel road in his truck and he turned into the drive and stopped beside the back porch. He got out and he looked up at me and he didn't say anything. He reached into the bed of the pickup and lifted out four roof jacks and a roofing shovel.

"Saddle up, cowboy," he called.

"We're going to need some plywood," I said.

"Today?"

"Presumably. There's some bad sheathing up here."

"For the love of frick," he said.

"And some three-inch deck screws."

"Deck screws . . ."

"And some eightpenny siding nails. Ring shank."

"Is there anything that's *not* broken in my house?"

"Too early to tell," I said.

Suddenly, from around the corner of the house dashed the adolescent Doberman that Paer had gotten from a neighbor just a few days before I'd arrived.

"Hey!" Paer yelled at the dog, which raced toward him and

then dodged away playfully. Paer looked up at me. "You weren't supposed to let him out."

"I didn't know he was out."

"He must have jumped the fence again," Paer said.

The tear-off went quickly, and it was one of the more satisfying things I had done in a long time. The old, brittle shingles and building paper came off the house easily and we pushed them down the slope and listened to them fall into the yard below, where the dog barked at each falling load. By noon the entire roof was bare except for a few remaining nails and the flashings. Paer took care of the nails while I worked on the flashings, which it looked like we could reuse. Then we swept the roof clean and went and straddled the ridge and drank some water. The day was hot but not mean-spirited and we hadn't been harassed by wasps at all. From the ridge of the old farmhouse you could see a re-markable stretch of wooded hills to the south and east. In the op-posite direction were the bottomlands, and we were up high enough that we could see the glimmer of the creek at a couple of bends. Paer's cows were lounging in the shade at the far end of the barnyard pasture. Paer was in a good mood and he kept looking at the broad, bare roof and you could feel the pride in him. He'd moved out here only last week, and he'd called me a few days later.

We made some final inspections and calculations—doing math with a piece of chalk right on the bare sheathing of the house—then came down from the roof and put the dog back in the pen. The dog was still angry with the big piles of shingles in the yard, and he didn't want to go in the pen, but he had no say in the matter. We got in Paer's old Ford pickup—a recent purchase—and headed out the driveway. A minute or so down the gravel road, Paer was looking in the rearview mirror and I could tell he saw something so I turned around and looked be-hind us and there was the Doberman, chasing after us.

"Wait," I said, "we don't want him to get lost."

"He won't."

"We should stop."

"He does this. He's done this before—he has to learn his lesson."

"At least you could speed up," I said.

Paer accelerated.

Though we were pulling away from the dog, he continued pursuing us without flagging. He was the kind of dog where you knew that there wasn't much activity going on in his brain, just little twitches and flickerings existing within a good-natured sphere of perplexity and instinct and appetite. I watched him as we drew farther away from him, and his pace remained the same. He was a strong dog—I gave him that. He was certainly inhaling a great quantity of dust, which was impressive in its own way, though sad. His black body faded back, back, back, until he was just a speck of motion in the distance, a bead of activity. We turned a corner and lost him.

At the lumberyard we got the plywood and fasteners we needed. We loaded the truck and then idled sixty feet down the shoulder of the street to Cort and Corene's house. The shade here was deep and welcome. I went into Cort's workshop to get another hammer. Paer went in the house to get us some soda. When we met back in the truck, we opened our sodas and drank and Paer started the truck. "Mom wants us to drive to the pool and pick up Gracie," he said. We crossed town, crested the little hill behind the school, passed the cement tennis court—with grass growing in its cracks—and came to the pool. The pool was busy. We got out of the truck and leaned against the chain-link fence and observed the swimmers and sunbathers. We were outside the pool and this made us both superior and inferior to the people inside. Finally, we saw Gracie and called her over.

"Why don't you guys have shirts on?" she asked.

"We're shingling the farmhouse," Paer said. "It's hot."

"Well, you look like *workers*," Gracie said.

"We are workers," Paer said.

"I like your hat," she said to me. I still had the cowboy hat on.

"He's been wearing that thing all day," Paer said. "It's unexplainable."

"Your mom said we're supposed to take you home," I said.

"I don't think I'm ready to leave," Gracie answered.

"Still, those are the orders," Paer said.

"Then you can tell Mom that I'll walk home."

"We're not a messenger service," Paer said.

"I'll just walk home," she resolved.

"We don't have time to fuss around, Gracie," Paer said.

"I'm not fussing. I'm just *saying*," she said.

"You are fussing," Paer said. "Come on, we have to go."

"Give me a drink of your soda," she said to me.

The fence was too high to pass the soda over, so I poked the neck of the bottle through the fence and Gracie drank from it.

"We do kinda need to get moving," I told her.

"Only if I can come out to the farm with you guys."

"No," Paer said.

"Why not?"

"We're working."

Gracie looked to me. "Don't you want me to come, Leo? I could supervise and make lemonade. And serve crackers and cheese."

"You'll get bored," Paer said, "and then you'll complain and then we'll have to waste time bringing you back to town."

"I won't get bored," she said. "I promise!"

Paer looked at his feet and dug at the ground with his toe for a moment.

"Promise promise promise!" Gracie said.

"I sometimes wish there were such a thing as melon soda," Gracie said, sitting on the truck's bench seat between me and Paer. We were headed back to the farm.

"General melon flavor," I asked, "or specific melon flavor?"

"Either," she said. "No, wait—specific."

"Cantaloupe?" I asked.

She scrunched her face in disgust.

"Honeydew?" I asked.

"Possibly. *Maybe*."

We had stopped by her house and waited in the truck while she put some shorts on over her swimming suit. But her hair was still wet.

"What about muskmelon?" I asked.

"Muskmelon?" she said. "I don't know anything about it."

"How about ogen melons?"

"You're making that up."

"I'm not, I swear."

"How about baba*looba* melons!" Gracie said. "If we're going to make up fake melons! How about tinky*tonky* melons!"

"How about the casaba melon?" I asked.

"You're making that up, too."

"Look it up, baby. It's a real melon."

"How do you know?" she asked.

"I just do. I'm older than you and smart as a whip."

"What, do they have melon class in high school?" she chided.

"Here's one for you: Charentais."

"Charentais *what?*" she asked.

"It's a kind of melon. It's a French melon."

"You haven't even mentioned watermelon yet!" Gracie complained.

"That was next," I said.

"Well, *that's* my favorite melon. *That's* what I want. Watermelon soda."

"Sounds good," I said.

We came around a bend in the gravel road and there was something in the middle of the road up ahead and it was moving and it was black and it was idiotic. It was the Doberman. All the time we'd been in town, he'd been running after us. Granted, his pace had flagged. But another couple of miles and he would have made it to town.

"The dog!" Gracie said.

"This is what he does?" I asked Paer.

"This is what he does," Paer said.

Paer stopped the truck. The Doberman, ecstatic with having found us, tried to jump in Paer's window. He got his front legs hooked inside the window and he held himself there while his rear feet scraped and scurried against the door. Then he fell and he jumped back up again and held himself there again and tried desperately to lick Paer. On the third attempt he made it into the cab of the truck and Gracie screamed and tried to hug him and his feet were everywhere and his slobber was being flung about and he started barking with joy. It was too much for everyone. We put him in the bed of the pickup and Gracie and I turned around and watched him as we drove the rest of the way to the farm.

"Maybe you can help us," I told Gracie. "Because Paer and I are having a heck of a time coming up with a decent name for the dog."

"Oh, I'll be good at this," Gracie said. "Let me think."

The dog was wobbling all over the bed of the pickup, falling down whenever the pickup turned a corner or changed speed.

"Normally I wouldn't let him ride with us," Paer said. "Because it just encourages him."

"You make him follow you back home?" I asked.

Paer nodded.

"Okay," Gracie said, done thinking. "How about Dirk?"

"Dirk," I said, trying it out.

"Or now I'm thinking Stephen," she said. "Definitely Stephen."

"Stephen . . . ," I said.

"No! Stephano!" Gracie said. *"Stephano . . ."*

"Stephano," I said. "Wow, you are good at this. Stephano."

"How about let's just go with Stephen," Paer said. And we all agreed.

"Well done," I told Gracie, and I shook her hand. "You're a good dog namer."

"Well," Gracie said, "I'm a big fan of names."

Gracie and I were still watching Stephen through the rear window. As we turned into the farm's driveway, Stephen tumbled over and banged into the side of the pickup bed.

"Ouch," I said.

"Wow," Gracie said. "Stephen's dumb."

The afternoon moved forward. Paer and I got the building paper put down, then the flashings, and then we started hauling the bundles of shingles up the ladders. Gracie watched us, with Stephen sitting contentedly beside her. Then for a long time we worked without talking, putting down course after course of shingles. The sun was hot, but it began to sink lower and lower. I didn't have a watch on, and neither did Paer, but we knew we didn't have much time left, and we were hungry. Intermittently, we could hear the barking of Stephen and Gracie's voice calling him or ordering him around. We had hours of work left yet.

At a certain point I looked up because I hadn't heard Paer's hammer in a while, and he was lying faceup on the roof, feet braced against a roof jack, arm over his face.

"Heck," he said.

I put my hammer in my belt loop and put my hands on my hips. I wished I had something to wipe my face with.

Then, from below, there was the sound of a car coming in the driveway. Paer and I looked at each other.

"Gracie?" I called.

There wasn't any answer. Two car doors slammed.

"Gracie?" I called again.

"What?" she yelled from far away.

"Who's here?" I called.

She didn't answer. Maybe she didn't hear me. But then one of the ladders moved a little bit and started bobbing. Someone was coming up. Paer sat up.

Soon Uncle Cort's head rose into view and then his torso and he stopped there and looked at the roof.

"Holy mackerel," he said. "You boys did this all today?"

"I'm afraid we're not going to finish before dark," I said.

"Sure you are," Cort said. "Because I'm going to help."

And he did. We worked steadily now, reinvigorated because we had reinforcements and because the end was within sight and because the daylight was slipping away. We could sense the gateway of nighttime approaching and we knew we could beat its arrival. We smelled charcoal smoke and Cort told us Corene had brought the grill out from town and was going to fix us some burgers and franks and all the fixings. It was the Fourth of July, after all.

"It's the Fourth?" I asked, surprised.

"Yes indeedy," Cort said, hammering away.

"You made me work on a national holiday?" I asked Paer.

And then, anticlimactically, we were done. We stood on the roof and observed the fruits of our labor and that was that.

"This'll last twenty years," Cort said.

There were no shingles left over. Exactly zero. Just a few scraps. We'd figured it perfectly and we'd made no mistakes.

———

When we got down from the roof we put down our hammers and took off our tool belts and we looked at ourselves and we were filthy. The grill was smoking away in the side yard and Aunt Corene came out of the house carrying a bowl of potato salad and she smiled at all of us and when she looked at me she gasped.

"Leo!" she said. "Where'd you find that hat?"

I took the cowboy hat off and looked at it. "It was in the attic," I said.

"That was your father's hat," Corene said. "Your father wore that hat all the time."

"Oh," I said. I had felt a connection to the hat, and now I knew.

"When I came out of the house just now," Corene continued, "for a second I thought you were him. You looked exactly like him then. I thought I was seeing my big brother again."

She put the potato salad on the card table. Cort and Paer were filling their mouths with potato chips.

I hugged Corene and she hugged me back.

"Okay, okay," she said as we released each other. "Now dinner's not ready, boys." She swatted Cort's hands away from the chips. "So get lost for fifteen minutes and let a lady work in peace."

While the burgers cooked, Cort drove Paer and Gracie and me down through the fields to the creek. We three stood in the back of Cort's pickup, leaning up against the cab, resting our palms against the smooth roof, feeling the air of the evening slip past us. We drove down into the bottomlands and into the shadows and here the air was cooler and we lit a sparkler for Gracie and she held it with one hand, keeping it as far from herself as possible, a little bit scared of it. We came to the creek. The bath in the farmhouse wasn't functional yet, so Paer and I stripped down to our shorts and got into the creek. I waded in and then made a dive forward and the water was refreshing and I emerged and realized that I had still had my hat on when I dived and now it was floating about ten feet away. I dunked myself again, rubbing my scalp, then retrieved the hat. I slicked my hair back and put the hat back on. We were too tired to flail around, so we just kind of floated there while we watched Gracie run up and down the gravel bar with sparklers in each hand. After a few minutes, Stephen arrived—tongue flapping—having followed us from the farmhouse, and we let him ride with us in the back of the pickup as we drove back up to the farmhouse, except that we left the pickup bed's gate open and as we mounted the short little hill below the barn Stephen started sliding backwards out of the pickup and his feet could get no purchase on the metal truck bed and he fell right out the back end. A split second later he was up and chasing after us and when we got to the farmhouse and stopped the truck he made a spectacular leap into the bed of the pickup and he knocked Gracie down and Gracie was laughing and we all got out of the pickup but Stephen for some reason was scared to jump *down* from the pickup, so Gracie asked me to lift him down, which I did.

Then we ate, and the sun was just then going down.

"I bet it's been ten years since anyone had a picnic out here," Corene said.

I lifted my bottle of root beer. "Here's to more picnics," I said.

Afterward, Cort and Corene sat on the front porch swing—which Paer and I had hauled out from the barn and cleaned just two days ago—and Gracie and Paer and me went up the ladders onto the roof for a final time. I carried Gracie up by letting her ride piggyback. It was dark now and we perched on the ridge and from here we had an unobstructed view of most of the horizon and we could see, from all quarters, the fireworks of celebration. They were small blooms of sparks that barely rose above the horizon, and most of them were so far away they were silent, but they were beautiful.

I took off the hat and put it on my knee and I felt my hair

and my hair was standing straight up. It had dried like this after being in the creek.

"Feel my hair," I told Gracie, and I bent toward her.

She touched my hair.

"Oh," she said, *"nice."*

Ten

THE FARMHOUSE ROOM I WAS SLEEPING IN WAS AUNT CORENE'S old bedroom. It was big and white and bright. I woke up because the sun was already coming in and because it was so quiet it was difficult to sleep. There weren't any window shades or drapes or anything, and the only things in the room were my cot, my backpack, and a floor lamp. I looked at my watch and it wasn't even six yet, but I was awake for good. Paer was driving me home this morning, which was probably another reason I couldn't sleep. I was restless.

I dressed and put on my cowboy hat. I made a mug of Paer's instant coffee and took it out onto the front porch and I sat there and sipped the coffee. I'd never tasted anything like it. It was like drinking liquefied ashes. I dumped it out and set the mug down. I could hear a car rambling down the gravel road and soon enough it passed the farm and the old coot at the wheel waved at me and I waved back and I had no idea who he was. He had a funny countrified wave where he kind of pointed at the sky in my direction.

I wondered how many times my father had waved from these steps.

I decided to walk to the creek, so I got my fishing rod and tackle box and headed out the back door. I passed Stephen's pen and he was sound asleep. He had stopped jumping out of the pen since Paer had chained him to the stump in the middle. He was cozied up against the stump like it was his pal. The sight of it was touching.

The grass was dewy and by the time I reached the creek my feet were wet. There was a mist on the surface of the creek, and the water beneath the mist was glossy and dark. I sat and watched the water, waiting to see if the bass were feeding on the surface. They didn't seem to be. I looked in my tackle box and the lures weren't interesting to me at the moment. I laid several of the lures out onto the gravel beside me and I looked at them and then I started looking at the rocks that surrounded them. I picked up a rock. It was a round black rock with a white stripe running through it. I picked up another rock, one with elusive sparkles in its grain.

And here was a smooth rock shaped like a cookie with a thumbprint on its crown. And here was a rock that was white and porous like bone. Here was a rock with a hole through it. And this one was just layers. Layers and layers. And there were more rocks. Rocks on rocks. Rocks under rocks. Rocks beside rocks. There were large rocks about the size of my feet. Then medium-sized rocks that fit in my palm. Then small rocks. Then pebbles. Then grit. Then sand. That was the progression. The whole acre-sized gravel bar was nothing more than a mound of rocks deposited here by thousands of years of floods. Had anyone ever touched this rock? Or that rock? Or this one?

The sun was warming the back of my neck as I was crouching there, looking at the gravel. I wasn't sure how long I had been here. Twenty minutes? Then there was a movement and I looked up and thirty feet away stood a doe and her fawn. The doe was drinking at the edge of the water and the fawn stood beside her.

Their tails flicked. They didn't seem concerned about me and the doe drank leisurely and then put one hoof into the creek and stood like that for a while. The fawn sniffed at the water and then at the air and then the doe began fording the creek and the fawn followed. They moved like light and they made no sound and they climbed up the far bank and went into the trees.

As soon as I got to the attic I realized how dark it was up there so I went and got the flashlight and then returned to the attic. I dragged the box that I hadn't opened into the light below one of the windows. The sun was coming in the window at a low angle and though it didn't do much to light up the attic, it did illuminate the thousands of bits of dust hanging in the air.

The box was big and it was heavy and it was taped shut. But the tape had dried up and come loose, so it came off easily. I opened the box.

The box was full and I saw immediately that it contained my father's treasures from when he was a child and teenager. There were some toy cars. There was an old Mitchell fishing reel. There was a thick stack of track ribbons, rubber-banded together. There was a wallet embossed with an eagle. There was a cigar box full of arrowheads. There was a small geode. There was a—

A car door slammed outside. I froze, startled. I leaned over and looked out the window to see who was here. Then I looked back at the box. I hadn't touched anything in the box. I had merely observed some of the items that were sitting at the top of the box. All kinds of stuff was buried in the box, out of sight. I folded the box close and pushed it back to where I had found it and I headed downstairs.

To my surprise, Paer was awake and he was already outside talking to Grandpa when I got there.

"Where have you been?" Paer asked.

"I was in the attic," I said. "Checking the job from the inside."

Grandpa was leaning against the open door of his car. He drove a huge American sedan now and lived three towns over where they had two grocery stores and a Wal-Mart. He'd moved off the farm after Grandma died eight years earlier.

"When's your all's phone going to be hooked up?" Grandpa asked. "Because I can't be driving over here every whipstitch."

"Supposed to be connected this week," Paer said.

"Hmph," Grandpa said. He was looking up at the roof, at our fine shingling job. But Grandpa didn't give compliments. A lack of criticism was the closest he ever got to a compliment, and apparently the roof passed muster, because he didn't say anything. He looked back at Paer.

"You know Clyde Seidel what lives down on the south branch?"

"Sure," Paer said. "I know his kids."

"You know how he has these contracts to supply premium beef for those grocery stores?"

"No," Paer said.

"Well," Grandpa explained, "he has these contracts to supply premium beef for a chain of stores. I mean, he's not the only one, but he got in early and he's one of their biggest producers and he helps them coordinate new suppliers."

"Uh-huh," Paer said.

"Well, here's what's what: he lined up with them for Warren Olberding to run eighty head but you've heard that Warren got sent up to the hospital on account of a stroke?"

"Who's Warren Olberding?" Paer asked.

"Shoot, that's right. You probably don't know him. Anyhow, he's an old-timer and he won't be coming back to his farm anytime soon and Clyde just doesn't have the room for another eighty head and he's looking for help."

"Help moving them?" Paer asked.

"No, no, kid. Listen. I talked to him and he wants you to run them out here."

"Eighty head? We don't have the pasture."

"What you do is run them in the east fields, like I did when I had all those shorthorns."

"East fields?" Paer said.

"It would be good grazing. I've brushhogged them every year, and fertilized them once. It's good fescue."

"The fences are all shot, or mostly shot."

"So string some new wire. Put up fourteen-gauge. It'll do."

"The posts need replacing," Paer said.

"So throw in some posts," Grandpa said. "Throw in some posts. It won't kill you. Throw in some posts."

"When would these cattle arrive?" Paer asked.

"Thursday at the latest."

"Well, I can't do that," Paer said. "That's too soon."

"It gives you a few days."

"It's too soon."

"You don't want to do it?" Grandpa asked.

"No, that's not what I said."

"If you don't want to do it, just say it."

"No, I want to do it. It's just that I can't get the fence in quick enough. Lee's going home today so it would just be me, and maybe some help from Dad. I can't afford to pay any help."

"All right—if you don't want to do it," Grandpa said.

"That's not what I said."

"Well straighten me out and say what you mean," Grandpa said.

Paer shrugged.

"If you want to be in farming," Grandpa said, "you have to learn how to make things work and you have to jump when it's time to jump and you have to spit when it's time to spit and you have to take your opportunities when they come. You have to stick around until the last dog is hung. Or I don't want to hear about it. I don't want to hear about it."

"What about water?" Paer asked. "The windmill hasn't run in years."

"So fix it," Grandpa said. He looked at me and pointed. "Your dad could have fixed it. Anson could have fixed it. He would already be out there working instead of whining and fidgeting."

"I don't know anything about windmills," Paer said.

"Lee's dad could have fixed it. Anson could fix anything."

"We can do it," I said.

"He'd already be out there working," Grandpa said.

"We can fix it," I said.

"He could fix anything," Grandpa said.

"We'll be ready for the cattle by lunch on Thursday," I said.

"He could do anything," Grandpa said.

"We'll do it," I said. "We'll have the fence in and water running and we'll be ready."

"That's not what Paer's saying," Grandpa said. "I'm not hearing that from Paer."

Paer looked at me. "You have to go home today," he said. "I can't keep you here. I've already kept you longer than I should have."

"It's just a few extra days," I said. "This is a big deal. I can help you. We can do it together."

"This is a good contract," Grandpa said. "It's a big contract. We didn't have these kinds of things when I was farming."

"It's too big an opportunity to turn away," I said to Paer.

"If you farm smart and you play it right," Grandpa said, "you'll get in good with these people and next year you'll run a hundred head and the year after that you'll run a hundred and fifty. That's more than I ever ran, I tell you."

"We can do it," I told Paer.

"Okay," Paer said, and he smiled after he said it.

Fifteen minutes later, I was driving the tractor east toward the windmill, a trailer full of tools behind me, and in the corner of my eye I saw something on the road and I looked over and there was Paer, driving his truck toward town to pick up the fencing supplies. Our paths were parallel, though he was going much faster than me, of course, and we waved big waves to each other and the morning sun was bright and clean and Paer's truck dipped out of sight and the dust cloud in his wake slowly dissolved.

By the time I saw him come back, I was down off the windmill platform, and by the time he came out into the field in his truck, I was standing at the trough with my hands under the pipe, and cold, fresh water was gushing out. The windmill was turning silently in the breeze and I cupped my hands in the water and drank and Paer came and did the same and now we knew that we could do it, that we'd have the fence ready on time, come what may.

Eleven

"MAIL!" I YELLED INTO THE HOUSE FROM THE BACK STOOP. There was no answer. I yelled again. I thought Paer was inside. I was pretty sure he was inside. We'd stopped back up at the farmhouse to get some more fence posts and Paer had gone into the house to use the bathroom. But he wasn't answering me and I looked down at the barn and he was already back down there putting posts into the pickup.

"Mail!" I yelled down at him.

He stopped. "What?" he yelled back.

"The mail's here!"

Paer had been waiting for his first piece of mail ever since he'd moved in. I had just seen the mailman's station wagon pull away.

"You get it!" Paer yelled.

I walked out the short driveway and the gravel was crunching under my boots. It was already a hot day and it was only going to get hotter and Paer and I were in the final stretch of fencing—a day before the cattle would arrive—and instead of getting tired and bogged down we were actually doing the work faster than before. We were speeding up and I was already worn out though it was only midmorning.

I opened the big rusty mailbox and inside its cavernous belly was one little letter—the size of a small card. I took out the letter and closed the mailbox. The letter was from Gracie.

A car was approaching and I turned and looked and it was Freeda Sweeney's pickup. She stopped beside me. Her passenger window was down and we looked at each other through it.

"So," she said, "my grandpa has been saying all week that he's been seeing the ghost of Anson Peery out at the old Peery place and I've been wondering all week just who the heck Anson Peery is and why his ghost is suddenly wandering around in broad daylight and just how clinically insane *is* my grandfather and finally I asked my mother who Anson Peery is and she told me."

"My father," I said.

"Leo Peery's father," Freeda said.

"Who I resemble a great deal," I said.

"And add that to the fact that my grandfather is mostly blind and mostly delusional, and I put two and two together and so I had to drive over myself and see this ghost for real and decide whether this ghost may or may not actually be Leo Peery. In the flesh."

"I don't think I'm a ghost," I said. "Because why would a ghost be so hot? Why would a ghost sweat so much?"

"My money says you're not a ghost either."

"I don't know how to prove it, though."

"I do," she said.

There was a pause.

"What if I pick you up at six?" she asked.

I agreed.

She put the truck into gear. "Nice hat," she said.

Moments later, though, as I walked back down the driveway,

I opened up the letter from Gracie and it complicated matters. I'd forgotten that Gracie was coming tonight.

Dear Leo and Paer,

Mom says that if I mail this today it will get to you tomorrow and that is the day when I am coming out for the sleepover which we have been planning which I am looking forward to to my ut most. So here is a listing of some things and ideas maybe we can do tomorrow by which I mean today, being the day you are receeving this note. Or we can decide later but here it is.

> *swim (in creek)*
> *float in iner tubes in creek*
> *roast weenies ~~in~~ at creek*
> *(no fishing allowed)*
> *watch tv*
> *have popcorn*
> *or samores*
> *stories*
> *joke contest or joke-off*
> *talk about our favorite books*
> *give Stephen a bath*
> *teach Stephen to sit*
> *teach Stephen to shut up*
> *skip stones at creek because I know how good Leo is at it*
> *no singing*
> *catching fireflies*
> *look for fossils*
> *look for arrowheads*
> *those leftover fire works we got*
> *fake tatus (how do you spell tatus?)*
> *ect ect ect and ect*

So I will see you and Mom says to say I'm bringing my sleeping bag and the cot and plenty of food.

Your cousin and sister
Gracie Frances

P.S. And I'm bringing the VCR too. Your little tv + VCR = fun.

I stopped in the driveway after I read the note, then I went on down to the barn.

"What was in the mail?" Paer asked. I gave him the note. He read it and laughed and then he put it in his pocket. "That's a keeper," he said. "My first piece of mail at the farm. A letter from Gracie. Mostly a *list*."

Sometime after two Paer and I returned to the farmhouse. Paer started putting the tools away. I wandered into the farmhouse and I felt light-headed. The day had been too hot and we had worked too hard. I could feel the heat in my body. It was deep inside my body, not just on the surface. I rubbed my scalp and my hair was wet with sweat. I rubbed my eyes. My *eyes* were hot.

I got a bottle of water from the fridge—we were still afraid of drinking the tap water—and I stumbled into the bathroom and turned on the shower. We'd just fixed the shower yesterday. I got out of my boots and jeans and I stepped into the shower and the water was shockingly cold. It was what I wanted but it was somewhat hard to take. My skin felt like it was burning, even as I stood in the cold water. I opened the bottle of water and drank it right there in the shower. I couldn't drink it fast, just little sips, and I could feel its coldness sliding down into me and then disappearing. I was pretty sure I'd never had a drink in the shower before and it was strange but I was just trying to cool down. I felt a little bit nauseated.

Finally, after standing in the cold water for at least ten minutes, I turned off the shower and dried myself off. I wrapped the towel around my waist and looked into the mirror above the sink. I was still hot, still heated through to the core, and as I stood looking at myself in the mirror I watched the beads of sweat form on my face. That's how fast it returned. It came immediately and I could see it forming. I shaved and then gathered my dirty clothes and carried them to my room. Then I went back downstairs in my towel and sat in front of the only fan. Paer came in. I could hear him in the kitchen getting a bottle of water and then he came into the front room where I was.

"You okay?" he asked.

"Fine," I said. "You?"

"Your face is red," he said.

I grunted.

"I mean really red," he said.

"But we're done," I said. "We did it."

"Yep," Paer said, and then for a while we didn't say anything. He was standing in the fan's breeze and I was sitting in it. Finally, he left and went into the bathroom and I could hear the shower come on.

I made myself stand up and go upstairs. This took effort. I put on some shorts and then I carried my cot down to the living room and put it right in front of the fan. I lay down and the fan was right there, inches from my head, and it drowned out all noise and the breeze wasn't cool, particularly, but what was important was that it wasn't hot.

After a while I heard Paer come into the room and he had brought one of the lawn chairs—a lounge chair—and he put it beside me and lay down.

"Oh, mama," he said.

I didn't have the energy to speak. I sensed the approach of oblivion and I wasn't going fight it and in a minute or two I was asleep.

The first thing we did when Gracie arrived was eat. Though I didn't actually feel hungry, I don't think I had ever been so happy to see food in my life. Corene had made fried chicken and Paer and Gracie and I spread an old quilt on the front yard and had a picnic there.

"Slow down or you'll eat the bones on accident!" Gracie said.

"But bones are good," I said. "Crunchy."

"You guys are crazy," Gracie said. "I think you sweated out your *brains* today."

Corene had also sent us biscuits, slaw, pickles, blackberry pie, fresh peaches, and a jug of mint iced tea. The jug sloshed whenever you picked it up.

We ate everything. And we finished the tea.

Gracie persuaded Paer to let Stephen out of his pen so that he could join us in our festivities at the creek. So we put Stephen in the back of the truck and drove down through the fields toward the creek. When we got down into the bottomlands and came around the little spur of woods, we could suddenly see the eastern pasture. All our new fencing was there and both me and Paer were admiring it. The metal poles and new barbed wire were so shiny that in some places they were sparkling. In the back of the truck, though, Stephen suddenly seemed to be angry at the sky and he was barking at it.

Gracie knocked on the back window to get Stephen's attention but it didn't work.

"What's wrong with our dog?" Gracie asked.

At the creek he stopped barking at the sky and started, instead, running at breakneck pace up and down the gravel bar, chasing nothing. But perhaps he was smarter than he looked, because his antics started a game in which we three tried to catch him. He was very good at this game and he dodged us again and again, even when we worked in concert, and whenever we got tired and took a short breather, he would stop and look at us in a begging kind of way, wanting to play some more.

"Hey, Gracie," I said, when the game was finally over and we were all trying to catch our breaths. Even Stephen was tired and he had wandered slowly to the creek's edge and stuck his snout in the water. He wasn't actually drinking, just snorting around.

"Hey what?" Gracie said.

"How would you feel if Freeda Sweeney came and joined our party for a little while? Because I talked to her today and she sounded very interested."

"Hm . . . ," Gracie said, cocking her head.

"Very," I emphasized.

"I think there are two advantages there," Gracie said. "First, there are too many boys at this party and so Freeda would add another girl. Second, I like Freeda."

"Well, I think she's going to swing by the farmhouse pretty soon and I can drive up and meet her and tell her to come down here. And while I'm up there I could throw the inner tubes in the back of the pickup."

"Shoot—we forgot them, didn't we?" Gracie said.

Freeda's pickup turned into the driveway just as I arrived. We talked and then she headed home to pick up her swimming suit.

Back at the creek, Paer was fishing the water at the bottom of the gravel bar, and Gracie was standing up to her waist in the water at the top of the gravel bar. There didn't seem to be any fun being had.

I got out of the pickup and unloaded the three big black inner tubes. One of them rolled away like a wheel until it landed in the water.

"Leo," Gracie said, "I said no fishing and look what Paer's doing."

"Paer, you're breaking the rules," I said.

"He hid his fishing rod under the seat and then he got it out when we weren't looking and then as soon as you left he started fishing."

"I don't know what we're going to do with him."

"Let's *shunt* him."

"Shun him? Okay. Sounds fair."

She yelled in Paer's direction: "We're shunting you!"

"Did you hear that, Paer?" I asked.

"He hasn't even caught anything," Gracie said. "So ha."

"Serves him right," I said.

"Where's Freeda?" Gracie asked.

"She's running home to get her swimming suit and then she's coming here. She'll be here in, like, two minutes."

"Well let's start swimming anyway."

I took off my shirt and shoes and made a mad dash into the creek, charging Gracie. The excitement and splashing attracted Stephen and he rushed in after me. Gracie fled into the deeper water.

"No getting me!" Gracie protested, as I swam inexorably toward her. "No getting me!"

"If I can't get you, how are we going to have fun?" I asked. I stopped swimming after her. I put my feet down and could barely touch the gravelly bottom.

"I don't know, but you can't get me!" Gracie said.

"Can you touch the bottom there?" I asked her.

She stopped swimming and began treading water, then she paused for a moment and she sank a little bit in the water and then started treading water again, more frantically than before. "No," she said. She was a fantastic swimmer.

Suddenly Stephen's bony legs were clambering all over my shoulders and head.

"Hey!" I yelled. "You're going to muck up the water!" I turned his body and pointed him back to shore. Miraculously, he went straight to shore and got out. He stood there dripping. It was somewhat pitiful.

"Why doesn't he shake off the water?" Gracie asked.

"Shake!" I ordered him. He faced me, eager but uncomprehending.

"Shake, Stephen!" Gracie said.

Paer walked up to Stephen. He put down his fishing rod. His other arm was wrapped around the errant inner tube.

"Shake, dimwit," Paer said.

And Stephen shook.

"His master's voice," I said.

Paer wiped his face with his T-shirt. "I just caught a little bit of dog mist."

"Let's do something and stop talking," Gracie said.

"What do you want to do?" I asked.

She was swimming toward me now. She shrugged as she swam. "Something fun," she said.

"How about rocket?" Paer said.

"Rocket!" Gracie said.

Just then there was the noise of a motor nearby and Freeda's pickup rolled into view on the gravel bar and turned toward us. She parked nose to nose with Paer's pickup and got out.

"Let's get this party started," she said.

"We're just now doing rocket," Gracie said.

Freeda came over to the edge of the water. She dropped two beach towels. She was wearing a black two-piece swimsuit. "I'm not familiar with 'rocket,'" she said.

132

"Then watch," Gracie said.

Paer was in the water with us now. We all moved to a section of the water that was just about the right depth—about four feet deep.

"Who's the first launcher?" I asked.

"I am!" Gracie said.

"No—who's the first *launcher*," I said, "not *launchee*. You're always the launchee. You're the designated launchee."

"She's my sister," said Paer, "so I say I'm the first launcher."

"But what you're overlooking," I countered, "is that I'm in love with her."

"Yes, but *how much?*" Gracie asked.

"Yes, how much?" Freeda asked from shore, spreading a towel.

"Plenty," I said. "More than enough."

"Really?" Gracie said.

"Don't get me started," I said.

"Why doesn't Freeda decide who the first launcher is," Gracie suggested.

Freeda was reclining on her towel now. We looked to her. "Hm," she said. "Family first."

"Ha!" Paer said, gloating.

"I'm family, too," I said, but it was a weak argument and no one even responded. I moved away, giving Paer and Gracie some room.

Paer crouched down in the water so just his head was out. Gracie hung on his back.

"Ready?" Paer asked.

"Yeah," Gracie said.

Paer ducked underwater and Gracie quickly repositioned herself so that her feet were on Paer's shoulders. She crouched there, trying to keep her balance.

"This doesn't seem safe," Freeda said.

"Oh, believe me," I said, "it's not."

After a moment of stillness Paer suddenly sprang up, shooting out of the water. At the same time, Gracie sprang, too, and the result of all this springing was that Gracie was launched into the sky maybe eight feet. She screamed and landed just in front of Paer. She surfaced and was laughing.

"Rocket!" she said.

Freeda clapped. "Pure genius," she said. "Who invented this game?"

"Leo did," Gracie said.

I nodded, accepting the honor.

"Leave it to the lifeguard to invent dangerous water games," Freeda said.

"Hey," I said, "I didn't just invent rocket, I *live* rocket."

"Uh-huh," Freeda said.

"I *am* rocket," I emphasized.

"I bet you couldn't rocket me," Freeda said.

"Don't make me come over there."

"You wouldn't know," she said, "what to do once you got here."

Moments later, me and Gracie met in the launching area. Paer had gotten out of the water and was talking to Freeda. Me and Gracie floated face-to-face.

"You ready for this?" I asked softly.

"I am!"

"'Cause we're going to give them a show."

"I know!"

"'Cause you're going to *fly*," I said.

"I'm ready."

"Okay. You sure?"

"Yes."

"Sure sure?"

"Yes."

"Good. It's going to be great."

"I know."

"I'm bigger than Paer," I said.

"I know."

"And I'm stronger," I said.

"I know."

"And before whenever I launched you I don't think I was ever really trying to launch you as high as I could."

"Uh-huh," she said, nodding.

"But this time I will."

"You will!" she said. "Good."

"So you're ready?"

"Uh-huh," she said, smiling.

I looked to shore and Paer and Freeda weren't paying attention to us.

"We're ready!" I called.

"Hey, watch us!" Gracie said.

"Okay, kids," Freeda said.

We positioned ourselves in the water and I ducked down. Gracie held on to my shoulders and her knees were against my back.

"Here we go," I said, and then I inhaled and went under. I felt Gracie clamber onto me, her little feet curved against my shoulders. I braced my own feet on the creek bottom, making sure I had a solid footing. Gracie was in position and I waited just a moment until she was stable, then I launched.

I could tell immediately that everything was perfect, that never before had she been launched like this. I shot out of the water and Gracie left my shoulders and went airborne and I watched her rising, rising, her arms and legs moving against the blue evening sky. And whereas normally she yelped or screamed with joy whenever she was launched, this time she was silent, and it was hard to say how high she went, but it's fair to say she went very high, perhaps too high, and she landed on her back twelve feet away and I swam toward her and she surfaced and I saw that her eyes were wide with fear.

My heart broke.

She was dog-paddling frantically, splashing. We met in the water and she clung desperately to me and I swam for the both of us. We were out in the deeper water.

"Are you okay?" I asked.

She nodded. Her head was against mine and I could feel her nodding.

"Did you swallow some water?"

"No. I don't think so."

"You didn't hurt anything when you landed, did you?"

"No," she said. "It stung."

"I'm sorry I launched you so high," I said.

"It's not your fault. I told you to."

"I didn't mean to scare you."

"It's okay," she said. "It didn't scare me. Just a little."

"I didn't mean for it to scare you," I said.

"I didn't know that it would be like that," she said. "I didn't know."

"I'm sorry."

"I know," she said.

"I won't ever do that again," I said.

"I know," she said. "It's okay."

"All right," I said.

"Yeah, but boy . . . ," she said, and now she was smiling, "but boy, I was *up* there. I was *up* there, wasn't I?"

The sun came in. It angled down into the creek bed, lighting the gravel bar, the water, the leaves. Our faces were bright. The evening was still hot and the water felt refreshing. I took the three big inner tubes and strung them together so that they formed a loose flotilla, then me and Gracie and Freeda floated in them. The current was lazy here, and it would slowly scoot us down the creek, moving us from the head of the gravel bar to the bottom of the gravel bar in about fifteen minutes. Then, whenever we reached the bottom of the gravel bar I would get out of my tube and wade upstream, dragging the entire flotilla back up the creek, where we would start our journey again. We didn't talk much and sometimes our eyes were closed and sometimes they were open. I breathed through my nose and felt the sun on my skin. There was no breeze now and the stillness was infectious. Paer appeared to be asleep onshore. And Stephen, bewildered by but not scared of our flotilla, followed us onshore, watching us the whole time.

Finally, at a certain point my inner tube bonked into Freeda's and we opened our eyes and our faces were mere inches apart and we didn't startle and we didn't blink. Our tubes began slowly drifting apart again and Freeda smiled.

"Hey," Gracie said. "What's that there?"

I turned my head to look at her. She was looking into the water.

"What's what?" I asked.

"At the bottom of the creek, it's like a big ball or something."

I paddled my tube over in her direction.

"I don't see anything," I said.

"Look right there."

The water was waist deep there, and finally I did see the outline of something. The way I could see it was that it was like a big shadow blotting out the gravel at the bottom of the creek.

I slid out of my tube and put my feet down.

"What is that thing?" Freeda asked.

"Hey, Paer!" I called.

His head snapped up immediately. Maybe he hadn't been asleep.

"Come down here," I said.

"It's not going to eat us, is it?" Gracie asked.

"No," I said, poking the thing with my toe. I knew what it was. "It's not going to eat us."

"What is it?" Freeda asked.

"It's a geode," I said.

"A geode!" Gracie said. "That's like the luckiest thing you can find."

"That's not a geode," Freeda said. "It's too big. Geodes don't get that big."

"This one did," I said. It was about the size of a big beach ball. "I've never seen one this big," I said.

"How big?" Paer asked from shore. He'd walked down to where we were.

I was holding on to the inner tube flotilla. But now I let it go so I could hold my hands apart and show Paer how big the geode was.

"Hey," Freeda said as the flotilla started to drift away. "Don't abandon us to the whims of the river."

"Well, either I can take care of the flotilla or I can get this geode out of the creek, but not both."

"You can get it out?" Gracie asked, lighting up at the idea. "You can get it out? But it'll weigh too much."

"We can get it out. But only if you want it, since you're the one that found it."

Gracie was now ten feet away, floating slowly downstream. I noticed that the air all about us was like velvet all of a sudden. The sunlight was low and golden and the humidity was soothing. The time for swimming was passing.

"I want it!" Gracie said.

With the help of a crowbar and some rope, me and Paer rolled the geode to shore, but once it was out of the water, it was much more difficult to handle. Maybe it weighed two hundred or two hundred and fifty pounds. Maybe it weighed three hundred pounds. We all looked at it. We were all out of the water. Gracie was wrapped in a towel. We looked at the geode. It was like a big gray head of cauliflower. But inside, we knew, it was hollow, and its inner surface was covered with crystals.

"How are we going to crack it open?" Gracie asked. "Let's crack that puppy."

"How about let's worry about getting it up to the farmhouse first," Paer said.

Stephen seemed to be scared of the geode. He was cowering behind us.

Paer and I tried to lift the geode together. It was hard to get a grip on it, and even harder to lift it those first few inches. But we did. We could do it. But we dropped it almost immediately. We couldn't carry it more than a few feet.

"We could go get the tractor," Paer suggested. "Scoop it up with the front loader."

But instead we just backed the pickup up to it and hefted it into the bed.

It was time to say good night to the river. The air was cooling off. The light was leaving us. Gracie didn't want to go. She was desperate to hold on to the day. She started running with Stephen, then she started skipping stones. Freeda joined her, then Paer. I was sitting on the tailgate of Freeda's pickup watching. Gracie turned to me.

"Skip stones with us, Leo!" she cried.

"I think it's time to go home," I said.

"Just one stone," Gracie said.

"Okay," I said, "but I want it to be a really nice skipping stone. You have to find me a really nice skipping stone."

Gracie scurried off, scanning the ground for a good stone. I went and stood near Freeda and Paer. Gracie came back and handed me a smooth, dark stone. It was about as big as my palm and as thick as the tip of my thumb. It wasn't particularly circular, but that didn't matter.

"This is great," I said. "This is one of the best skipping stones I've seen in a long time."

"Skip it!" Gracie said.

"Look at it," I said, "how it has the perfect heft and a perfectly flat surface."

"Skip it!" Gracie said.

"And how when you rub it against your cheek it has that nice slightly chalky feel—not hard and cold. I like it."

"Skip it!"

"It's going to skip beautifully."

"Leo!"

"It will be as beautiful as a poem."

Gracie slapped my shoulder.

I stepped to the water and observed the water. The upper pool was still and shimmering. I threw the stone and it sang on the water, skipping big skips at first, then medium skips, then small skips. It was going through the whole range of skips. And then as it slowed and slowed it stopped skipping and started kind of *plowing* forward, cutting a wake into the water. You could hear it, even though it was far away. And then it sank and was gone.

Gracie cheered. "That was like *ninety* skips," Gracie said.

"Wow," Freeda said, looking at me.

"It was hard to count, but I think it was about *ninety* skips," Gracie said.

Freeda was still looking at me. She said, "I didn't know people like you existed."

We drove home. I rode with Paer and Gracie rode with Freeda. It was dark enough that we almost needed our headlights, but we didn't use them. We moved through the lower fields, passing alongside the dark stand of corn. And on our other side was pasture, and from the pasture—from the wild mixture of fescue grass and red clover and daisies and Queen Anne's lace—from that pasture rose hundreds upon hundreds of fireflies, blinking and bobbing and burning little arcs into the air.

And Paer surprised me. He was driving and looking at the fireflies. And he said, "July . . ."

Twelve

IT WAS ABOUT AN HOUR LATER. WE HAD SPREAD OUT OUR sleeping bags and blankets and pillows in the front room, making for one huge sleeping area, and we were all lying there watching the little black-and-white television, which was sitting on the floor underneath the front windows. We were watching a recording of one of Gracie's favorite shows. It was an animated show about bunnies, birds, and a wide and surprising assortment of rodents, most of whom were generous and kind, but some of whom—particularly a ragtag group of disgruntled rats—were basically out to ruin everyone's fun. For some reason, this whole woodland-creature saga was set in medieval times.

When the episode was over, Gracie sat up. "It's time for some popcorn, I think," she said. "Before we start the next episode, which I warn you is intense."

"How could it get more intense than the rat scheme to drown the prince by sabotaging his pleasure boat?" Paer asked.

"Oh, it gets more intense," Gracie said. "Believe you me."

I volunteered to make the popcorn.

"What I'm thinking would be perfect," Gracie said, "is that if each of us had our own private bowl of popcorn. And we can enjoy it that way."

"What size of bowl?" I asked.

"Medium size of bowl," Gracie said.

"I think all we have is cereal bowls," I said.

"That's smaller than I was thinking," Gracie said.

Freeda rolled over. "Why don't you make one big batch and put it in that huge bowl," she said, "and then we'll each be able to refresh our small popcorn bowls whenever we want by dipping them into the big bowl."

Gracie was nodding. "Let's go with it," she said. "It's kind of a group bowl plan."

There was a noise across the room. Something was brushing the screen from outside. The windows were open and something was brushing against the screen. We looked over there. I could see a vague shape.

"Stephen!" Gracie said.

He was sniffing the screen, looking in at us from the porch. I could identify the gleam of his wet parts: two eyes and a nose. Gracie went over and sat down by the window.

"Hi, boy," she said. "Tell me something new."

It was hot in the kitchen. I wasn't sure I could sleep unless the house cooled down. I heated some oil in the big pot and then I added the popcorn and stood there waiting. I was sleepy and worn-out. It felt like it was about two in the morning, but I knew it was maybe only ten-thirty. I shook the pot as the popcorn popped and then I turned the popcorn out into the big metal bowl. It was pretty popcorn. Large popcorn. Fluffy popcorn. It merited attention. But I decided I should make a second batch, so I put some more oil in the pot.

"We're thinking we're going to turn on the AC," Paer called from the front room.

"Why are you telling me?" I asked. "I'm just the cook."

I could hear them closing the windows in the front room.

"Close the windows in the kitchen, Leo!" Gracie called.

"There aren't any windows open," I answered. I measured out some more popcorn kernels.

And then I heard a brief and shuddery kind of rumbling. The huge air conditioner that had been bought by Grandpa in the sixties had never been removed from the window in the front room. And when Paer and I had tried it out a few days ago, we were surprised to find that it still worked, and could cool the entire downstairs, even if it did sound like a jet.

But before the air conditioner actually got up to speed, it cut out, and all the lights in the house went out and everything was quiet.

"Oops," I heard Paer say.

We'd blown three fuses this week, and we'd used our last spare one already. In fact, we'd taken the fuse out of the upstairs circuit to use in the downstairs circuit. The old thirty-amp service panel in the basement only had two circuits.

So that was that.

Well, Freeda left. Which wasn't so surprising.

Then what we did was carry our cots outside. It was cooler out there, and it was a fun sleepovery-type thing to do, and Gracie was excited about it. Besides, Paer was worried about the sweet corn. He'd plowed and tilled the old garden plot way back in the spring, long before he moved out here, and planted it with sweet corn, hoping to sell it at farmers' markets come July and make a few hundred dollars. To keep the raccoons out he'd put an electric fence around the garden, but now with the electricity out, the fence was dead. And the corn was mere days from maturity and the raccoons were dying to get at it.

So we each put our cot on a different side of the patch. And Paer agreed to let Stephen run free, in hopes that he would deter the coons. And just as I was getting snuggled into my cot, Paer came around the garden in the dark and he handed me a rifle. It was his .30-.30.

"Do I really need this to protect myself from raccoons?" I asked.

"Well, why not?"

"I don't think we should have guns out with Gracie around."

"Just put it under your cot and forget about it," he said.

"But a .30-.30?" I asked. "I just want to scare the coons, not turn them into *mist*."

He left and came back and gave me Grandpa's old .22. He took the .30-.30. I checked the .22 to make sure the safety was on and that there wasn't a bullet in the chamber. Then I put it under my cot.

A few minutes later, close to sleep, I heard Gracie call from the other side of the corn patch: "I need to tinkle."

I had the flashlight, so I walked barefoot around the corn. She was sitting on her cot.

"Do you want to go inside or outside?" I asked.

"I think inside," she said.

We walked to the farmhouse, the light of the flashlight fanning out in front of us as we crossed the side yard. Stephen followed us, curious. All the crickets and bullfrogs and peep frogs in the world were clamoring in the night, but it was soothing somehow. It was supportive.

We neared the back stoop and I smelled something.

"Do you smell that?" I asked Gracie.

"Smoke," she said.

I opened the back door and a big puff of it came out. I slammed the door closed. "What the . . . ," I said.

"What's smoking?" Gracie asked.

"Stay here," I said. I headed toward the living room window. Stephen was on my heels, excited by my tone of voice. I shined my flashlight into the living room and it was just a little smoky in there, like fog. I heard Gracie's bare feet running away across the lawn toward Paer.

"Paer!" she called.

For some reason, I knew I was to blame for whatever was burning. Did we even have a garden hose? I knew there wasn't a fire extinguisher.

I stood on my tiptoes to see in the dining room window. Stephen barked. There was hardly any smoke in the dining room.

But the kitchen was full of it. Something was burning in the kitchen and Stephen was barking and barking. Then I figured it out.

When I came back out of the house holding the popcorn pot, Paer and Gracie arrived. What had happened was that I'd left the pot on the burner—it was a propane stove, not electric—and the oil had smoked up the whole house. Paer shook his head and walked back toward the corn patch.

While Gracie used the bathroom I went around the house opening windows. The place needed to be aired out. Then we returned to the corn patch. I told Gracie good night and I tucked her into her cot and asked her if she was afraid and wanted to sleep over by me and she said no, that she wanted to help guard the corn by maintaining a thorough perimeter. She actually said "thorough perimeter." Then she consoled me about the burnt oil.

"Almost anyone could have made that mistake," she said.

I walked around the corn patch to Paer.

"You really should put smoke alarms in there," I said.

He grunted in his half sleep.

"They're really cheap," I said, "and you need at least one upstairs and one downstairs."

"Tomorrow," he said into his pillow.

"And first thing in the morning we'll replace the fuse panel. That thing can't be safe, and how can you live here if you're blowing fuses every other day?"

"I can do it by myself. You need to get home."

"One more day won't matter," I said. "It has to be fixed. We know it's not safe."

"I can do it by myself," he said. He was still talking into his pillow.

"We'll go to the library in the morning and research it."

"Listen, back off. I know you can fix anything. I said I'll do it myself."

"Okay, okay," I said. "I'm just saying. I can help."

"We know you can fix anything. We're all very impressed."

Trying to sleep under the stars was distracting. All that immensity, that open space, that coldness and silence—all of it was right overhead and though my eyes were mostly closed I kept getting little glimpses of the sky that would wake me up. And then it began to seem that I could see the stars through my closed eyelids. How was one supposed to feel cozy in the face of such a thing? Stars, space, galaxies! Events and explosions and collisions that happened millions of years ago, blazing away.

Plus my cot wasn't level.

My mind was not at rest, but eventually I entered the tunnel of sleep. I was too tired to do anything else. But when a hand touched my bare shoulder, I was awake immediately. I was calm and I looked up and saw Freeda. I sat up.

I must have slept at least an hour. Stephen was asleep under my cot, lying on the rifle. His muzzle was twitching—he was dreaming doggy dreams. Freeda and I walked away from him and I was glad he didn't wake up. I was barefoot and wearing only my cutoffs, and I looked at Freeda and she was barefoot, too. I felt separate from myself but not scared or driftless. The night around us was still and comfortable, but it was also uncontained. The moon was up. We were in a different territory, a different domain than we'd been in just a couple hours ago. It was night. Summer night.

She led me across the yard and then over to the edge of the woodlot. I saw a dark form there and soon enough recognized that it was her horse. It was Harrison.

As we rode Harrison away from the house, suddenly Stephen was with us, trotting alongside.

"Stephen," I said, "the best possible thing you can do right now is just stay put. Guard the corn."

I wasn't sure he comprehended this. Freeda stopped Harrison. Stephen stopped and looked up at us.

"Git," I said.

He licked his nose.

I got down from Harrison and told Freeda I'd be right back. I took Stephen by his collar and started leading him away. Then I realized I didn't really need to lead him—he'd follow me wherever I went. So I let go of his collar and he immediately turned around and started walking back toward the horse. He walked slowly, glancing back at me, knowing he was doing something wrong.

"I know that to you a horse looks like a big dog," I said. "But you're going to have to trust me that it's not."

He stopped for a moment, considering my argument.

"It's a horse," I said. "And to him a dog is just a thing underfoot."

Stephen started moving away again. So I hooked my fingers under his collar and led him all the way to his pen. By the time we got there I was practically dragging him. I clipped his collar to the chain that was tied to the stump, then I patted his head.

"Someday, boy, you'll understand," I said. "Or probably not. But don't feel bad."

He tried to lick my wrist.

"I promise I'll let you out first thing when I get back."

We rode bareback, down into the creek bottom. Down there the fireflies were still rising, but not in the same numbers as before, and not with the same energy. It was as if they were dreaming and flying at the same time. We got to the gravel bar where we had spent the evening and then we splashed across the creek. The stars and the segment of the moon were reflected in the creek water. We heard something splash in the distance. For a second I saw how similar the night sky and the water were—how they were really both expressions of the same facts. There was beauty in this realization, but I lost it all almost immediately.

We came up out of the streambed and into a long, low pasture that stretched slowly up a hill. It smelled good here, like a field in a story, a nighttime meadow. We followed the creek upstream and I held Freeda around the waist.

"Wait," I said, "I don't even know your middle name."

"Yes, you do," she said. "My middle name is Freeda."

I thought about that.

"Wait," I said, "I don't even know your first name."

"Catherine," she said.

We moved out of the landscape that was familiar to me and into foreign fields. But I realized where we were—we were getting close to Freeda's farm. In fact, we were probably already on her family's land. We were still riding right next to the creek and I wasn't sure where we were headed. But finally she turned Harrison down into the creek bed again, and he walked into the water and this time the water was deeper than where we'd forded the first time and the water came up and embraced my feet. Then Harrison climbed out of the water and we were on a long, humped gravel bar, one of the biggest ones on the entire creek. I recognized it. I had canoed this creek so many times. And over at the edge of the gravel bar, where the gravel merged into the tall weeds and trees along the riverbank, there was a huddled mass, a dark mound. It was an outpost of shadow. We were passing close to it and Freeda pulled on the reins and Harrison stopped.

"What is that?" I asked. There wasn't quite enough moonlight.

"It's Paer's jeep," Freeda said.

It was. I saw it was.

"Oh, jeez," I said. "How long have you known it was here?"

"A while."

The jeep was upside down, its wheels pointed skyward, and in the darkness I could not make any judgment about what kind of condition it was in, but it was partially buried in the gravel, and there seemed to be weeds growing from its underbelly.

"Do you think I should tell him it's here?" she asked.

"No," I said. "Probably not."

"Okay."

"It's sad is all."

We moved upstream a bit, fording a riffle and then wading up a shallow pool until we came to the next gravel bar. This one was smaller and when we got down from Harrison I liked the feel of the tiny, tiny stones on my bare feet. They were almost like sand. And there was the sound of the water moving down the riffle, coursing around the rocks gently.

There was a sleeping bag laid out here, and Freeda pulled me down onto it and she started unbuttoning her shirt. But the buttons made popping sounds. They weren't buttons at all, they were snaps. The shirt was a Western-style shirt.

"Snaps!" I said, and I reached up to help her undo them, but she pulled the rest of them open with one motion. She tossed the shirt aside.

"Are you flirting with me?" I asked.

"I waited and . . ." She was kissing my chest and shoulders. "I waited through that whole little girl party. I waited . . . I waited all night."

She was tugging at my fly, mostly unsuccessfully.

"Take these off," she said.

"How can I say no to that?" I said.

"That's not an option," she said. "You don't have any options here."

I took off my shorts.

"Everything," she said, nodding at my boxers. "Now."

I obeyed and I was soon bare to the night. I could feel the boundary between me and the night and I could feel the slightest of breezes moving down the stream. I reached for Freeda but she had leaned away, searching for something nearby. She dropped a condom onto my chest and I opened the packet and sat up a little bit. I unrolled the condom onto myself, then closed my eyes and stretched, arching my back, curling my toes into the gravel, and then I reached tenderly for Freeda, but to my surprise she pushed me down roughly. Her clothes were gone and the next moment, without any guidance, she moved onto me.

"That," she said. "That."

While in the shadows, the horse breathed.

Later, we were in the water. We moved in the water and we were wet.

"Look at me," Freeda said.

We came out of the water and she wrung her hair and I could hear the water falling onto the gravel. We were wet and we didn't want to get the sleeping bag wet and so the second time we lay on the gravel itself. We lay in a soft part, in a sandy part just at the edge of the water and when my knees sank into the sand they felt water. There was water just beneath the surface of the sand. It was holding me there. Freeda and I were together a second time and this time she didn't close her eyes and she was looking up at me and smirking and then she said filthy things and she slapped me. I responded and part of my response was that I put more of my weight on her and she kept talking and now her eyes were closed and I knew I would win and she moved her head from side to side so I put my head against hers and held her still and she continued talking but I was pressing the breath out of her and she could only whisper and whimper and then her words started falling apart—she was losing control—and then she was silent.

But we weren't done.

When finally I returned to my cot, it felt uncomfortable to me. The darkness was going to be over soon and I was afraid it would start to get light before I was asleep and I knew that there would be no real sleep tonight, no real comfort. The dawn would come and the sun would rise and with it would come the heat. But for now I was cold. I was shivering. Or shuddering. It was hard to say which. I was shaking and I didn't know what to do about it. I smelled my hands and they smelled like the creek. My hair was a bit wet. My legs were aching. My knees were scratched. My lips were bruised. I was shaking so much that my old army cot was creaking, its frame was creaking. But I made myself keep my eyes closed. I was afraid of the dawn and I didn't want to know it was coming. There was a gigantic silence in the air. But some birds somewhere were starting to call, some harbingers of dawn. I made myself breathe evenly and deeply and this seemed to calm my body. My shuddering became a shivering. And the shivering became a quivering. And the quivering went deeper and deeper inside me until I could feel it no more. It merged with my heartbeat, deep inside.

So, one dreams.

Suggest a table. Seeking dusty plates. Trying to wipe. Or dipping them in creek. Where else? The creek. With fish swimming only half-submerged. Their scales are drying out. So dive! Get wet! Not my problem. Is it?

There's Mom, downstream. At a bend downstream. She doesn't see me. Expressions of noontime. But I'm fully clothed. But to reach her I must swim in my clothes, which is a heavy, slow kind of swimming. I list. I tilt. I'm supposed to be a good swimmer. The creek is supposed to be shallow almost everywhere. I should be able to wade most of the way, but I can't. The water is deep for some reason. And the current should be helping me but it isn't. So now you can see that the water is stagnant. Mom, though, is out of sight. There are deer. They're not Mom. They are woodland creatures. They can disappear into the woods and then reappear behind you. Sneaky.

I'm not going to succeed today, but I keep trying.

In the water, at the bottom, there I see it: my bike. It is renewed. It is reborn. All is forgiven. Oh, please forgive me. I didn't mean it. I wasn't thinking. I will have scars for life, see, both internal and external. See? Here, here, and here. Scars. It being difficult to reach the bike. It is in a deep pool, and I have had enough of being wet. So I must devise a thing with rope and a big hook. I have two hooks to choose from and I choose the red one. I can see how beautiful the bike is, but truly it doesn't belong at the bottom of the creek. So it's like fishing, except that I'm trying to hook the bike and the hook keeps slipping off the frame. Finally, though, I hook the wheel. It's later in the day and

I'm starting to worry about nightfall. Having to walk home in the dark. Or ride my bike! But in the dark? Not pleasant. Come here. Come here. Come here. Gotcha.

Pulling the bike out of the water is an act without effort. The bike is rising toward me, rising for along time, until finally it is here. It is in the air again. It is gleaming, sparkling, sheeny. It is my bike. It is my bike. And I will look at it as long as I please. Until Mom touches my shoulder. It's surprising. Where'd she come from?

There you are, I say. I wasn't sure you saw me, I say.

I didn't, she says. Until I happened to turn around, she says.

Oh, I say.

But I'm here, she says.

Good, I say. That makes me glad, I say.

She kisses my cheek.

Well, I say. I'm glad, I say. But look, I say. I found my bike. It was in the creek and I got it out and it's all okay, it's all fixed. Maybe it was never hurt, I say. Maybe it was spared, I say. Look at it. How beautiful it is, I say. A machine.

But when we look at it, it is rusty, bent, incomplete. Crashed. Dead. Remember: I killed it. It will never live again. I touch the bike. It turns out to be floppy. This is a final blow. It is rusty, bent, incomplete, dead, and floppy.

Oh, I say. And I'm crying. Let me search again, I say. Mom, I say, let me look in the water. This isn't the bike I just pulled out.

If that's what you have to do, she says.

I can do better, I say. I can.

I dive into the water. I go down, down, into the realm. The feeling of the water pressing on my eardrums. The suggestion of a current. The way shadows are darker underwater, the way bubbles sound coming out of your nose. I can't reach the bottom. I know the bike is there if I can reach it. It's darker down there than I thought. But I can see my own face for a moment, just a moment. I'm kicking. Hard to swim straight down. Hard even for a lifeguard. I'm a good swimmer, but this is hard. How long will I be able to hold my breath? Well, it's worth it. I'm going down, see. See?

But it burns. Inside. It burns inside. You hold your breath too long. You deny yourself breath. You can't do it forever. I am getting deeper and deeper, but it is hard to say how deep. There is a whining in my ears. Will this damage my eardrums? An ache, yes, fine—I'll accept that. But pain? Permanent damage? I'm not sure I'm making progress. Will I give up? What is that noise? There is something approaching from far away. I hear it. I stop kicking my feet. I turn around. What's wrong? What is that noise? I head back to the surface of the water, but it is night outside now and it is hard to determine what is up and what is down. But I know I am headed the right way. The sound is getting louder, even as the ache within my chest grows worse. I'm kicking as fast as I can. Why is the surface so far away? I should wake up. Gracie is screaming. That's Gracie. Gracie is screaming. I hear her. She's real, not a dream. She's real.

Wake up.

Wake up! For Gracie!

I do. My eyes are open. I'm breathing. The morning is bright. I am sweating in my sleeping bag. I'm blinking. The sun is up, up in the sky. I'm kicking off the sleeping bag. It's twisted around me somehow. Gracie is screaming nearby and finally I am up and running. Where is she? I run past Paer, who just now raises his head. I run across the lawn toward the house.

"Gracie!" I call.

I'm closer. I come around the house. I hear her. I run past the shed. I know where she is. I run. Behind the shed is Stephen's pen. Beside the pen is Gracie, still screaming. And Stephen—

I stop. Just for moment. I see.

"Fuck," I say.

I go to Gracie. Only a few steps away. And she's standing close to the pen, close to the fence. She's standing close to Stephen, who is dead. He jumped from his pen one final time. But this time he was attached to his chain. And the chain was long enough to let him get over the fence, but not long enough to let him land on the other side. So he hung himself. And Gracie found him.

What do I do? I pick her up. She is not that big. I pick her up and I take her away. I remove her. I walk fast. I walk away. I walk away from the pen, from Stephen, and I don't know where I'm walking and Gracie's scream has become a wail. She is crying, wailing, and I am walking and talking to her. I'm carrying her. I tell her I'm sorry. I am sorry. It was an accident. We should have been more careful. It's not her fault. And it's not Stephen's fault.

I'm holding her and still walking. Her body is small. She is young. She is very young.

"I'm on your side," I tell her. "I always will be."

Thirteen

"WELL," AUNT CORENE SAID. "LET ME THINK ABOUT THAT."

We had burgers in hand, but as soon as we entered the car wash, we both stopped eating. Corene put the car into neutral and we waited there for several seconds before the track pulled us forward with a jerk. We approached the spray nozzles and the cabin of the car grew dark. Comfortably so. The water was loud against the sheet metal of Corene's sedan and I put my hand on the window and I could feel the force of the spray. And now the smell of the car wash came through the air-conditioning vents. There was a floral soapy smell and a suggestive musty smell, both of which were pleasant and both of which complemented the other.

There were suds on the windshield, sliding down, clotting. It was pretty. My skin in this light looked smooth and brown. Now a curtain of dangling blue and white strips of fabric was swaying in front of us, and now it was brushing the hood. It covered the windshield and blotted out our view of the world.

Everything was quiet for a moment. "It's been a long time," Corene said. "But I can't say that it's not sad for me to think about him."

"I know," I said.

Then hidden nozzles began shooting a second shower of water and soap onto the car and it was too loud to converse over. Then came another curtain of wagging fabric, a rinse, a wax spray, a delicate misty rinse, and finally the giant hot-air blower, which seemed so powerful there was the feeling that we might be blown backwards into the car wash. But we inched forward, the blower blew, the exit shone before us, and the sign gave us the green light and Corene pulled forward and the attendant dried our windows and gave us a thumbs-up. Corene waved to him and she idled across the lot and put the car in park and we both picked up our burgers again.

"But basically," she said, "the way I want to answer your question is to say that he was like you. Your father was like you."

Which didn't help. Which made me want to ask, well, what am *I* like?

My phone rang, somewhere beneath me on the couch, and I rolled over and found it and answered.

"Are you asleep?" Jenny said.

"No," I said. "I was," I said. "I fell asleep watching TV."

"It's not even ten yet."

"I know. I got up early."

I sat up. I was on the couch in the basement and the television was muted. I had called Jenny this afternoon, just after Corene had dropped me off, but Jenny had said she was busy.

"I don't mean to be a *bother*," she said.

"No, no," I said. "Let's do something. I want to see you."

"So what should we do?"

"I don't know," I said. I was groggy. There were giraffes on the television and their tongues were startlingly long. "It doesn't matter."

"Well, you can't come over here because my parents are having some kind of function. With people."

"Hm," I said. I was flipping through the channels and I came across coverage of the Tour de France. *Peloton! Peloton!* I said.

"What?" Jenny said.

The conversation went nowhere and we made no decisions and no resolutions except that Jenny would come pick me up in twenty minutes. So our wandering and nonproductive phone conversation had become a literal wandering. We meandered through town, uninterested in any destination that came to mind. I felt tired. I felt displaced. The streets of my own town were unfamiliar. I had been gone more than a week. Most of me was still back in Charbourg.

After we'd wandered a while, Jenny started talking on her cell phone with E. B. From this end, the conversation was unexciting. E. B. seemed to be doing most of the talking, so that Jenny's side of the conversation went like this: "Uh-huh. . . . Yeah. . . . Sure. . . . I know, I know. . . . You mean last night? Oh. . . . No. . . ."

So I ignored it until I heard her say, "I'm with him right now. We're driving around."

Pause.

"Nothing," Jenny said.

Pause.

"Nowhere," Jenny said.

Then E. B. apparently pitched a plan to Jenny and Jenny listened and considered it and I couldn't figure out what the plan was. "Okay," Jenny said, "we're, like, at the corner of Hoyt and Edgewier, so we'll be there in two minutes."

They said good-bye and Jenny hung up.

"Be where?" I asked.

———

We parked several doors down from E. B.'s duplex. Jenny turned off the van and I looked across at her in the dark and she looked at me for a moment, then she reached for the door handle. We walked down the middle of the street. The neighborhood was quiet. There was a lot of on-street parking here. The trees were small. The whole neighborhood was only twelve years old. The sky above the neighborhood was orange—the city lights reflecting off of low clouds. I remembered when this neighborhood was built. I remembered the sound of bulldozers audible from our backyard.

We walked through the muggy night air and then we turned up the sidewalk to one duplex. They all looked the same.

To my surprise, the door of the duplex opened and E. B. stuck her head out.

"Hi, girlfriends," she said.

"Hi, princess," Jenny said.

"Yick," E. B. said.

"Yick what?" Jenny said.

"It's muggy out here," E. B. said.

"Bleck yick blurg," Jenny said.

E. B. laughed. "Hi, Leo," she said.

"Hi," I said. I was suddenly self-conscious. I was aware that Jenny and I were being seen together. Not that this was really a date, per se. And not that we hadn't been seen together by E. B. dozens of times when we dated last year. And not that we hadn't been seen by other people on our date at the end of June. But those people had been strangers.

"The story," E. B. said, "is that my mom is knocked out. I'm not saying she's a heavy sleeper, but she's not a light sleeper, either. She's somewhere in the middle. But she worked a huge banquet last night and only got three hours of sleep."

We went inside and the house was dark and there was the ticking of a clock. We crept up the entry stairs and turned down the short hallway. There was a night-light in the kitchen, and another in the bathroom. And at the end of the hallway we entered E. B.'s room and she closed the door. It was dark in here and we all went to the far side of the room and sat under the window. There was some light coming through the window, and we were partially hidden behind the bed if E. B.'s mother happened to open the door.

"One of the questions," E. B. said, "is what would my mom do if she caught us?"

"She might ban me," Jenny said.

"Yes, but what about Leo?" E. B. asked.

We were all whispering.

"I'm going to suggest," I said, "that it probably depends on what she catches us *doing.*"

"Yes," Jenny said.

"Good point," E. B. said.

We all nodded a while.

What we did was body tricks. Jenny, for example, could touch her nose with her tongue.

Then E. B. asked us if we could curl our tongues. I could. Jenny couldn't. E. B. could. Then E. B. did this thing where she curled her tongue and then *whistled* through it. I'd never heard such a thing, and me and Jenny burst out laughing. Then E. B. suddenly slapped her hand over her mouth and held up one finger with her other hand. We shut up and listened. There was a noise outside E. B.'s room. A door shut. A fan started whirring.

"She's in the bathroom," E. B. said. "You guys lie here," she said, pointing at the floor. She got into the bed and Jenny and I lay together beside the bed. After a while, we heard the bathroom fan stop and then there was a long silence and then we heard another door close. We continued to wait. I'd met E. B.'s mom a few times, and she was nice but maybe a little tense. She was a sous-chef at the big hotel downtown.

Finally, after enough silence had passed, E. B. rolled over and looked at us from above. "Coming down," she said. And she flipped her covers off and clambered down onto the floor, wedging herself between us. There wasn't much room back there.

"Where were we?" she said.

"You just whistled through your tongue," I said.

"Right, right," she said. "And are you impressed?"

"Yes," I said. "I'm all hot and bothered."

"You sure your mom can't hear us?" Jenny said.

"Oh, she's probably already asleep again," E. B. said.

"I don't know . . . ," Jenny said.

"Okay, we've all done a trick except Leo," E. B. said. She was propped up on her elbow right next to me. I was lying by the bed, E. B. was lying beside me, and Jenny was third.

"I don't have any tricks, I don't think," I said.

"Don't play coy with me," E. B. said. "Out with it!"

She poked me.

"Maybe we should go," Jenny said.

"I'm not double jointed," I said. "I can't wiggle my ear. I certainly don't have any tongue tricks. You both did tongue tricks."

"Can you make any interesting sounds?" E. B. asked. "Interesting sounds would be acceptable."

"Sounds?"

"Like, can you make a drip noise with your mouth?"

"In fact, I can," I said. And I made a drip noise with my mouth.

"Cool," E. B. said. "Is there a drip in here?" she asked, looking toward the ceiling, holding her palms out like she was wondering if was raining. "Is there a drip in here? 'Cause I just heard a drip."

I made another drip.

"I think that's your special purpose in life," E. B. said. "To make that drip noise."

"They teach it to all lifeguards," I said. "It's not special."

"Well, downplay it if you want, but I'm blown away," E. B.

said. She craned her neck and looked at Jenny. "Aren't you impressed, Jenny?"

"Mm," Jenny said.

"Wait," I said. "I can do this other thing. This other body noise."

"Don't josh me, man," E. B. said. "Don't bird-dog me. Don't yank my toupee. Don't suck the helium out of my balloon."

"No, really. Listen." I pulled up my shirt and I plopped the pad of my index finger onto my belly button. The resulting noise was a modest but endearing plop. I repeated it a few times.

E. B. was transfixed. "Belly button noises . . . ," she said, listening. "Belly button noises!"

Jenny sighed an exaggerated sigh.

E. B. took my shoulder and looked into my eyes. "Leo," she said, *"teach me."*

I explained the technique but she couldn't quite get a satisfying plop and so I had to demonstrate on her and she was ticklish whenever my fingers touched her but finally she calmed down and I made a good plop and she smiled. Then she winked at me.

"It's all about landing the finger so that it's perfectly centered on the belly button," I said. "That ensures a good seal, which is key to a satisfactory plopping noise."

"Maybe my middle finger will work better," she said.

"Whatever is most comfortable for you," I said. "Now try again."

And this time she succeeded and her eyes widened. "This is the best thing anyone has ever taught me," she said. She kept plopping.

"I aim to please," I said. "That's my motto."

"I think we're going now," Jenny said.

"My question for you, Leo Peery," she said, "is whether you are a belly button virgin."

163

"A whatzit?"

"A belly button virgin."

"I'm not kidding," Jenny said.

"How would I know if I'm a belly button virgin?" I asked.

"What are we, in second grade?" Jenny said.

"Has anyone," E. B. said, "ever done this to you?" And she reached over and poked her finger into my belly button. It was ticklish and cozy at the same time. I flinched.

"Sheesh!" I said, a bit too loudly.

"Well," E. B. said. "Are you or aren't you?"

"I guess I'm not any*more*," I said.

We laughed, then we both sighed. Jenny propped herself up on her elbows and was staring at us.

"Oh, I wish I'd known you when I was young," E. B. said to me. "Think of the fun we could have had."

"Yeah," I said.

Jenny sighed through her nose.

"What did your mom make for the banquet last night?" I asked. I was comfortable, lying on the carpet, looking up at the textured ceiling.

"You really want to know?" E. B. asked.

"I do," I said.

"Well, she made some mousse cakes. One chocolate and one hazelnut. And she made a genoise with a kumquat syrup and a white chocolate glaze. And she did these strawberry crêpe things."

"I didn't know she was a pastry chef," I said.

"She's not," E. B. said, "but she can make anything. And it was a dessert banquet. These people only wanted desserts served. There were twenty different kinds of desserts."

"A dessert banquet! Wow. . . . I didn't know there was such a thing."

"I know, I know!" E. B. said. "It's amazing. I want a dessert banquet at my wedding!"

"Me too," I said. "I want a dessert banquet at your wedding."

"My mom made seven of the desserts. There were two other chefs."

"What else did she make?"

"A blackberry tart with crème fraîche."

"What kind of crust are we talking about?" I asked. "Pâte brisée?"

"Yes, but it had a big cinnamon punch in it—cinnamon actually in the crust."

"Yum," I said.

"How do you know what pâte brisée is?" she asked.

"I just do. What else did she make?"

"Some coffee crème brûlées. And some pears poached in Riesling."

"You're killing me," I said.

"No, you're killing *me*," she said.

"No," Jenny said, "I'm the one you're both killing."

Fourteen

WHEN I ARRIVED, I WAS SURPRISED TO FIND JENNY WAITING FOR me under the trellis.

"The parents are still asleep," she explained. "And I didn't want you to wake them up with the doorbell. As if they won't be in bad enough moods with their hangovers."

She was wearing her tennis whites, but she looked bleary.

"How long did people stay last night?" I asked.

"Well, I woke up at three," she said, "because there was some kind of sing-along going on."

"Yikes," I said.

We passed through to the courtyard. There were several pairs of shoes and sandals in the pool. Some were floating, some were sunk.

"I don't even want to think about what this means," Jenny said.

"It means that there are Republicans all over the county waking up this morning and saying to themselves, 'Now, where the bric-a-brac are my *shoes*?'"

Jenny laughed.

"'Where in the bric-a-brac are my *penny loafers*?'"

And some patio chairs had been left in the middle of the tennis court. We relocated them.

I sat on the courtside bench and opened my tennis bag. "I brought a new can of balls," I said.

"That's very nice," Jenny said. "But it's my court, you're my guest, and I insist we play with the home equipment."

She opened the lid to the big foot locker and I got a glimpse of all the cans of balls packed in there. She took out one can. Then she got us each a bottle of water from the little courtside fridge and we both opened our water and drank and then we put the water back into the fridge to keep it cool and we walked onto the court. Though it was only nine o'clock, the heat of the day had already announced itself.

"What's with your outfit?" Jenny asked, stretching her arms.

I was wearing cutoffs and an old T-shirt.

"Do you think that by deriding my clothes you can gain some kind of psychological advantage?"

"The thing is," she said, "I don't even need a psychological advantage."

"If that's what you need to tell yourself . . . ," I said.

"It's just that you look . . . well. Well, I'm wondering which trailer park you wandered off from."

"That's it," I said. "Let's get this game under way."

We were well matched on the court. Historically, I had won every match, but only by a narrow margin. A typical set would be 4–6 or 5–7. On the court, Jenny had finesse, intuition, versatility, and a remarkable backhand. She also put more spin on the ball than anyone else I knew. She had been the cocaptain of the tennis team last season. I, on the other hand, had quit the tennis team after sophomore year. But I didn't quit because I was bad. I was a solid baseline player. I hit the ball with pace, had great foot speed, and a devil-may-care brashness. I also had a golden serve.

In my first service, I hit three aces in a row. I could see that it was upsetting Jenny. She didn't mind losing to me, but she hated my aces.

In my second service I hit an ace and Jenny screamed at the ball as she lunged for it. She dropped her racket in the attempt.

"Do you want me to back off the serves?" I called.

"No!" Jenny said, picking up her racket.

"You sure?" I asked.

"Serve!" she said.

So I served, putting a little extra juice into it, and it rocketed straight at her and it jammed her and the ball ricocheted off her knuckles. She shook her hand in pain, then sucked on her knuckles.

"Sorry," I said.

She glared at me.

"Serve," she said.

"Thirty–love," I said.

I took a breath and cleared my mind, then went into my routine. The serve was beautiful, and it flew at her and I was sure it was another ace. But she somehow managed to get a backhand on it, despite being off-balance, and she grunted when she hit the ball and the combined velocity of my serve and her vicious backhand sent the ball back to me so fast that I wasn't prepared. The ball was coming right at me and I must have hesitated a split second, and the ball bounced off the court and came toward my waist and I tried to get the racket there but it was an awkward shot and the ball hit the frame of my racket and bounced up and smashed into the bottom of my chin. It was like getting punched.

I bent over. There was a buzzing, burning sensation where the ball had hit.

"Thirty–fifteen," Jenny said.

"Can I have a second?" I asked.

"Thirty–fifteen," Jenny repeated.

And that was the last conversation of the match, which I lost in straight sets. After hitting me with the ball, Jenny changed. She played with a new energy. She was fast and cunning and I could never get the court position I wanted. She rushed the net often, surprising me every time. Instead of being overwhelmed by my fast shots, she used the power in them to fire them right back at me, plus her usual spin. And whenever I would finally get myself set up and comfortable on the baseline, she would pop these weak little bloopers over the net, and they would drop in for a point.

She was mad. That was all. She was angry. And she beat me. For the first time ever, she beat me.

On my way home, I went to talk to Leland. His auto shop was just off Avery Avenue, not far from home, on a little dead-end street. I pulled up and saw that all the bay doors were open—he'd never had air-conditioning—and as I walked across the pavement I could hear the radio playing inside the garage. Leland listened to an AM station that played big-band music.

I stepped into the garage and looked around. As usual, there were a few cars being worked on at the same time, and Leland was nowhere to be seen. He was the only mechanic here—he always was, except during the school year when I worked ten hours a week.

"Leland?" I called.

"Who's that?" I heard him say.

"Where are you?"

"I'm up in the business of this Volvo," he said.

I walked toward the 240 station wagon and I saw his legs peeking out from underneath.

"What's going on down there?" I asked.

He slid out from underneath the car. He had a torque wrench in one hand.

"Who's that I'm looking at?" he asked.

169

"Hi, Leland."

"Who is this man?" he said. "Who is this *stranger*?"

"What're you doing under there?" I asked.

"Leo, you know fine and dandy what I'm doing back under there."

"Mostly napping?" I said.

"Bingo," he said.

"What year?" Leland asked.

" 'Eighty-four," I said.

We were sitting in the little office, which was primarily a storage room for stacks of Chilton's manuals and old invoices.

Leland nodded. "That was a good year," he said. He gestured to the wall and there was a calendar, faded and curled, displaying May of 1984. It was a Corvette calendar.

"But like I said, it's been in storage for maybe sixteen years."

"A Supra?" he asked.

I nodded.

"Black?" he asked.

"How did you know?"

"Because I remember the car. I serviced it for your mom. But I thought she sold it a long time ago."

"No, it's sitting in our garage."

"Is the garage climate-controlled?"

"Yes."

"What about the fluids?"

"We took care of them every couple of years."

"Mm hm," Leland said. He sipped from a can of store-brand soda.

"And now I want to revive it."

"Want to sell it?"

"No, I want to drive it."

"You'll like it," he said. "You know I'm not partial to the

170

Japanese cars, but the MKII is a sweet piece of locomotion."

"I'm going to have to take it apart, look in every nook and cranny."

"That you are."

"And I don't have the right tools at home," I said.

"Uh-oh—I see where this is headed."

"I need a dial indicator, a bunch of pullers, an engine stand, a ridge reamer, a ring groove cleaner—"

"Uh-huh."

"And most of all I need a lift."

"You're saying you don't have a lift at home?"

"No, Leland, I don't have a lift at home. Do you?"

"And you're waltzing in here like the prodigal son and wanting to take up my floor space with some pet project?"

"Exactly."

"Okay," he said. "You can do it."

"Of course I can. As if there was any question."

"Well," he said, "you know my motto."

"I do," I said.

"Fixing cars for whitey since 1971."

"I thought it was '72."

"'Seventy-one. But tell me, how many miles are on this scrap heap?"

"Just over four thousand."

"Four thousand?"

"Yeah."

"Oh, heck," he said. "This'll be easy. Even for you."

"Thanks," I said.

"Even for a *lifeguard*."

"Hey, man. Don't give me that. Three-quarters of the year I'm a mechanic."

"Well, I'm looking at you now and I'm seeing a lifeguard," said Leland. "And since you're going off to college soon, well, I know you're not going to be commuting back just to work part-time for an old hound like me. And I know you're not going off to a hotshot university to study car repair."

"I'll always be a mechanic," I said. "I had a great teacher and I have grease in my veins."

"Hm," Leland said.

"Metaphorical grease," I clarified, "not real grease."

"Have you decided what you're going to study yet?" he asked.

"The jury's still out on that one," I said.

"Well get yourself a new jury," he said. "That's my recommendation."

I shrugged.

"How's your mother?" he asked.

"I don't know," I said. "She's fine," I said. I shrugged.

"That reminds me. You know something I heard the other day?" Leland said.

"No, what."

"I heard someone say that doctor is just a fancy word for mechanic."

I nodded. "I guess that's about right."

"I never taught you anything," he said. "I just want to be clear about that. I just gave you access is all. And tools."

Mom was actually standing in the driveway when I pulled up. She rapped on the windshield. I got out.

"Leo!" she said. "I told you I had to be at the hospital at one, and here you are rolling up at twelve-fifty-five!"

"I'm sorry, sorry. I forgot."

"This meeting is important," she said.

"I know. I'm sorry. Here, go." I gave her the keys. "Go. I'll walk to work. They won't mind if I'm fifteen minutes late."

She got in the car.

"I don't mean to be snippy," she said. She started the engine.

"It's okay," I said. "Go! It's okay."

"It's just that this new administration has us cornered."

"Go, go, go."

"I think they hate doctors. I think they actually hate doctors. But who they really hate is patients."

"Good luck," I said.

"Thanks, honey. I'll see you later."

She shut the door and backed out of the driveway.

I went in the house and the cat was on the counter, licking a bowl of tuna salad.

"Okay," I said, removing her from the counter, "if you're going to pilfer our food, go ahead and *eat* it. Don't just lick it. That's just affected."

I put the cat down and she sat there and I realized she was just waiting until I left so that she could get back on the counter.

"Bad kitty," I said. "Bad, bad, bad."

She was looking at me with a bunch of attitude.

"Bad *Kitty,*" I said emphatically. "That's right," I said. "*That* Kitty had a capital K."

I dumped the tuna down the disposal.

Upstairs, I checked my answering machine. There was one hang-up, which was odd. I changed into my swimming suit and I grabbed my whistle and my sunglasses and my hat. I looked at myself in the mirror and then I went into the bathroom and put on sunscreen.

As I walked toward the pool, a car slowed beside me and honked. It was Greg. So I ended up being on time for work anyway.

On my break, I looked around the busy pool. I was looking for a quiet corner. On the far side of the pool was one of the sun-bathing decks. Though the pool was busy, this deck was only sparsely populated. I wandered over there. I pulled one of the lounge chairs close to the chain-link fence and I sat there and looked up the long lawn. There was not much activity in the park today. It was just a bit too hot. The trees at the crest of the hill were still. The cicadas were droning in the distance.

"How much do you love summer?" someone said.

I looked to my left. There lay a girl, sunbathing on her stomach, her arms against her sides. She was lying on a large beach towel, and she was looking at me with only one eye. Her other eye—the one against the towel—was closed. She was about my age.

"I don't know," I said.

"Sure you do," she said. "Think about it. I can tell by the way you walked over here and how you were looking up the hill just now."

"The way I walked?"

"You walked slow and you looked at your feet a couple of times."

"I like being barefoot. I could feel the hot concrete. And in some places it has that nice rough texture."

"See," she said. "I could tell you loved summer."

I'd certainly seen her before, but I couldn't place her.

"Love is such a strong word," I said.

"That's why I used it," she said. "I picked that word out. I meant that word." She adjusted herself a little bit so that she was now looking at me with both eyes. I felt like she was waiting for me to say something. "What if," she finally said, "you asked me the same question?"

"The summer question?" I said.

"Yes."

"Okay," I said. "How much do you love summer?"

"Beyond measure," she said.

I smiled. It was a nice answer. "Why?" I asked.

"Why beyond measure or why do I love summer?"

"Both," I said.

She propped herself up on her side. She was pretty. I had already known that, but now it was more evident.

"Come sit over here," she said.

I started dragging my lounge chair toward her. It made a horrible noise on the concrete.

"Wait," she said. She reached into the canvas tote beside her and pulled out another beach towel. She threw it to me and I caught it. I walked to her and spread the towel near her. I lay on my stomach and crossed my arms underneath my head. I faced her. She was in a similar position.

"Good," she said. "Now tell me what the rules of summer are."

"The rules of summer?"

"That's right."

"You didn't answer my question about why you love summer so much."

"I'm trying to. Just follow me for a moment."

"Wait—I know who you are. You're Stacy Freese."

"And you're Leo Peery."

"But we've never really met before, have we?"

"Not really," she said.

"But you know who I am?"

"Well, apparently you know who I am, too. It's not a very big town, is it?" she said.

It was obvious why I knew her. Stacy Freese was at the pinnacle of the A-crowd. But in many respects she transcended the A-crowd—transcended the entire system—because she was above their pettiness. She was gracious and smart and personable. Seeing her here was somehow shocking, though. That's why it took me so long to recognize her. Here she was, alone, enjoying the sun. She was genuine, and that's why everyone liked her.

"Let's get back to it," she said. "Tell me what the rules of summer are."

I thought about it. "I'm not sure there are any," I said.

"Exactly," she said. "And the boundaries dissolve. The old patterns are irrelevant."

"But that makes it sound like chaos."

"It's not chaos because it is contained. It's part of a cycle. And it's both destructive *and* creative."

I shuddered. "What are we talking about here?" I asked. "What are we discussing?"

"We're trying to approach it too directly, aren't we?"

"Maybe so."

"I don't normally talk like this," Stacy said. "Really I don't. Just so you know. But we have a connection."

I smiled. Then I nodded, which felt odd because of the position I was lying in. My head moved inside the nest of my arms.

"But look at what we're doing right now," she said. "How we're talking. How we've never met each other, but because it's summer we can talk like this. You came over and lay down and it felt natural, as if we've known each other for years. That's summer. Summer opens the world."

"Yeah," I said.

"Or like this," she said. "Look at my hand. Look at this." She held out her hand, rotated it in the sun, closed it, opened it, flexed it, moved her fingers individually. "The back of my hand. The front of my hand. The palm. The fingers. The knuckles. The fingernails. The tips of the fingers. The little tips. I see it. I feel it. I move it. There's no thinking involved. The sun is warm on my hand."

I held out my own hand, moving it like she was moving hers.

"I see it," I said.

"When it's summer," she said, "I don't even think about the other seasons. I forget them. They don't exist. And when it's not summer, I don't think about summer. I forget about summer. The winter is like a tunnel and you just move forward and eventually you escape. Spring is change. Autumn is acceptance. But summer is . . ."

"Summer is summer," I said.

"Yes."

"Summer is a realm," I said.

"That's it," she said. "That's it exactly."

I smiled again. I sighed through my nose. Our conversation had ended. There was an easiness to it. There wasn't any pressure to keep talking. We looked at each other and I watched as Stacy's eyelids slowly narrowed. She was sleepy. So was I. The sun was warm on my back. The concrete was warm beneath me, through the beach towel. My nose was close against the skin of my arms, and that skin smelled good. And my arm hairs were blond—bleached by the sun.

Then, from across the pool, the PA system crackled and Wanda's voice came through it: "Mister Leo Peery, report to the pool house. Mister Leo Peery, please report to the pool house. Your break is over, slick."

I entered the pool house and I was feeling sleepy. I was feeling detached.

"Leo, Leo, Leo," Wanda said.

"Lee-o," Pepper sang.

"Leo, Leo, Leo," Sam said.

"Leo, Leo, Leo, Leo," Wanda said.

"Uh-oh," I said.

"We were waiting for you, Leo," Sam said. She was leaning across the counter.

"Leo, Leo, Leo," Pepper said.

"Oh, boy," I said. "I can tell that something's going on, but I don't know what it is." I looked at Becky. She was the only one who hadn't said my name. She wasn't even on duty today. Apparently she was just visiting.

"We arranged," Wanda said, "so that Greg and Thayler would be on duty at the same time so we could talk to you alone."

"Is this some kind of intervention?" I asked. "Because I swear I've given up gambling."

"We've got a proposition for you," Sam said.

"Okay, first off, that's illegal."

"Not that kind of proposition," Pepper said.

"Talk to me," I said.

"Look at us," Wanda said.

"I can do that," I said.

"I mean, look at us," she said again. "Aren't we wonderful?"

"Yes," I said.

"Me and Pepper and Sam and Becky? Aren't we wonderful?"

"You're all splendid. An embarrassment of riches."

"We know," Pepper said.

"I know you know," I said.

"We *like* you," Wanda said.

"I like you, too," I said.

"And we don't like many boys," Wanda said. "But we really like you."

"I'm starting to get scared, girls," I said. "So tell me what's what."

"Okay," Wanda said.

"Give me the heads-up," I said. "Because I'm getting worried here."

"Don't be worried," Pepper said.

"What's the deal?" I asked.

"The deal," Sam said, "is that tonight is our girls' night out."

"Uh-huh," I said.

"Doesn't that sound like fun?" Wanda asked.

"Yes," I said. "Good for you."

"All the sudden I'm shy," Sam said.

"I thought we agreed that you were going to ask him," Wanda said. "Since it was your idea in the first place."

"I'm shy all the sudden," Sam said.

"Do you want me to leave?" I asked.

"No, no, no," Sam said.

"No!" Pepper said.

"No," Wanda said. She nudged Sam. "Go ahead," she said.

Sam shook her head. "I'm sorry," she said. "I just got shy."

"It's okay," I said.

"Okay, I'll do it," Wanda said.

"Do what?" I asked.

"See," Wanda said, "tonight me and Pepper and Sam and Becky and Rachel and Valerie have our girls' night out. All the girl lifeguards. Of course, Rachel and Valerie aren't working today, so they couldn't be here to ask you, but Becky was nice enough to come by just for this."

"Thank you, Becky. I guess."

"And what we're doing," Wanda said, "is asking you to come with us."

"Come with you where?" I asked.

"On girls' night out," Wanda said.

"I'm missing something," I said. "Because the title implies that I'm not invited."

"We're bending the rules for you," Sam said. "We want you to come."

"Oh," I said.

"There's going to be all kinds of frivolity," Pepper said.

"Well, I do love frivolity," I said.

"So that's what we wanted to ask you," Wanda said.

I looked at Becky again. "Becky," I said, "you haven't said anything this whole time."

"Come," she said.

"You're all wonderful," I said. "And this is a great honor. This is a wonderful, happy thing."

"We won't let you say no," Sam said.

"Do it for us," Wanda said.

"Do it," Pepper said, "for the Commodore."

Commodore Wilbert E. Longfellow, the father of modern lifeguarding, was a figure we often evoked. We also frequently swore on his grave.

"I don't know, girls," I said.

"I'm going to pretend I don't hear you waffling," Wanda said.

"Our happiness depends upon you," Pepper said.

"See, that's just out of whack to begin with," I said.

"We'll pick you up at eight," Wanda said. "Pepper's driving."

"It's just that I'm busy tonight," I said.

"You are not," Wanda said.

"I am."

"You are not," Wanda said.

"I am."

"Who with?" Wanda said.

"Yeah, who with?" Pepper said. "You're not busy."

"Why don't you like us?" Wanda said.

"I'm with Jenny," I said.

"Jenny?" Wanda said.

"Yes," I said.

"Jenny who?"

"Jenny Previer."

"Jenny Previer?" Wanda said. "You guys broke up a long time ago. Decades ago."

"We're back together," I said.

"I don't believe you," Wanda said.

"I swear," I said. "It's tedious but true."

"But," Wanda said, "didn't you, like, ask her to prom and then turn around and ask someone else without even telling her?"

"That's a rumor based on almost nothing," I said.

"I hate Jenny Previer," Pepper said.

"Wait," I said. "I want to clear this up about prom. I'm tired of hearing the story mangled. See: I asked E. B.—Jenny's best friend—if she thought Jenny would say yes if I asked her to prom. I was *thinking* of asking her. But I decided not to. We weren't close this spring. So I asked Amanda Breckenridge instead. But E. B. told Jenny that I'd made inquiries and Jenny thought I was going to call and so she bought a dress and turned down a couple of other guys but of course I didn't call and she didn't go to prom and somehow I got blamed for the whole mess."

They were absorbing this. It was something they'd all heard about.

"You're too good for her," Wanda finally said. "End of discussion."

"I don't know what to tell you guys."

Wanda sighed. "We'll see you at eight," she said.

"I'm sorry, guys," I said. "I can't."

"Eight!" Wanda said.

Later, I was up in the first tower. The pool was still packed, and there were a lot of swimmers to keep track of, which was one reason it took me several seconds to notice the little kid calling up at me from the water just underneath me. This kid was with another kid, a scrawnier kid. They looked about Gracie's age. I recognized them as part of a group of boys that had been playing a frantic chasing game moments earlier.

"Seth says he can't breathe," the first kid said.

I looked at the second kid. He was pale and he was breathing through his mouth and he was frightened. He was breathing fast. I blew my whistle twice to attract Sam's attention. She was in the second tower and when she looked at me I patted my head and then pointed to the kid in the water. She nodded. I climbed down from the tower and put my rescue float aside and got into the pool. I squatted in the water so that I was eye level with the scrawny kid. His friend was already gone.

"What's your name?" I asked him.

"Seth," he said.

"What's your last name?" I asked.

"Stahle."

"Do you have asthma, Seth?"

He shrugged.

"Do you take any medications?"

"I don't think so," he said.

"Seth," I said, "let's head over to the ladder and then we're going to get out of the water."

"Okay."

"Is your mom or dad here?"

He shook his head.

"What about a brother or sister? Are you here with anyone?"

"No. My mom dropped me off."

He was still breathing rapidly. When we got onto deck, Greg met us.

"What we've got here," I said, "is that Seth is a little bit hyperventilated. And we're going to go sit over there."

Greg nodded and left us.

"I still can't breathe right," Seth said.

"We're going to fix that," I said. "I promise you that. It's real simple. There's nothing really wrong with you. You're just a little excited."

We sat on the bench.

"What's hyperventilated?" he asked.

"Well, it's an excessive rate of respiration which leads to a depressed level of carbon dioxide in the bloodstream."

He looked at me and I could see that my answer had simply frightened him more.

"What it means," I elaborated, "is that in about two minutes you're going to feel normal again and there's nothing really wrong at all. You just were playing so hard that you got all worked up. It happens to the best of us."

This he seemed to understand. Greg reappeared with a small paper bag and I showed Seth how to breathe into the bag and he did it and while he did it I told him the story of how I had hyperventilated while playing basketball in fifth grade and how after I felt better we went on to win the game anyway. When Seth's breathing had slowed down I had him put the paper bag aside and I asked him how he felt and he said he felt better. I checked his pulse and it seemed normal. He was calming down.

Greg came back over and stood in front of us. He was already writing up the incident report.

"Everything okay?" he asked us.

"I think we're good to go," I said. "Seth here is a real sport."

"Is he here with anybody?" Greg asked.

"No," I said.

"How are you supposed to get home?" Greg asked him.

Seth said his uncle was going to pick him up.

"Well how about we call your uncle and have him pick you up a little early," Greg said. "How's that sound?"

Seth shrugged.

"Maybe it's best if you go home and take it easy for the rest of the day," Greg said to Seth.

"I want to stay," Seth said. "I want to swim more."

"We can't hold that against him," I said. "If the man wants to swim, I say we let him swim."

So we released Seth. He got right back into the pool. Greg wandered down the deck, writing on his clipboard, and I climbed back into the tower.

But I watched Seth. At first the wandered back over to the group of boys he'd been playing with before, but they made no gesture of inclusion, no welcome-back motion, and he hung on the margins of their game. He slunk along the rim of the pool, and he traced his finger along the grout between the tiles. He turned, putting his back against the side of the pool, and looked out across the busy water. He seemed to me to be very alone. At one point, a beach ball landed in the water near him, and he picked it up, prepared to throw it back to the girls who were playing with it, but before he could even throw it one of the girls actually came and took it away from him without saying anything. After that, he turned back toward the tile wall and he seemed to stare at it for a long time. Finally, he left the wall and started meandering slowly and somewhat joylessly through the midsection of the pool. When he wandered near my tower, I called his name, but he didn't respond. He looked like he was daydreaming. His wandering was slow and a bit reckless, a bit inconsiderate of other swimmers. I called his name again, but he apparently didn't hear. The pool was loud. I thought about blowing the whistle.

Slowly, though, he was getting into the deeper water. He'd already moved from the three-foot section to the four-foot section. Even the four-foot section was almost too deep for him, and only his head and the tops of his shoulders were above water. And now he was getting close to the five-foot section, which dropped pretty quickly into the diving well, where the pool was fourteen feet deep. In fact, technically he was out of my section of the pool. He was in the zone that was surveyed by the second tower.

I stood up in the tower. Seth was facing away from me at the moment. He bumped into a swimmer and I could see the kid say something mean to Seth, but Seth didn't respond. I climbed down from the tower. I got Sam's attention and signaled her to cover my zone. She nodded, but then held her palms up in a gesture that meant she didn't see any problem, didn't know why I was leaving my tower. I walked down the deck, getting closer to Seth. Greg and Thayler came out of the pool house.

"It's that kid who hyperventilated," I said to Greg. I pointed him out. "Something seems wrong."

"He's a space case is all," Thayler said.

"Watch," I said.

I blew my whistle—one sustained blast. And nearly everyone in the pool looked at me. Everyone but Seth.

"See?" I said.

Greg's brow was furrowed.

"I'm going in," I said.

When I got to him, it was clear immediately that his eyes were not focused on anything. The water was almost up to his chin, and he didn't respond when I spoke to him. And when I touched him, he didn't react. I took hold of his arm but he kept walking slowly forward. I positioned myself behind him to pull him to the side of the pool, but as I put my arm around him his body suddenly clenched up—like all his muscles were contracting at once—and he sank immediately.

Fifteen

I CAME HOME AFTER ELEVEN. I COULD HEAR THE DOWNSTAIRS television, so I went into the television room and there was Mom, curled up on the couch, wearing scrubs. I could see that she was awake, but it took her a few seconds to notice me.

"Oh, hi, honey," she said.

"Are you okay?" I asked.

"Sure."

"Is there anything I can do for you?" I asked.

"Hm? No, I'm fine, Leo."

"Are you sure?"

"I'm fine. I'm tired. I'm running on empty."

"Are you sick, Mom?"

"Hm?"

"Are you sick?"

"No," she said. She stretched a little bit.

"Shouldn't you say something like 'Why do you ask?' or 'That's a funny question'?"

"Leo . . . ," she said. She sat up and turned off the television. "What are you talking about?"

"I don't know," I said.

"Okay then," she said.

"How'd the meeting go?"

"Can I tell you tomorrow?" she said.

"Okay."

"It's just that I've decided not to think about it tonight."

"That's fine," I said.

"I heard that there was a kid," she said, "who was brought into the ER from one of the pools this afternoon. Was he from your pool?"

"No," I said. "What was wrong with him?"

"Oh, he was fine. He'd had a seizure."

"Oh," I said.

I went upstairs and thought about going back downstairs and talking to Mom. But I heard the door to her bedroom close. And then my phone rang.

"Where were you all night?" Jenny asked.

"I had this thing," I said, "with work. Everyone from the pool went out."

"I thought we were going to rent a movie tonight," she said.

"Is that what we said?"

"Yes. You don't remember?"

"No, I . . . I . . . I do remember. But this thing happened at the pool today and I felt like I needed to go out with everybody afterward."

"What kind of thing?"

"This kid almost drowned."

"Oh."

"Some little kid," I said.

"Well why didn't you call me?"

"I don't know."

"Who'd you go out with? Thayler and Greg?"

"Uh, they didn't come. It was Wanda and Sam and a few other people. I don't think you know them."

"Okay," she said.

"I'm sorry," I said.

"Sorry for what?"

"That I didn't call you and tell you."

"Fine," she said. "Okay."

"It's just that it scared me. This little kid had a seizure right in my arms. It was brought on by him hyperventilating and we thought he was okay but then he started spacing out and he had convulsions right when I got to him and if I hadn't been right there he would have inhaled a lot of water. He could have died. But I was right there. I was watching him the whole time and I was right there. So, I don't know, I'm still a little bit shook-up. I don't feel like the day was a real day. It was like a made-up day. I feel made-up. I don't know how to say it, or what there is to say even."

"Who else?" she said after a pause. "Wanda and Sam and who?"

"Uh, Pepper."

"You know I can call Wanda and ask who all was with you."

"Wanda and Sam and Pepper and these new lifeguards Rachel and Becky and Valerie."

"I hate Pepper and I hate Sam," she said.

"I know."

"It sounds like it was just a bunch of girls."

"It was."

"Where were the guys? Why wasn't Thayler there?"

"The guys didn't come. I don't know."

"What'd you do?"

"When?"

"What did you and Sam and Pepper and all the other girls do?"

"We went to a movie and then we went for ice cream."

"Where?"

"Little Dean's."

"I don't like this," she said.

"I'm sorry."

"This isn't right."

"I'm sorry," I said.

"Stop apologizing!"

"What do you want me to do?"

"You should have been with me."

"I know."

"What are we *doing,* Lee?"

"I don't know."

"You know what? Forget it. What do we have, like, only five weeks left? Six? Something like that? What are you trying to do to me?"

"I know."

"I want you to talk."

"It was a confusing day."

"Keep talking," she said. "Surely there's more."

"What do you want me to say?"

"That's a stupid question."

"I'm just lost is all."

"You don't call me. You go out with, what, six girls. You go visit your cousin for ten days without telling me—the day after we, after we . . . You . . . You're gone for ten days without calling." She made a frustrated growling noise. "You know what?"

"What?"

"I don't want to talk to you right now," she said.

"Okay," I said.

"I don't want to talk to you right now."

"This kid," I said, "could have drowned. But I was right there. I was right there."

"None of this is right at all," she said.

"I did call you," I said. "When I was in Charbourg."

"You left *one* message. *One* message. You were gone ten days and you left *one* message."

"I thought I left two."

"One."

"It's my fault," I said.

"Keep going."

"It's my fault because when I go to Charbourg it's like being in a different world. I get sucked into it. It's a whole different world and I get sucked into it. I told you that there's no phone at the farmhouse. And I'd left my cell phone at your house."

"Wait—what's that mean that it's a different world, that you get sucked into it?"

"It's just that it feels so separate from home."

"So do you have a separate girlfriend in Charbourg, too?"

"That's not who I am."

It sounded like she put the phone down for a second and then picked it back up.

"I shouldn't have said that," she said.

"It's okay."

"I shouldn't have said that."

"Listen: I'm here now. I'm not going back."

"I'm going to feel better in the morning," she said.

She hung up.

In the basement, in the rear storage room, lay my bike. I looked at it under the fluorescent lights. This was really the first time I had looked at it since the day of the accident. I don't know how long I stared at it. It looked dead—it *was* dead—and the fluorescent lights did not flatter it. Finally, I touched it. I lifted it. I clamped it into my bike stand. And I started stripping off the parts, one by one.

They were almost all ruined. The carbon-fiber seatpost was cracked. The saddle rails were bent. The saddle itself was badly scratched. The handlebars were bent where they'd hit the asphalt. One brake lever was dangling. Both wheels were bent. The rear derailleur was bashed. The chainring was bent. One pedal was ruined, as well as the crank.

So when the work was done, only a few parts were salvageable, including the brakes, the cogset, one crank, one pedal, the stem, the fork, the headset, the bottom bracket, and the front derailleur. The chain looked okay, too, but it needed replacing anyway.

Then I turned my attention to the frame. The gleam of the brushed titanium tubes was as pretty as ever, even in this light. I ran my fingers along the tubes —the top tube, the head tube, the down tube, and the seat tube—searching for any nicks, dents, or buckles. I found nothing unusual. The seams all looked clean and unchanged. I turned my attention to the rear of the frame. The chainstay and seat stay were carbon fiber, and I was worried about the effect the impact had had on them. But the only problem I detected was a very small scratch on the chainstay. Even the derailleur hanger seemed straight. The final test was to check the frame alignment. To do this I tied a length of string to one of the dropouts and then stretched the string around the head tube and tied its end to the other dropout. I then measured the distance between the string and the seat tube. The measurements on both sides of the seat tube was identical.

In other words, the frame was okay. My bike could live again. My bike *would* live again.

Sixteen

E. B. PICKED ME UP IN HER MOTHER'S CAR. THE CAR WAS A little Japanese sedan, about ten years old, and it had an exhaust leak that sounded like a cat purring. I climbed in the backseat and E. B. looked at me in the rearview mirror. Jenny was in the passenger's seat.

"Where have you been keeping yourself, chief?" E. B. said. "I haven't seen you in days and days and days."

"Oh," I said, "I've been busy with this and that. And the other."

"The other!" E. B. said. "That's wild."

"He's been holed up fixing things," Jenny said bitterly. "It's demented."

"Fixing what?" E. B. asked, backing out of our driveway a bit fast and a bit crooked.

"Vehicles," I said.

"Like what?" E. B. said.

"You know that bike he destroyed back in June?" Jenny said. "He's trying to resuscitate it."

"You destroyed a bike?" E. B. said.

"I did," I said.

"Why didn't I hear this story?" she asked.

We were moving down the street, through the neighborhood.

"You did hear this story," Jenny told her. "Remember when he showed up at my house bleeding?"

"Oh, *that* bike," E. B. said.

"That bike," Jenny said.

"That bike," I said. "And I'm working on a car, too."

"When aren't you working on a car?" E. B. said.

"But this one's for me," I said.

We hit a small pothole and suddenly the car's horn started sounding. It was a crazy warbling kind of honking and E. B. shrieked and started hitting the horn pad with her palm. The horn stopped sounding.

"Jeesh," Jenny said. "Good golly."

"What was that all about?" I asked.

"It's been doing that—going off on its own," E. B. said.

"That seems abnormal," I said.

"It keeps you guessing," Jenny said flatly. She was full of sarcasm. "You never know when it's going to start blasting. It really adds a lively and interesting element to one's life."

"I guess the question is," E. B. said, eying me in the rearview mirror, "can you fix *this* car?"

Jenny said, "He can fix anything."

At the fairgrounds, we were directed to park in the big field outside the west gate. We rolled along quietly over the grass. We parked. I put on my baseball cap.

It was only the second night of the fair, but it had an air of permanence to it. It was basically the same fair that we had seen last year. We walked through the livestock barn. We looked at the huge draft horses. They were kind, and they looked down at us with a little bit of pity. Back behind the barn was an area where people were washing their horses, hosing them down and scrubbing them, getting them ready for competition. The evening sunlight was lighting up the mist that came off the horses. The horses that were being washed were Appaloosas and Arabians.

On we went.

We all had corn dogs and then we all had monkey tails and then we all had snow cones. We took our snow cones and went to the Ferris wheel and stood in line. The line was moving forward because they were loading the Ferris wheel and when we got up to the gate the man said there was room for two more people but E. B. said that she would squeeze in. The man didn't look like he was moved by this, but then E. B. held out her arm toward him, and said, "See, squeeze me. I'm squeezable." He didn't squeeze her, but he did let her in, and the three of us wedged ourselves into the seat and lowered the bar. Our hips were packed tight against each other. I was in the middle. I put my hands on the safety bar and I looked at my snow cone and it was lovely and vibrant, and I said, "Look at our snow cones," and we three held our respective snow cones together and admired them and then went back to eating them. That's when the Ferris wheel's engine whirred into action and we were hoisted suddenly into the air and the fair revealed itself below us and we looked at our feet dangling in space and then we were at the top of the wheel and the sky was ours and the night was coming, coming, coming.

A while later we were in the 4-H building and we were looking at jars of mint jelly, pear butter, peach chutney, homemade catsup, and dewberry preserves. Then we looked at the rows and rows of pickles. None of the canned goods had been judged yet, so it was anybody's guess which ones were any good. Then we moved on to the quick-bread tables and here we found the blue ribbon corn bread, the blue ribbon muffins, the blue ribbon biscuits, the blue ribbon doughnuts, the blue ribbon coffee cake, and the blue ribbon "other quick bread"—which this year was an Irish soda bread. Then there were several long tables that were empty but which had a sign on them that said "Tomorrow Cookies."

"Mmm—tomorrow cookies . . . ," E. B. said.

We bought a tub of kettle corn that was bucket-sized, and we carried it to the grandstand. We bought some drinks there and we sat down and watched teams of horses pull wagons around the arena. The drivers sat stiff-backed on top of the wagons. Then the judge asked the drivers to back the wagons up. This appeared to be difficult. The horses didn't like doing this. There were only four teams competing, but when the judge was handed a microphone he talked at length about the remarkable quality of this year's competitors. He was a man with an amiable Oklahoma accent, and you just knew that he was someone's favorite uncle. He kept talking. He made specific comments about each team. Finally, the winner was picked and the crowd applauded and the team took a celebratory lap around the arena. I got a warm feeling from seeing it.

Just after the wagon teams left the arena, there was some kind of cattle leak somewhere and about a dozen young steers came running into the arena. They sprinted across the middle of the arena, feeling their oats, kicking up their heels, and then they slowed and got all bunched up at the other side of the arena. They looked around, but they really didn't know what to do next. They were out of ideas, and they were burdened with small and unsophisticated brains. A couple of cowboys rode into the arena and headed toward the steers. Jenny asked me if this was planned, if this was an event of some kind, but I said it wasn't. The cowboys easily ushered the steers back the way they had come—yelling "Hya! Hya!" and "Hup!" all the way—and they hustled the steers through an open gate and the gate banged shut and the cowboys rode off at full tilt and exited at the other end of the arena.

There was scattered clapping.

Then some men rolled three barrels out into the dusty arena and set them up in a triangle pattern. The men carefully measured the distance between the barrels and made a couple of adjustments. They also measured the distance between the barrels and the fences.

"Are there clowns hiding in those barrels?" E. B. asked.

"No," I said.

"That's too bad," she said. "That's kind of a disappointment."

"We're here to be entertained!" Jenny yelled at the arena.

The announcer announced that now the regional barrel racing championship would be decided, a showdown between the barrel racing champions from fourteen counties. Only the top three finishers would go on to compete at the state fair in August.

Barrel racing is mainly a girls' and womens' event. And some of the racers tonight were small, and some were large. Some were teenagers, some were adults, and some were just girls. Some of the horses were great sprinters, while others were great cornerers. But since the object of the barrel race is to run a cloverleaf pattern around all three barrels without knocking over a barrel, only a horse with a combination of speed, acceleration, and agility would win. And the rider had to control all of it.

The horses were beautiful—the quarter horses, the Appaloosas, the Paints. There was even one Pinto. And the riders were good, but a great time was posted early and it looked like no one would match it. Everyone tried but failed. Finally the last competitor came out. She was referred to only by her number: 22. And her muscular stallion looked like he didn't have the finesse he needed, but as soon as he started running you could see that he was a champion, and that his rider knew what she was doing, and that the event was probably over. Number 22 and her mount took the turns fast and hard and they sprinted gorgeously between the barrels. They beat the best time by a full second, and the crowd cheered and the rider shook the judge's hand and there was still dust hanging in the air from her remarkable run.

"Who does she think she is?" Jenny said.

"She thinks she's a cowgirl or something," E. B. said.

"I'm pretty sure I hate her," Jenny said. "I'm almost sure."

"You know," E. B. said, "girls are supposed to grow out of liking horses when they turn twelve."

"Exactly," Jenny said.

"Exactly," E. B. said. "And I bet she's got a made-up-sounding name," E. B. said. "Some fake-sounding name."

"Precisely," Jenny said. "Like Marybeth Delilah."

"Yes," E. B. said. "Or April May June."

Of course, I knew the rider's name: Freeda Sweeney.

We were walking back to the car, and it was so dark we couldn't really tell where we were going. But we could see the dim shapes of the parked cars around us, and when a car passed and threw some light on the situation we realized we were pretty far from where we thought we were. Then we heard something. Something in the distance.

"Oh, Lordy," E. B. said.

We were hearing the sustained blaring of a car horn. Actually, this probably saved us several minutes of searching, because the horn led us right to the car. E. B. unlocked the car and started pounding the horn pad. But the horn kept sounding.

"Let me," I said. I banged on the horn a couple of times. It kept blaring. Then I knelt and searched for the fuse block under the dashboard, right by the driver's door. I took the cover off the fuse box and then I took the fuse puller from the lid of the fuse block. The cabin light wasn't throwing any light down there, so I felt for the correct fuse with my fingers. I pulled the fuse and the horn died.

"Praise be," E. B. said.

They asked what I had done and I explained it to them and they both remarked that they hadn't even known that cars had fuses.

"The only problem," I said, "is that the circuit that powers the horn is the same circuit that powers the brake lights. If I'm recalling correctly."

I put my foot down on the brake pedal and E. B. took a few steps backwards and looked at the brake lights.

"You're right," she said.

So we drove Jenny home without brake lights. Then E. B. took me to my house. She parked in the drive and turned off the engine and looked at me.

"You know what I want?" she said.

"No," I said. "What."

"Tomorrow cookies."

I nodded. "I think we all do," I said.

I told her to wait a second and I went and got the toolbox and then I came back outside. I had her move her car into the open bay of the garage so I would have more light to see what I was doing. I took off the steering wheel's center pad. I disconnected the horn and cruise control connectors. Then I plugged the horn fuse back into the fuse box. I took the horn plate assembly off the back of the center pad and I showed E. B.

"What's happening here is that there are these two copper plates, see. And these two plates are kept apart by this layer of foam. And when you press on the horn pad you compress the foam and the copper plates touch each other, thus closing an electrical circuit, which then sounds the horn. When you release the horn pad, the foam separates the plates and the circuit is broken. So what you've got here is some old, crusty, compressed foam that's not keeping the plates separated very well."

"Old, crusty foam," E. B. said. "That's embarrassing."

"So if you took this into the dealer they'd charge you ninety bucks for a whole new horn assembly, plus an hour of labor."

"What are you going to charge me?" E. B. asked.

"A nickel," I said. "Or maybe a dime."

"Cripes."

"But first we have to find some foam."

Which led us into the house. We looked in the utility closet. Then we looked in the craft drawer. Then we looked in Mom's sewing stuff. No luck. Finally, I remembered the little remnants of foam that were left over from when Mom reupholstered and replaced the foam in her reading chair last winter. E. B. and I found these remnants in the attic and then we took them to the garage and cut some nice slivers of foam with a utility knife. I pried the horn assembly's copper plates apart and rubbed away the old foam. It was glued to the plates but it came away really easily and the glue left the plates sticky so that the new foam would adhere just fine. E. B. and I arranged the new slivers of foam on one plate and then I carefully lowered the second plate down onto the first plate and then I reassembled the whole thing. When it was all done I had E. B. sit in the driver's seat and test it. It worked fabulously. The horn pad felt springy and lively again, whereas before it had felt hard and dead.

Then I decided I wanted to show E. B. my bike. So I led her to the basement and showed her into the storage room. And there was my bike, still clamped into the work stand. And it was complete again. I hadn't ridden it yet, but it was complete and it was happy and it was beautiful.

"I don't know anything about bikes," E. B. said. "But that's a pretty one," she said. "That is a gorgeous one."

"I know," I said. "Believe me."

Mom was out with Ruben, and as soon as E. B. left, the house felt large and lonely. I went to my room but nothing there appealed to me and I was not sleepy and so I went back downstairs. The doorbell rang and I went to the side door, expecting to see E. B. Or Jenny. But there was no one there. I walked through the house to the front door and I opened it. The heavy door swung smoothly on its hinges, and the smells of nighttime hit my face. And there, before me, stood Freeda Sweeney. Her pickup was parked on the street. And she was still wearing her Western wear from the fair. Her hands were in her back pockets, and she smiled and then inhaled and she was about to speak.

But I beat her to it.

"No," I said.

And I shut the door.

August

Seventeen

I WOKE UP BECAUSE MY HEAD HURT. I WENT TO THE bathroom and took four Tylenol and then got back into bed but I wondered if Mom was home so I went down the hall. The door to her bedroom was open. I went downstairs and looked in the garage and her car wasn't there. I stood there for a moment, then I went back upstairs and looked at my clock and it was exactly 3:00 A.M., which was the hour at which I always figured *very late* became *very early*. So I bridged the two. And I realized my stomach hurt, too. The food I had eaten at the fair was catching up to me.

I got back in bed and closed my eyes but aside from my head still hurting and my stomachache and the house being excessively silent there was something else wrong, some throbbing or pulsing and I thought I was imagining it or at least exaggerating it but finally I was so frustrated I sat up and opened my eyes and waited and sure enough, there was a firefly in my room, flying around and pulsing. He was impressively bright, but once I figured out that it was just a bug and not some kind of stroke or hallucination that I was experiencing, I tried to go back to sleep. But the firefly's pulsing was remarkably unnerving, not because it was too bright, but because it was always a question of when he was going to flare up next, and it never happened when I thought it would, and it was always a bit of a shock when it did happen. Like the phone ringing.

I sat up again and talked to him. "Little fella," I said. "Little fella." It was kind of a warning, but he didn't heed it.

I stood on my bed and tried to catch him but I couldn't see him except when he flared, so I turned on my light.

"Little fella!" I said. "Don't make me come over there!"

Finally, I did catch him and I took the screen off my window and released him but I didn't see him fly away or pulse and so I wondered if he'd escaped back inside or fallen down to the driveway or what. And I noticed that by opening the screen, I'd let in a couple of moths, who fluttered their way toward the shadowy apex of my bedroom's vaulted ceiling.

"Keep it quiet, boys," I told them, and I went back to sleep.

In the morning, I heard Mom moving about the house. I looked at my clock and it was exactly one minute before my alarm was set to go off.

There was a great smell in the house. Something was baking. Downstairs, I looked in the oven there were a dozen biscuits and the biscuits were puffy and almost done. Mom came into the room and said good morning and apologized for not calling me last night and telling me that she was staying at Ruben's. I told her it was okay and then I asked her if this meant she and Ruben were back together and she said that it meant nothing of the sort and then there was a muffled thud against the front door, and Mom said, "The paper's here," and she left the room. I poured myself some orange juice and I heard Mom open the front door and then she called to me and I went through the entry hall to the door and Mom was standing in the doorway, holding the paper in one hand and looking at something on the stoop.

"What is that exactly?" she asked.

It was pretty obvious.

"That," I said, "is a little pile of horse manure."

"What's it doing here?" Mom asked. "Who did this?"

"Oh," I said, "I'm sure it was just some neighborhood kids."

Eighteen

I GOT A LETTER FROM GRACIE.

Dear Leo,

I wanted to write a letter to you and Mom said she would help and so she is typing this into the computer while I talk and that is why it is printed out and the words are all spelled right and the grammar is so nice.

But what I wanted to express to you in this letter is an idea I have for Halloween. As you know, Halloween is a highly festive holiday and it happens to be my second favorite holiday after Christmas. I am still considering several different costume options, all of which are fantastic in their own way. For example: dust bunny.

You do realize of course that Halloween is less than three months away? It's best to start planning now.

Here's the idea I want to tell you about though. You take a big pumpkin, right? And then you scoop out all the goop and the strings and the seeds and then you carve it up as a jack-o'-lantern with a really big gaping mouth. Maybe with a couple of sharp teeth, right? Okay, and then you take a little pumpkin, okay? And you scoop out all the goop and the strings and the seeds and then you carve it up as a jack-o'-lantern, too.

And then comes the good part. You position this little jack-o'-lantern in the mouth of the big jack-o'-lantern so that it looks like the little jack-o'-lantern is getting eaten by the big jack-o'-lantern. See?

That's my idea, which I thought of. And the big jack-o'-lantern would have a mean face with sharp teeth and he would have an expression like he was biting down on something hard. And the little jack-o'-lantern would have an expression of fright or pain or both. Him being crushed and all. See?

Isn't that great?

Write to me and tell me what you think and also what is new with you. Me, I'm going shopping for school supplies this week and also sneakers.

Your cousin,
Gracie Frances

Nineteen

BEN SCHRIFF CALLED AND TRIED TO SPEAK GERMAN TO ME, despite my protestations. He was just home from German camp—he'd been there all summer. But the only thing I could figure out was that he was talking about some kind of colorful festivities, or a colorful feast perhaps.

"*Die Messe,*" he said. "*Messe, ja? Heute abend.*"

Was he talking about a knife now? "*Was?*" I asked. "*Worum handelt es sich eigentlich?*"

He growled, frustrated. "*Die Messe!*" he yelled.

"Okay, now we speak English," I told him. And he finally obeyed.

"The *fair,* my man," he said. "Let's go to the *fair.*"

"I've already been," I said.

"Well, we're going again."

"Are we really?" I asked doubtfully.

"Hey, buck up, buttercup," Ben said. "It's the fair's last night. This is what we're doing tonight. In good conscience, we cannot—no, we *must* not—sit idly by and allow these last glorious weeks of summer to slip through our fingers like so many grains of sand. It would not do. It would not befit us."

"I don't know," I said. "I think it would befit us just fine."

He convinced me, though, and he talked Jenny into it, too, and she agreed to drive. She picked me up in her minivan without even saying hello. Then we drove to Ben's neighborhood. He was sitting on the curb, waiting for us.

"So what's been going on all summer?" he asked when we were under way. "What's happened? What've you guys been up to? What's the news? What's the story? What's the deal? Tell me everything. Spill it."

"The thing is," Jenny said, trying to make a left onto Edgewier Avenue, "nothing happened. Nothing happened at all."

The fair was busy, the fair was bright. There seemed to be a lot of children in attendance—children without parents, without chaperones. A restless breeze pushed our hair, raised dust. The sounds of the sprint car races at the grandstand reverberated off of every cinder-block wall, every booth. And somehow, in the fray, we lost Ben.

In our Ben-bereft stupor we kept walking up and down the midway, hoping that these lights, these prizes would eventually attract him. For our part we avoided the game booths and rides and vendors, but at ten o'clock Jenny veered from the center of the midway, pulling me with her, so that I found myself standing before a cotton candy vendor who had not only attracted an impressive number of bugs to his lights, but who also did not seem to have the standard pink cotton candy but only yellow, green, and mauve.

"Lookit," Jenny said, tapping the glass that separated us from the sugar. She sighed.

"I'll get you whatever you want," I told her. "I will." I beckoned to the vendor man, who was loitering behind his booth.

"I'm smoking," he said.

Indeed he was, and the shadows in which he stood suggested what nothingness lay behind the midway's facade.

But suddenly Jenny was crouching. She was petting a mutt.

"Ben!" she exclaimed.

"That's not Ben," I observed.

"Sure it is. He's been turned into a doggie."

"That there hound is named Barrow," the vendor man said. He was back in the fluorescent-lit glory of his booth. "I wouldn't be keen on touching that hound."

Soon enough we were pacing the midway again. Jenny had her face involved with a patch of mauve spun sugar, which she found engaging or challenging enough that she used both hands to hold the stick. When a moth landed in her sugar Jenny simply tore out the chunk to which the moth was attached and dropped it. Ben the doggie put the moth and the sugar into his stomach. Jenny ate on.

"Don't get your hair in the sugar," I advised.

"I already did," she said. "And I like it."

"I'll eat your hair," I threatened.

"You will not."

"I will."

"Won't."

"Will."

"Can *not*," she said.

Her hair was marvelous—black and alive. It always was. And tonight it seemed like a lake.

"I'll swim in your hair," I said. "I'll get in there and swim around. I'll splash in there. I'll swim in the darkness, in the thick of it, in the depths. I'll dead man float, tread water. I'll make bubbles, or use a kickboard, or snorkel. Sidestroke, backstroke, breaststroke, crawl . . ."

For the first time since she'd gotten her cotton candy, she looked at me. "Good luck with that," she said.

Then here came Ben—the person—from behind the Blam-o! game. He held nothing in his hands, which seemed odd because earlier in the evening he had been carrying three stuffed animals.

"Where were you guys?" he asked.

"Here," I said.

"Oh," he said.

"Where were you?" I asked.

"Hither," he said. "Also yon."

"Fair enough," I said.

"Hither and yon," he reiterated, looking at the ground. He smiled and considered Jenny. "Well," he said, "if I were writing a newspaper article about our evening, I think the subhead would read, 'Fine Time Had By All.'"

We headed toward the parking lot and Ben related how he'd given his stuffed-animal winnings to some toddlers who'd been making spit pudding in the dust beside the beer garden. We got into Jenny's van, me in back, and Jenny started the van, and the dashboard started glowing, spreading light onto Jenny's lap, and Jenny let her head flop to one side, and said, "Ugh," and then she shifted into gear. Across town she dropped Ben off and then turned like she was taking me home. I was still sitting on the back bench seat and she was way up front and I felt ineffectual and she began humming. As we turned into my neighborhood, Jenny stopped humming and then turned on the radio and then turned it off. The houses were hidden back up in the darkness, and the street was wide and barren.

Jenny said, "I feel like that carnival sucked my soul out."

She pulled into my driveway, but she did not roll up to the patio. She just stopped there at the driveway's end, so that as I exited the van I had to contend with my own damn mailbox.

"Just say good night there!" Jenny said in a whiny way.

But I walked around to the driver's door. She lowered her window.

"Turn off the van for a bit," I said.

"I have to get home, Leo."

"Just for a bit."

She gave me a flat stare.

"Turn off the headlights, at least," I said.

She sighed and looked at the steering column. She appeared frozen, so finally I reached in and turned the lights off myself. She looked back at me. The seat belt was tight against her. I tried to lean playfully and puckishly into the window, but it was the wrong height, this was the wrong night, and the arbor vitae behind me scratched my legs.

"I had fun," I said.

"Uh-huh," she said. She started humming again. I waited. She played with the keys that dangled from the ignition.

"Wanna go on that hike?" I asked. "That hike to those river cliffs?"

"You know how hot it's going to be this week?" she said, by way of discouragement.

"We'll go early. We'll leave at eight tomorrow. *Seven*."

She blew air and rolled her eyes.

"I'll pack lunches," I said. "I'll make cookies tonight. I'll make sandwiches. Tiny sandwiches! Tiny *crustless* sandwiches!"

She tapped the dashboard clock. "I only have twenty minutes to get home."

"That TV show? That soap opera rerun thing?" I asked.

"It's not a soap opera."

"It only takes fourteen minutes to get to your house."

"Eighteen," she said.

"Fourteen," I said. "You think I don't know?"

"You think *I* don't know?" she said right back.

I raised my hands in apology. I looked down. I couldn't figure out what to say.

She turned on the headlights. I stepped back.

"I'll call you," I said.

And she shrugged.

Twenty

TWO MORNINGS LATER, I GOT MY FATHER'S COWBOY HAT OUT of my closet and I left it downstairs on the kitchen island. I wanted to make it look like it was left there casually, carelessly, so I went and got a soda can from the recycling bin and put the can beside the hat. I went upstairs to my bathroom and started brushing my teeth. As I brushed, I wandered back downstairs. I opened the door to the garage and I walked barefoot across the cool concrete. I looked at the Supra. I had just brought it home from the garage yesterday. I sighed through my nose, which is the only way you can sigh when your mouth is full of suds, and which is sometimes an extremely satisfying way to sigh.

I drove to Jenny's house and I tried the side door but the side door was locked. I walked into the backyard and then into the courtyard. The sun was overhead and the courtyard was bright and I tried the sliding glass door and found it locked, too.

"Are we expecting you?" someone said.

Mr. Previer was sitting in the shadows, reading the paper at one of the tables. He was in his suit.

I greeted him. "We are indeed expecting me," I said. "We're going shopping for college supplies."

"College supplies?" he said. "What's that mean? Ramen noodles? Instant cappuccino?"

"And lava lamps," I said.

He actually cracked a smile.

"Come sit," he said.

I hesitated, made a vague gesture toward the house.

"Sit for one minute," he said.

I went and pulled out one of the other chairs at the table. Half of me was in the sun and half was in the shade. Mr. Previer put his newspaper aside and took off his reading glasses. He folded his reading glasses. He rested his hand on the table, in the sunlight. The rest of him was in the shade. He was a larger man than me in all respects. He asked me when I was leaving for school and I told him and he nodded. He asked me what I expected to study and I said I hadn't decided yet, I had at least a year before I had to declare a major. He nodded some more. He said, "Mull it over." He said, "Hope for certainty."

"I always do," I said.

His hand moved on the table. It went from sun to shade, then back to sun.

"These negotiations at the hospital," he said. "I hope they're not making things uncomfortable for your mother."

"You'd have to ask her that yourself," I said.

"I've tried," he said. "She doesn't take my calls."

I didn't know what to say.

"I hope she understands," he said, "that this is not personal. It's business."

"I think that's perhaps exactly what she objects to."

He nodded. "I can understand that side of it," he said. "Maybe you can tell her that."

"Sure," I said.

"But without these new investors, the hospital would fold. And then who would we be helping?"

"I know," I said. "It's a hard situation."

"It's my job to bring the new money into the mix without disrupting the hospital's excellent quality of care."

I nodded.

"Your mother," he said, "is a great physician. She's a great woman and I respect her."

"Thank you," I said.

"We want to keep her on our team, believe me."

"This will all be over soon enough," I said.

"That's true," Mr. Previer said. He reached for his paper. He put his glasses back on. "We're going to miss you around here," he said. "Jenny's going to miss you."

"I'm going to miss her," I said.

He said, "Your life is starting."

That night, we were driving down a tiny blacktop, headed to a small town. Jenny was driving again. She was trying to fulfill her days-old and very arbitrary dream of visiting every Catholic church in the county. The fact that it was ten o'clock on a weeknight didn't deter her. She'd discovered that these country churches didn't lock their doors.

"Are you guys making out?" Jenny asked, looking in her rearview mirror, back toward where Ben and E. B. were sitting.

"No," E. B. said. In the passenger seat, I turned and looked back into the van, but it was dark.

"E. B. contends they're not making out," I said.

"She's a filthy liar," Jenny replied.

E. B. and Ben weren't interested in each other, but they were the kind of people who liked to grapple, and they grappled well together. Now, from the back of the van came the sound of somebody blowing a raspberry on someone else's skin—a neck, arm, or belly.

"I'll pull this van over right this minute!" Jenny threatened.

"Repeat that," I asked E. B.

"She told me she was wasting too much ink on you in her journal, and I said, 'Dirty thoughts, Jenny?' and she said 'Ugh, well, I don't have much control over them.'"

"Ugh?" I said.

"Yep."

"What kind of 'ugh' was it?"

E. B. and I were sitting on the steps of St. Stanislas. Ben and Jenny were inside, sneaking through the dark to touch the altar.

"I don't know how to characterize this ugh," E. B. told me.

"It seems to me that she's been saying 'ugh' a lot recently," I said.

E. B. picked up my hand and bit the heel of my palm.

"You're the fun stuff, Elizabeth Biddle," I said.

"I'll lick your eyeball!" she joked.

"I'm waiting," I said.

"I bet you are."

Above us, the wind was suddenly moving in the elms. The church sat on a ridge and we could see the scattered lights of the farms in the valley.

"You're such a well-balanced person, E. B.," I said. I had my arm around her. I put my nose against her neck. She smelled nice, like paraffin. Maybe it wasn't a smell at all, but an absence of smell. "You eat a balanced diet. You're smart—"

"You're smart," she said.

"You're pretty and you dance so well."

"I know."

"And you're nice to people. And you tell me which books to read. And you're a beautiful swimmer."

"I'm a fish," she stated.

"Yes," I said. "And you stop to help turtles cross the road."

"Are you proposing to me?" she asked.

"Absolutely."

Ben and Jenny appeared and Jenny showed us the candle she had stolen. As we drove back toward town we put down the windows and turned off the music. In town, everything seemed bright. My hands were orange in the streetlights.

In the end, as it so often did, it came down to me and Jenny in her van. We had dropped off E. B. We had dropped off Ben. On other nights, other times, other years, we had dropped off Evan, we had dropped off Wanda, we had dropped off Easley, Thayler, Robbie, and Kit. We had dropped off Jen Eagleton, Jen Powell, and Jen Guilford. We had even dropped off Tom and Fay, those idiots.

We drove in silence. The traffic in town was sparse. The stars were muted, hidden in the haze. There was no breeze here. There was no breath.

When we'd dropped Ben off, he had done a handstand as we pulled away. When we had dropped E. B. off, she had kissed my hand. But those things were past, they were memories, they were done, and now we were headed to my house. The path was clear, the distance small. We were in the van on a calm and muggy August night. Now we were in the van alone. Here we were. Here we went. Jennifer Previer. Leo Peery. The night was over. Tonight, there was nothing before us, nothing in front of us. There was no remedy now. There was no backing out.

We had two weeks.

At home, I walked through the dark kitchen. The cowboy hat sat there, undisturbed. But the soda can had been removed. I took the hat and I felt it. The straw was so worn it was soft.

Suddenly I heard movement in the dining room. There were lights on in there. I looked at my watch. It was nearly midnight.

"Leo?" Mom called.

I went and stood in the door to the dining room. Mom and Ruben were sitting at the bare table, holding hands.

"Hi, Ruben," I said.

"Leo," he said.

Then there was a moment when the confusion inside of me cleared and everything turned to fear. I would flee. I must flee.

"Ruben and I have a couple of things we need to tell you," Mom said.

But I was already moving, already on my way. I mumbled my good night and imitated a casual and everyday kind of bedtime shuffle, heading toward the stairs. Behind me, there was no immediate reaction. I would make it. I would escape. I started up the stairs.

"Leo?" Mom called.

Then I did that thing where you yawn and talk at the same time. "See you in the morning," I said, ascending, ascending. My throat tightened and I could feel my pulse in it.

I continued my act upstairs, feigning sleepiness and late-night befuddlement. I padded into my room and passed through the darkness to my bedside. I turned on the lamp. I sat on the bed. I was surprised to see the cowboy hat in my hands. I put it on the floor. I got up and closed the door to the bedroom. Then I came up with an even better idea and I got up and opened my door and crossed the hallway and went into my bathroom and shut the door. I turned on the lights. Then I turned on the exhaust fan. I leaned on the vanity and I waited. I could not hear any sounds outside my room. But it was unlikely I would hear anything over the noise of the exhaust fan.

I stood nervously for a while. Then I turned to the sink again and hurriedly brushed my teeth. I smiled and looked at my clean teeth and then I splashed some water on my face and then dried it. I turned off the exhaust fan and listened. I opened the door to the bathroom and did a fake bleary-eyed shuffle to my room. I closed the door behind me and then I heard the muffled closing of a car door outside and I looked out my window and saw Ruben's coupe moving away down the street. I turned off my light and got undressed in the dark. I climbed into bed and I found that I was shivering. I curled up and put my head under the covers and I remained still for a very long time.

Sleep, it turned out, came easily, as if it were just part of the act. It was the final part of my retreat, the final layer of safety.

But something intruded. There was a noise. There was another noise. I woke. I listened. It was late. I had been sleeping a while. I rolled over and continued listening. Suddenly, something small hit my window. I got up. I was unsteady on my legs. I went to the window.

There stood E. B. on the lawn.

I pulled on my jeans and walked down through the house, into the basement, and out the French doors. But when I stepped onto the patio, which was cool beneath my bare feet, I couldn't see E. B. Then she hugged me from behind and led me down to the gazebo. We sat cross-legged, facing each other, on the bench inside the gazebo. She had walked the dark path through the ravine to get to me. In the middle of the night.

"Do you know why I'm here?" she asked.

"I don't think so," I said.

"Do you know how your girlfriend feels right now? I just talked to Jenny for two hours."

"She's not my girlfriend," I protested.

"Stop it."

"I'm just stating facts," I said. "I think it's clear."

"Leo, she's hurt."

"We're all hurt. The *world* hurts."

"Stop it for just a second, okay?"

"What did I do?"

"How did you say good night to her tonight?"

"I said good night and I got out and that was it."

"She says you jumped out, mumbled good night, and were gone."

"I guess that's right."

"Well that really hurt her."

"It's not like that's how I really wanted it to be," I said. "I wanted it to be different. I always want it to be different."

"Mm-hm."

"It's August," I said. "This whole thing is done."

"Thing? You're calling it a 'thing'?"

"How come she's all bent out of shape when she's worse than me?"

"She's not worse than you."

"She is!"

"This isn't a contest."

"The other night she shrugged when I said I'd call her. She doesn't take me to her house anymore. She's sullen and sarcastic. Come to think of it, she didn't say good night to me tonight, either. And she never says hello anymore."

"She's waiting for you, Leo. She's just waiting. Do you know how much I'm sticking my neck out for you? She's been waiting for years, and she finally thought you were going to move forward and you didn't and now she thinks you're withdrawing and I thought I had to tell you because I'm not sure you get it. I've been watching this since, what, fifth grade? Standing by and watching. I mean playing sweet and clean will go so far, but with Jenny you'll have to do more."

"Oh, so it's all my job?"

"You're using the circumstances as an excuse to avoid what you *want.* And to avoid what you fear. I'm just telling you what I see. I mean, sometime you're going to have to push her up against a wall and kiss her. Then that's something."

It seemed E. B. was missing some vital information about what had transpired between Jenny and me.

I shrugged.

"You know . . . ," E. B. said. "You know, if you . . . I don't think you know. I mean, if you did that to me, well, jeez, forget it. If you kissed . . . if you did that to me, forget it, I'm yours. You don't even know that. Dammit, Leo, you don't even know that."

Now I was distracted. I couldn't focus. What had happened? What was being said? I realized that E. B.'s foot was in my lap, and my hands were on it. Had I pulled it there? Had she put it there? And why was it shoeless and sockless?

I looked at her foot and her lap. Then I kissed her foot. I could think of nothing else to do. So I kissed the arch her foot, and then I said, "But it's you I like."

For a long moment there was no sound, no movement.

"This," she said, "is when I leave."

"I'll drive you home."

"No," she said. "Okay," she said.

"Let me get my keys."

"Wait, no," she said, thinking. She looked at me. "Walk me home."

E. B. was a long person. She was tall for a girl, but she didn't seem tall. She seemed long. And though she was thin, she didn't seem skinny. She seemed long. She was long and it was beautiful.

But the path was dark.

"I can't see," I said. She had confiscated my flashlight.

"I can," she said. "Close your eyes."

I closed my eyes, she took my hand, and on we walked. She guided me gracefully, and I felt at ease. When finally we stopped I opened my eyes and could see bits of sky through the forest's canopy.

"This is halfway," she said, "and I'm not guiding you farther." She let go of my hand and gave me back my flashlight. "Now what are you going to do?"

"I'm going to walk you the rest of the way," I said, puzzled.

"No you're not," she said. "What are you going to do?"

She was standing close, but not touching me.

"What am I going to do," I said, buying time. "I'm . . . going . . ."

"What?" she said.

"I don't know," I finally admitted.

"You don't know?" she asked.

"Right."

"Okay," she said. "Good night." She walked away.

I stood wondering for a while. I was in the night. I turned on my flashlight and went home.

At breakfast, Mom told me about her cancer and her engagement to Ruben.

Twenty-One

SHE, THOUGH, HAD TO BE AT WORK IN TEN MINUTES. SHE left. I finished my cereal and drank a glass of orange juice. I sat on the patio. I fed Kitty. I took a shower and cut my fingernails. I read the mail.

When noon approached, I changed into my swimming suit and sorted through the T-shirts on my floor and found one that didn't seem too dirty. It was a black T-shirt and on its front it said PLUS ONE. I didn't know where I'd gotten it and I didn't know what it meant. I applied sunscreen to my face, neck, and arms. I noticed that I had forgotten my ears, but I was running out of time and so I put the tube of sunscreen in my pocket. In my room, I saw the cowboy hat sitting on the floor and I picked it up. It would keep my ears from getting too much sun.

I went to the garage and got in the Supra. I looked at my watch. I wasn't as short on time as I thought. I paused in the driver's seat. I looked at the gauges and I looked at the dashboard. I touched the stick shift and I touched the radio dials. I looked at the cowboy hat in the passenger's seat. And I decided to leave the car at home. I decided to walk. I would walk to the pool. I wanted to walk. And I would leave the cowboy hat at home. The hat did not belong at the pool.

It took me the usual fifteen minutes to walk to the pool. I walked through the shade and I walked through the sun. I was only two or three minutes late.

I entered the pool house and I greeted Greg and Rachel and Becky and Thayler and they welcomed me and were kind and jovial and lighthearted. We dispersed and prepared the pool for opening. There were decks to hose down, filters to clean. Bugs and leaves would be skimmed. The diving well needed vacuuming. The pH would be checked. The water temperature would be recorded. The logbook would be updated. The weather report would be checked. The pump equipment would be monitored.

And my first duty of the day, with Greg, was to raise the flag. We did it as always with the solemnity of two good ex–Boy Scouts, and we didn't say a word, and I think it is fair to say that we were both comforted by this small bit of routine ceremony, this ritual.

The flag, for its part, hung limp, listless.

I sat in the tower, within the red shade of the parasol. Color moved me and moved inside me. It moved in a flowing kind of way. Words did not have color, but people did. Their faces did. Their hands did. A smile was color. A bare forearm was color. The lawn had color. The sky had color. It was what I noticed. Sounds were distant. My sense of touch seemed remote. But color stood out. The pool, below me, had color. The wind, somehow, had color. It all felt new. I was seeing, and the sights were passing directly into me and filling me. There was a drifting feeling. There was a sense of fullness. But what kind of fullness? Something had been crowded out.

The afternoon was a fine one for swimming, and yet there

weren't as many swimmers as there should have been. We only had two towers occupied. At three-thirty I was up in the north tower as some minor cumulus clouds approached. I watched the clouds and waited, but nothing happened, no lightning, no thunder, no looming darkness. The clouds drifted over harmlessly, beautifully, tracking northeast. I felt tired, though, and restless. So finally I blew my whistle anyway. "Clear the pool!" I called. Rachel, in the far tower, looked at me and I pointed to the clouds. She blew her whistle, too.

Greg came out onto deck and when I climbed down he was there watching the clouds. "Jeez," he said, nodding. "Sure. Sure, sure."

Twenty minutes later, as if my will had directed the cosmos, we were pinned down by a lovely little thunderstorm. As it waned, Greg sent me and Thayler home. Thayler and I walked south along Point Street. Thayler had a tendency to follow me without invitation, and we soon passed the street where he should have turned for his house. He talked on and on about what skateboard he was going to buy next, and which one was the best and why and who had told him what and so forth. This was one of his standard topics, and he wasn't going to buy a new skateboard ever, and he knew I didn't like that stuff. Then, in the light, warm rain, E. B. appeared on her bike and she pulled alongside us and patted her handlebars and I hopped on and off we rode, off we rode. I had been delivered.

The gutters were running with nice rivulets.

"It's a good rain," I said.

"That's why I'm out in it," E. B. answered.

Soon the sun came out, and here came Jenny's van. She stopped.

"Get in," she said. She was on her cell phone with someone.

"What's the destination?" I asked.

"Blah blah blah," she said. "Just get in."

We opened the back and put E. B.'s bike in.

"No," Jenny said into the phone, "it's just E. B. and Leo."

We headed off.

"Can we turn off the AC?" I asked. I was cold because I was wet. And it wasn't hot outside.

"It's summer, isn't it?" Jenny replied. Then she went back to her phone conversation. I asked E. B. who Jenny was talking to and E. B. shrugged. "Maybe Jen Powell?"

"But the thing about living here," Jenny said into her phone, "is that it could be anywhere. Anywhere in the Midwest. It's that bad."

"I don't think that," E. B. whispered.

At Wal-Mart Jenny amassed an assortment of meaningless junk: film, hair gel, Post-it notes, candy, neon pens, a yo-yo, and gum. She wandered slowly, chatting all the while on her phone. E. B. and I gave up and went and sat on the curb.

"You guys look married," Jenny said when she came out.

"We were just talking about going to the park," E. B. said. That was a lie. We hadn't been talking at all. And we all knew Jenny didn't enjoy the park. Me and E. B. liked the park—the swings, the trees, the quarter-acre sandbox.

"I have to eat dinner with my parents anyway," Jenny said. She drove us to the park. We got E. B.'s bike out of the van, and Jenny drove off. That easily were we rid of her.

We turned and walked to my house. We ate cold sesame noodles in my room. When we heard Mom's car pull into the driveway we grabbed cards, lawn chairs, and candles and went into the lower part of the yard and played gin rummy. The light faded. Fireflies rose, and then were gone. Clouds moved back over the city. Then it was too windy to light the candles. Then it began to rain. We retreated to the gazebo. The wind died, the rain set in, the thunder rolled along. We lit the candles and played more gin. We weren't speaking much. After an hour of play, we were tied. "We're in balance. Halfway. A middle point," E. B. said, and this time I kissed her, she kissed me back, and we didn't return to the house until the rain let up, well after eleven. I drove her home in Mom's car. I drove back to my house. I went upstairs to my room. I went into my bathroom and blew my nose. My hair was mussed. My hands were warm. I went downstairs and got a glass of water. I listened for Mom, but she seemed to be asleep. I looked out into the dark of the yard. I turned on the floodlights and the yard looked unengaging, very wet. I turned the lights off and checked the doors and went back upstairs. I undressed and got into bed and I entered sleep quickly and my sleep was deep and I was not worried and I did not dream.

Twenty-Two

E. B. AND I DROVE OUT OF TOWN. THE WIND WAS LOUD IN THE car, E. B.'s hair was blowing around her face, but she was smiling, smiling, watching the landscape, turning every now and then to look at me. And I was driving. I was in third gear, I was in fourth gear, I was in fifth gear. The instrument panel was there for me. The seat held me. In my mind, I pictured all the parts of the engine. They were working. They were refreshed, revived. They were reliable. The pistons were sliding, the spark plugs were firing, the camshafts were rolling, the injector was spraying, the fuel pump was pumping, the valves was jumping. The crankshaft, the oil pump, the air filter . . . All of it.

The Supra was reborn. I did it all.

We moved through the countryside, and E. B. expressed the same sense of release and possibility that I was feeling. We reveled in this shared experience, this connectedness. The sun was setting—it was setting earlier these days. And we commented on that, too.

We pulled into the gravel parking lot. Through our open windows, we could hear the music coming from inside the roadhouse.

We parked between two dusty pickups and when we got out of the car E. B. kissed me and we stood by the car for a while. I was leaning against the car and E. B. was leaning against me. No one would see us here. No one would know who we were, know who we were fleeing.

"I'll tell you what I like," E. B. said.

"What."

"Gravel parking lots," she said. "White gravel parking lots."

I nodded. "They're nice. They're notably nice."

As we walked toward the restaurant, I squeezed her hand. "Know what I like?" I asked.

"No. What."

I said, "I like the cut of your jib."

Inside, we were seated at a table in the corner. The previous occupants had just left—they'd walked past us as we were led to the table—and the table was covered with their dirty plates, glasses, napkins, and silverware. We sat there for a long time and the music was both loud and muffled. E. B. pointed up and I looked above us and there was a big black speaker bolted to the wall just above our table. The music was twangy to an extent that I don't think I had ever heard, but I understood that it was part of the setting, part of the place. The dim red lighting was otherworldly enough to obscure the plain fact that we were not natives here.

"Do you think we have to eat off of their plates?" E. B. asked loudly over the music. I shrugged. The table still hadn't been cleared.

E. B. said something about a menu. I couldn't make out what she said. We didn't have a menu. I leaned forward and asked her to repeat what she'd said.

"Maybe there aren't menus," she said. "Maybe everyone knows what the choices are."

"Maybe," I said.

"Or maybe the menu is posted somewhere."

"What?"

"Maybe," she yelled, "there's a chalkboard or something with the menu on it."

We looked around for such a board. Then three things happened almost simultaneously. First, the music was turned down to a more reasonable but still very-present level. Second, a busboy appeared and swept the remnants of the previous occupants' meal into a plastic tub with one motion. Third, a waitress—let us call her the waitress of the sloppy French braid—sprayed our table with some kind of cleaning solution and then wiped it clean and dropped two napkin-wrapped silverware sets onto the table, along with one menu. We looked at the menu and we turned it over to look at the back but there was nothing there.

"I love this," E. B. said. "This menu is great."

"How so?" I asked.

She pointed out a couple of regionalisms, the likes of which we would never have encountered in town. One of these was a simply a pile of Fritos topped with chili.

We talked our way through the menu, absorbing it and mulling it over. Then we became aware that our waitress was with us again. She had not announced her presence but was simply standing by with her pencil to her ticket pad. We ordered and then handed her the menu and she was still standing there.

"Thank you," I said.

The waitress said, "What're we drinking?"

"Oh," I said. I shrugged and looked at E. B. "What are our choices?"

In one breath she said, "Bud Bud Light Busch Busch Light Coors Coors Light MGD Miller Lite Pabst Icehouse Leiny and uh Coke Diet Coke."

"Coke," I said.

"Pabst," E. B. said.

The waitress scribbled this and was gone. I eyed E. B.

"What?" she said.

"*Pabst?*" I said.

"It's part of the experience," she said. "It goes with the food."

"Gross," I said.

E. B. went in search of the facilities and I stretched my legs out under the table. Our drinks arrived. The beer was set in front of me and the soda was set in front of E. B.'s chair. I switched the drinks and tasted the soda. It was mostly ice. A new song came on and the lights above the small dance floor brightened and these two things apparently were some kind of signal, because suddenly several couples began dancing. Most of them seemed to come from the bar section of the room.

When E. B. came back, she sat down and pushed her beer bottle away. Her face was changed, serious.

"What's wrong?" I asked.

"Look at the bar," she said.

I looked. "What am I looking at?" I asked.

"Don't you see him? He's the tallest one there."

I looked again. The dance floor was blocking my view across the room, and the moving bodies and the dim lighting made it difficult to get a clear view of any single person at the bar. But as the dancers shifted about the dance floor, I saw a tall man leaning against the bar near its end. He had a good three or four inches on everyone, and the back of his head looked familiar. Then he turned so that I could see his face.

It was Mr. Previer.

"Oh, holy," I said. "Our luck."

"We should go," E. B. said.

"Who's he with?" I asked.

"I didn't see."

"Did he see you?" I asked.

"I don't think so."

I nodded.

"Should we go?" E. B. asked. "We should go."

"I don't know what to do," I admitted. "I plead ignorance."

"Then let's go," she said, shifting her chair to get up.

"Wait," I said, reaching for her hands.

The song ended and there was clapping and hooting.

"I say we stay," I said.

And whistling.

"That's what I say," I said.

A new song started, but many of the dancers were leaving.

E. B. smiled at me. "Okay," she said.

"Kiss me," I said.

And we leaned across the table and kissed, only to be interrupted by the arrival of our meals. We looked at our hot food. It was gorgeous in a simple way and it was a welcome reinforcement.

"Wow," I said, looking at my plate. "That's a lot of gravy."

"This food will be restorative," E. B. said.

"That's good news."

We picked up our silverware and started our work. But I noticed that Mr. Previer wasn't at the bar anymore. I couldn't see him anywhere. Then I saw him. He was heading in our general direction, two bottles of beer in one hand.

"Watch it," I said. "He's incoming."

E. B. turned around to see. The hostess was showing him to a table. The table was only twenty-five feet away. The hostess wiped the table for him. He set his beers down.

"You know what I'm going to do?" I said.

"No," E. B. said.

"I'm going to will him to look at us."

E. B. looked at me. "Really?"

"Why not? I don't see why not."

She smiled. "Let's both will him to look at us."

"It's a deal."

And so we kept watching him, waiting. He sat in the booth. He slid one of the beers across the table. He loosened his tie—of course he was wearing a tie—and then, as if on cue, he looked directly at me and E. B. Our shared glance was not a long one, but it was long enough. He clearly recognized us, and he was puzzled. But he was also, it seemed, embarrassed: because the woman who arrived just then and slid into the booth opposite him was twenty years his junior, and she was clearly not Mrs. Previer.

"Ha," E. B. said when the moment was over and we went back to our meal. "Ha," she repeated.

"I guess so," I said.

"What's it mean?" E. B. asked me when we got back to the car.

I told her I didn't know what it meant, but that it was likely Mr. Previer wouldn't tell Jenny. And even if he did, what did it matter? I noticed E. B. was crying.

"I'm an easy crier," she said.

"That's not a bad thing," I said.

She smiled, wiping away the last tears. "It's kind of like getting a face massage," she said.

I comforted her and we sat for a little while and then I started the car. We backed away, the gravel popping beneath the tires, and we accelerated down the narrow road. The moon was up and the road was empty and open. The car drove smoothly and we rode at first with the windows down because the night air was soft. It had a hint of coolness to it, too—a touch of September.

I rolled up the windows. The sunroof was still open, but it was not loud.

"What's your favorite month?" I asked E. B.

"This one," she said.

We were in the hills and the road moved up and down and there was grace in it.

"These hills," I said, "were shaped by the glaciers."

"I love these hills," E. B. said.

Back in town, we forgot that the bridge on Central Avenue was closed. So we had to turn back north and cross the river on the highway. This route took us past the new produce market, which appeared to still be open.

"Pull in here," E. B. said.

It was only a few minutes until the store closed, but we went in and E. B. sized things up quickly. I simply followed her. She nodded at several things, as if she approved of them—a few varieties of early apples, some melons, raspberries. But then she stopped suddenly in front of a display of peaches.

"Oh," she said. "Red haven peaches."

She picked one up. She smelled it.

"Wow," she said.

At her house, I sat at the kitchen table and watched her work. She turned on the oven and got out a baking sheet. She set a pot of water on the stove and turned the flame to high. She got out a roll of parchment paper and cut two big squares from it.

When the water was boiling, she dropped two of the peaches into it. She removed them a minute later and put them into a bowl of ice water. Then she peeled them. The peels slipped off. She didn't even have to use a knife.

She cut the peaches into segments and arranged the segments on the two pieces of parchment paper. She sprinkled brown sugar over the peaches, then squeezed a little lemon juice on, too. She got some butter from the refrigerator and placed two dabs on the peaches. Then she folded one of the peach-loaded parchment papers in half. She folded and crimped the edges of the paper so that a pouch was formed. She repeated this with the other paper and then put both of the pouches on the baking sheet and put them in the oven.

"Not long now," she said.

"My heart is full," I said.

Her mother was still at work. E. B. smiled at me.

"Smell my fingers," she said.

I did. There was peach, lemon, and brown sugar.

"Well," I said, and then I told her the detailed account of how I had killed my bike. I told her how I was responsible for Stephen's death because I had forgot to untie him. I told her how I had saved the kid at the pool. These were things I hadn't really talked about with anyone, and she listened and she absorbed them and her responses were comforting.

Then she said something that no one had said in a long time. She said, "Tell me about your father."

I hesitated.

"You don't have to," she said.

"I want to," I said. "But I have to sort it out for a moment."

"My father left us when I was four," she said. "And I've always visualized it happening as if it were just some really simple event."

"Like how?" I asked.

"I've always—" she said.

I waited.

"I've always pictured it like, you know how when a blackjack dealer's shift is over, he kind of wipes his palms together and then shows his open hands to the players?"

"Yeah."

"And then he walks off. That's what I picture. Like: here's Dad with me and Mom. He's sitting on the carpet, playing with me, and then he stands up, wipes his palms together and shows them to us, and then he walks away."

236

"Oh, Elizabeth," I said.

She shrugged.

"There's really nothing else to tell," she said.

The room was filling up with the smell of the baking peaches.

"I just think about the glaciers," I said. "And how they came, and how they shaped everything, and how they left. The land was beneath them, then the land was free again and the sun shone down and there were new rivers and new valleys and new hills."

She was listening.

"And the weather," I said. "The summer thunderstorms. The winds in the winter. The mists. And there was the farm. And the creek. And my father always had a simple haircut—his mother cut his hair—and they didn't have money. He built a new chicken coop when he was ten and the raccoons never bothered the hens again. He trapped in the winter and he hunted in the spring and autumn and in the summer he fished. He got a scholarship and was the first person in our family to go to college. Then he went to medical school because his goal was to fix things, fix people. After his residency he took a fellowship in the East and at the end of the fellowship his mentor offered him a place in his practice but he wanted to come back to his home state. So he did. And he met Mom and they got married. He bought her a sports car to celebrate the end of her residency. That same year I was born and they moved into a new house—our house—and he died. Then it was just me and Mom."

The timer on the stove beeped.

"But," I said, "I'm leaving soon."

"How'd he die?" E. B. asked.

"Kidney disease," I said.

"Did he get a transplant?"

"Yes, his sister, my aunt Corene, gave him a kidney, but it didn't last."

"What was his name?"

"Anson," I said.

"Your middle name."

"Yes."

"Are his parents still alive?"

"My grandpa." I nodded. "You know where I feel most comfortable and closest to him? It's kind of obvious."

"Where."

"The farm," I said.

"Then we should go there," she said. "I'd like you to show me."

"Really?"

"Soon."

"That's actually a great idea," I said. "I promised Paer that I'd visit before I leave. And I guarantee we won't bump into anyone we know out there."

The peaches came out of the oven and E. B. put one of the pouches before me and then cut a little flap in the top and I opened the flap with my fork and the steam came out along with the smell of the cooked peaches and when the peaches had cooled slightly we ate and it was extraordinary.

It was like eating summer.

Twenty-Three

"I DON'T WANT YOU TO TELL CORENE," MOM SAID.

"I don't understand."

"I just don't want you to tell her!"

"She's on our side, Mom. We can help you. I don't understand this secrecy. We can help you."

"How? How can you help? Are you oncologists all of a sudden? Are you faith healers?"

"Stop it."

"I'm just asking," she said. "I want to know. It's my right to know. It's my right."

She was leaning over the sink and she seemed out of breath. I was standing over by the windows, eating an apple. I didn't have shoes on yet, even though it was noon. Mom was going in to the office to do charts. I walked to the counter and put my apple down.

"Mom," I said, "when did you know?"

"That's hard to say."

"When? May?"

"It took a long time to be certain."

"June?"

"Later in July."

"So the CA 125 test I saw in June didn't tip you off?"

She stared at me. "I don't want to know how you saw that," she said.

"I'm not going to tell you. I can play the secret game just as well as you can."

But she made the connection on her own. "You . . . ," she said. "You were in my office. You left the front door unlocked."

I'd forgotten about that.

She moved across the room. "I'm going to work," she said. And she went into the garage.

I looked at my apple on the counter, and the exposed flesh was already turning brown. I walked out the side door and onto the concrete of the driveway, but Mom was already accelerating down the street.

A few hours later, I was in the woods, wading through underbrush. Gracie was somewhere up ahead of us, and E. B. was several feet behind me. I stopped and waited for her to catch up.

"I'm sorry," I said.

"About what?" she asked.

"The heat, the humidity, the bugs, the brambles."

"Pshaw," she said. "I can take it."

"It's possible that Gracie is leading us on a wild-goose chase."

"Well, I love geese," E. B. said.

"Where are you guys?" Gracie called.

"Er," I said, "we're right here."

"Where's 'right here'?" she asked.

There was noise up ahead, as she came walking back toward us. She came within view of us.

"So, let's make an *effort,* people," she said.

We were climbing the ridge on the east side of the farm. The slope was increasing, and it was getting difficult to steer clear of all the poison ivy. The day's humidity was oppressive, and my clothes were starting to cling to me. Finally, Gracie stopped in a small clearing and turned around. She looked puzzled.

"That's it," she said. "I'm lost."

But we urged her on, and several minutes later we crossed a tiny streamed of mossy rocks. It wasn't even really a streamed. There was no water, and it was only a couple of feet wide. We were back along the side of the ridge where it started bending east. Gracie had crossed the streambed without stopping and so I called to her and brought it to her attention. I held up a mossy round rock to show her.

"This looks suspicious," I said.

"Oh," Gracie said, hurrying back toward us. *"Oh!"*

She led us up the slope. It was quite a scramble, and it kept getting steeper. We were using saplings as handholds. We called this part of the farm the bluff, and we didn't come here very often.

"I *told* you," Gracie said, ahead of us. "I *told* you I found the spring."

Then suddenly we were there. We were deep in the old-growth forest, high above the floodplain. The canopy here was thick, and little sunlight was reaching the ground. The air was still and quiet. There was a shelf of limestone jutting out nearby, above a mossy bowl of land, and at this end of the bowl was a small spring.

Gracie knelt and touched the clear water.

"Feel it," she said.

E. B. and I crouched. The water was cold. The bottom of the spring was sand and the sand was bubbling in a few places where the water was rising. Granted, the output was little more than a trickle, but it was a still a happy sight. I remembered that Grandma used to talk about it, and that she always had a bottle of springwater in the refrigerator. She would give us a drink from it on hot summer days and she always told me that when my father was a boy, it was his job to keep the jug of spring-water full. Aunt Corene had confirmed that that was true, but she said she'd never known exactly where the spring was. And Grandpa was no help.

But here it was. Gracie had found it several days ago—somehow, miraculously—and now we were kneeling at it, drinking. And E. B. bent over it and dipped her hair in it. Gracie did the same. Then they wrung out their hair.

"I think," Gracie said, "that we three will keep this a secret."

"Yes," E. B. said.

Gracie was sitting there, staring into the spring, mesmerized, eyes unfocused, face relaxed. "And we will know about it," Gracie said, "and we will always know that it is here, and we will remember it even when we are far away, and we will keep it inside of us, hidden. Because that will make us strong."

We decided to take a more direct route back to the farmhouse. We came down off the bluff. Finally, at the edge of the woods, we were suddenly confronted with a barbed-wire fence. I recognized it immediately. It was the fence that Paer and I had put in so quickly back in July. And in front of us was an arm of the pasture, and at the northern edge of the pasture—where the sycamores along the creek spread shade—we saw part of the new herd of cattle. It was the first I'd seen of them, and they were beautiful and healthy.

"If we cross the field," Gracie said, "will the cows eat us?"

I told her no, the cows wouldn't eat us.

"Will they charge us?"

"No," I said.

She thought about this. "Will they feel *affronted?*"

E. B. and I looked at her. Here was Gracie, my nine-year-old cousin, employing advanced vocabulary.

"Now why would they feel that?" I asked.

She said that they might feel affronted because we would be tramping across their territory without their permission. I assured her that they were very generous with letting people tramp across their territory, and that in general they were pleasant and generous creatures who wished no ill will to anyone.

So we crossed the pasture. The wind was moving in the middle of the pasture, and the cattle watched us.

When we got back to the farmhouse, the girls went inside to the air-conditioning. Paer wasn't home yet. I walked through the backyard and down to the barn pasture. The wind was blowing through the barn, and as I walked past it I could smell the old hay in the hayloft.

I walked past the pond and down toward the shade at the end of the pasture. I could see Paer's herd there. These were the cattle that Grandpa had given to Paer for graduation. They were all standing in the shade, chewing their cuds. The cows looked good, and the calves—who were finally putting on some size—looked good, too. Paer had recently given his herd ear tags. In their left ears they had tags to help repel flies. In their right ears they had numbered identification tags.

After a while, I heard someone walking toward me through the dry grass. I looked back. It was Paer. He must have just arrived home. He was working in an insurance office in Charbourg now, and he still had on his work clothes. We greeted each other and then stood side by side, looking at the cattle.

"Which one was the knuckle-ankled calf?" I asked.

Paer pointed. "It's number 64 there."

"That's what I thought," I said. "But he looks great."

"He *is* great."

"You wouldn't even know that he'd had a problem," I said.

"Well, we fixed him."

I nodded.

"I've got some bad news," Paer said after a moment.

"What's that?"

"Gracie lobbied Mom to see if she could stay at the farm tonight. And Mom agreed."

"That's fine," I said. "That's okay. I've already talked to Gracie about not mentioning E. B. to anyone."

E. B. was here surreptitiously. She'd done the classic cover-up: she'd told her mother that she was staying at her friend Carrie's house for the night. And if E. B.'s mom called Carrie's house looking for her, Carrie would call us on my cell phone and E. B. could call her mom right back.

"It's just that we can't party or anything if Gracie is staying over," Paer said. "And you guys won't get much privacy."

"That's okay," I said. "We don't care."

"There's a party at Denise Landon's tonight."

"You can go if you want," I said. "Why don't you go and we'll stay with Gracie?"

"It's not a big deal," Paer said. "We don't have to go out. Anyway, Glen Sands has been making noises for a while now, and I don't really want to run into him."

"Making noises?"

"He's itching for a fight. He's an idiot."

I didn't know who Glen Sands was. But Paer was usually mixed up in one dispute or another, so I didn't even ask.

"Well let's steer clear of him then," I said.

"Did you see anyone as you came into town?"

"No," I said. "Wait, I did see Freeda."

"See, that's just the kind of thing we don't need," Paer said.

"Oh, it was fine. She just drove past as I was gassing up. She didn't stop and chat or anything."

"Well, it's just extra incentive to lie low."

"Sounds good to me," I said. "How about a trip to the creek?"

Paer shrugged. "It's a little low. Fishing's not any good."

"I didn't bring my fishing stuff anyway."

We turned and started walking back up through the pasture. The grass was dry and there were legions of grasshoppers. They fled before us, to the best of their ability.

"Look at you, all dressed up," I said, good-naturedly. Paer looked good in his nice clothes.

"Ah, it's a living," he said.

"If you had a choice," I said, "assuming you could make a decent income either way, would you work on the farm or in an office?"

He thought about it. "I actually don't know," he said.

The creek was lower than I'd ever seen it. We walked to the tip of the gravel bar and looked at the stagnant pool above the riffles.

"Ick," Gracie said. She was in her swimsuit, but the murky brown water was not appealing. "I'm not getting in that," Gracie said.

"What's that stink?" E. B. asked.

"A little bit of stagnation," I said.

"I told you guys," Paer said.

"I'm not getting in that," Gracie repeated. "It's like an old puddle."

Gracie made me perform by skipping some stones. E. B. clapped and Gracie kept saying, "Just wait—the next one will be even *better*." Paer fished and hauled out a twelve-inch large-mouth with little lesions all over. We spent a good twenty minutes in what Gracie called a fossil hunt contest, which really just amounted to us each shuffling aimlessly across the gravel bar, looking at our feet. We found nothing except an old pull tab from a soda or beer can, which Gracie thought was quite exotic. Finally, we broke out the box of fireworks that Paer had bought half-price after the Fourth. The bottle rockets proved to be basically the worst bottle rockets ever. Their fuses would sputter and then they would explode immediately, without achieving any altitude. One bottle rocket did the whole thing backwards—it exploded and *then* it jetted into the air. The big rockets were better, but it was still just light enough outside that it was impossible for us to appreciate their showery sparkles, their blooming colors, their comet tails, and their floral sprays. We did, however, enjoy their multiple reports.

The sun eased down into the crimson haze.

We got back to the farmhouse about dark and we slumped on the old couch in the living room. The couch was a classic avocado color and Paer and had picked it up for free somewhere. It was springy and very long and it didn't smell unpleasant at all, although its surface was slightly abrasive. We sat there in the brisk wind created by the old air conditioner and it felt like we were in a different territory all of the sudden and the light was yellowish, and Gracie said, "August is too *much*." Then she said she was hungry.

We all were.

We had a short discussion about what food was on hand and then unanimously decided to go get food in town. We finally agreed we would go get burgers at the drive-up place in Charbourg. But despite this decision, we all just continued to sit there, semicomatose. There was no move to go. The old air conditioner breathed ceaselessly upon us and I, for one, let my eyes close.

"Wait," Paer finally said. "Let's not go to Charbourg. Let's go to Reed's Point."

"Why?" I asked.

"We won't run into anyone we know in Reed's Point."

"There's the Dairy Barn in Reed's Point!" Gracie said. "We could eat at the Dairy Barn."

Somehow, this sparked us and we got up and went outside

and we decided to take the Supra and E. B. and Gracie piled in back and I drove and Paer sat beside me. He brought along some of the bottle rockets, and as we drove he lit them and then held them out the window. Normally, this worked well, and the bottle rockets would fly off in whatever direction he pointed them. This was classic summer fun. But with this particular batch of half-price dud bottle rockets, it was not a fulfilling activity. Paer would light them and they'd blow up as he held them. It didn't hurt him, and it wasn't even that loud, but it was significantly disappointing, again and again. He would just end up holding a smoking red stick. Finally, he gave up.

To get to Reed's Point, we had to drive north, cross the creek at one ford, go along a long desolate stretch of road, cross the creek again at Blank's Ford, and then turn onto a county blacktop and ride another ten minutes. We were quiet on our ride. After we crossed Blank's Ford we came up on the Landon farm and we looked out at it because we knew there was supposed to be a party there tonight. But it was too early. The party didn't exist yet.

It is remarkable what foot-long chili dogs, fries, and chocolate malts can do for morale at ten-thirty on a muggy summer's evening. We ate at the picnic table that was in front of the Dairy Barn, and hardly any traffic drove by. As we sat there, the Dairy Barn closed, and the lights went off inside, and the lighted sign above us went dark and we still had just a little bit of eating left to do, so we ate in the semidarkness. Reed's Point was the kind of town that had one streetlight, and it was about a stone's throw away. The town was too small to have its own school. And in the environs of Charbourg, to say that someone was from Reed's Point was an insult, even if it was true.

We headed home after eleven, and I let Paer drive. E. B. sat up front with him and me and Gracie sat in the back. Gracie was quiet and she was clearly sleepy and by the time we turned onto the gravel roads again and passed the Landon farm, she was asleep, leaning against me. And the hour was late enough that the party at Denise Landon's was under way, and we could see the cars and pickups parked up and down their long driveway. We passed without slowing, and we said nothing.

Down in the creek bottom, the air was cooler, but it also felt closer. It felt a little too close. There was also a rivery, ripe smell in the air. We crept along the pitted lane, following the tree line, and then made the abrupt turn down the creek bank. Our headlights spread across the water, but the water resisted illumination and remained black and separate. The trees on the other side of the creek, however, caught the light and revealed themselves to us.

Blank's Ford was a long and narrow ford. The concrete slab was only about twelve feet wide, which felt precariously narrow when you were crossing it. Veer a couple of feet to the right and your wheels would slip off into the upper pool. Veer to the left and you would tumble over the two-foot drop. Normally, about five inches of water covered the ford. But tonight there was only an inch or two in the middle of the ford. A trickle. A gleam.

Our wheels had just touched the water when I heard a new sound—a sound other than the noise of our own engine and the spraying of the water. It was the pronounced rasp of a hot rod downshifting. And almost immediately, two headlights came around the bend on the opposite shore, and turned onto the ford. It was a pickup, and it was going fast—or at least fast for a narrow gravel road.

"Whoa," Paer said.

Paer stopped the car and the truck slowed and finally stopped but not before we were eye to eye with it. Headlight to headlight. The dust from its wake billowed toward us. I leaned forward, trying not to wake up Gracie. The truck idled loudly. Though common courtesy dictated that the truck should back up because we were the first on the ford, it made no move. We couldn't see into the cab of the pickup, but the pickup's high headlights were aimed right into our faces. They could probably see us.

"Shoot," Paer said.

"Just go ahead and back up," I said.

He shifted into reverse.

"Yeah, well," he said. "That's Glen's pickup. Glen Sands."

We were moving slowly backwards now, and the truck was moving forward at the same speed, a little bit too close.

"He's not going to recognize you in this car," I said.

"Maybe," Paer said. "I just don't think we want to do this right now." He backed us all the way to the start of the ford, and then he backed us onto the edge of a gravel bar so that the truck could pass.

"Do what?" E. B. said.

"Glen is bad news," Paer said.

"Don't want to do what right now?" E. B. asked.

The truck moved forward slowly and then it stopped directly in front of us, blocking us in. Glen leaned out the driver's window and glared at us. He was a ruddy guy, and he was big.

"Paer!" he called. It was good-natured and sinister at the same time.

Paer waved genially.

"Wait," I said. "Who *is* Glen Sands?" I wanted some clarification. I was getting an odd swirling sensation in my stomach.

"What do you mean?" Paer said. "You don't know?"

"No. Why would I know?"

"Because he's Freeda Sweeney's boyfriend."

"Boyfriend?" I said. "What boyfriend?"

"Yes, boyfriend. Of two years," Paer said, incredulous. "You didn't know?"

"Oh, hell," I said.

"Who's Freeda Sweeney?" E. B. asked.

But now we noticed that Glen Sands was out of his pickup, and he was walking toward us. And from around the front of the pickup came someone else. It was Freeda.

"That's Freeda Sweeney," I said.

"Let's just play it cool," Paer said.

"Whose car is this?" Glen asked, coming up to Paer's window.

"Hey, Glen," Paer said. "What's up?"

"Let me out," I whispered to E. B.

"Why?" E. B. said.

"Just let me out," I said.

"This your car?" Glen asked Paer.

"Do you like it?" Paer asked Glen.

Glen looked at the car again, as if to decide whether he liked it. He was holding a can of beer.

"It's my car," I said.

"Oh, yeah?" Glen said, peering in at me. There were no head-lights on us anymore, so it was pretty dark in the car.

"Yeah, it's mine," I said.

"Sweet," Glen said. He drank from his beer. Freeda was standing a good ten feet away, arms crossed.

Finally, I was out of the car. E. B. was with me. I nudged her toward the rear of the car. I started around the hood.

"Yeah," I said. "I fixed it up this summer. It only has four thousand miles. All original."

"Can it move?" Glen asked.

"Oh, it can move," I said. "Dual cam six. Great tranny. And it can really hold the road."

Paer got out.

"What year's your Chevy there?" I asked.

"Seventy-nine," Glen said.

"Three-fifty?" I asked.

He nodded, just barely.

"I'd love to peek under the hood," I said, "but, see, we're taking Gracie home 'cause it's late and she's already asleep in the backseat there."

Glen nodded, smiling slightly. He took another drink.

"This your cousin?" he asked Paer.

"That's him," Freeda said.

"Hey, Freeda," I greeted her. "You guys going up to Denise's?"

"You're Leo Peery?" Glen asked. We were both standing in front of the car.

"Yeah," I said. "I don't think I remember meeting you before."

He put his beer on the hood of the Supra.

"I'm Glen Sands," he said.

"Hey," I said. I put out my hand.

But then, in the gloom, I was hit in the cheek with a fast punch and there was a huge whooshing sound and I saw the stars streaking above me and I was falling sideways and backwards and suddenly my head thunked something with a really loud thunk and after that I felt fine. I was lying in the gravel and I felt the gravel with my hands and I could see that Glen was saying something and that Paer was yelling at him and even though I couldn't hear anything I felt fine so I got up and looked at the hood of the Supra and there was a dent there and I looked at the dent and I realized that this was my dent—the dent made by my own head—and I kept looking at it and it meant a great deal to me for some reason, it meant a lot, that dent. And I looked up, and I said, "I'm okay. What's a little— What's a little—" and then E. B.'s arms came around me from behind and I passed out.

Twenty-Four

AND THOUGH I WAS UNCONSCIOUS, E. B. WAS THERE.

I lay prone on my back, staring up, my arms outstretched, my eyes open, very open. I could see all around me, as if my eyes were seeing in all directions at once. I could even see through my own body. And behind me lay E. B., in a position identical to my own, and she was supporting me. I could feel her. I could see her. Our breathing was synchronous, and we were together in the darkness.

Above us, the stars had come loose, and I watched them as they drifted down like snowflakes, falling toward us. And the stars passed through me. But E. B. caught them. They adhered to her body, eventually covering her in a fine layer, and in this way the stars were sandwiched between us.

It was a glimpse of the future, I realized, a process that would take many years.

And I understood it to be permanent.

Twenty-Five

"I'D LIKE TO CARRY HER," I SAID.

We were back at the farmhouse, sitting in the car. The night was quiet there. Gracie, to her credit and our relief, had slept through the entire Glen Sands episode, and was sleeping still, and now we were discussing whether we should wake her so she could walk into the house or whether we should carry her.

"Let me do it," Paer said.

He and I carefully lifted her from the backseat and then Paer took over and carried her across the dark yard toward the stoop. Gracie's hair hung down and she was still completely asleep. E. B. held the door open for Paer and he went into the house, being careful not to bump Gracie on the doorframe. He disappeared into the darkness of the house and E. B. closed the door. When I got to the stoop, I stood one step below E. B. Thus, our heads were at almost exactly the same level, whereas normally she was four inches shorter than me.

Paer reappeared in a few minutes. He had put Gracie in his room, in his bed—which was the only real bed in the whole house. And his room had a new air conditioner that was much quieter and more comfortable than the one downstairs. Paer sat on the stoop and opened a can of beer.

"I don't know, I don't know . . . ," he said, looking into the dark. Then he took a drink and looked at us. E. B. and I were still just standing there, holding each other. "You okay?" he asked me.

"I'm fine," I said.

"You were out for at least a minute," he said.

"It was pleasant," I said.

"We could . . . ," Paer said. He took another drink. "We could go up to Denise's. He'll be there. We could—"

"Paer," I said, interrupting him, "me and E. B. are going home. And you should just let it go."

"Are you kidding me? He doesn't deserve to get away with that."

"Listen to me, Paer—"

"He doesn't."

"Listen: *I'm* letting it go. It doesn't matter."

"It does."

"It doesn't. Not to me. You matter to me. E. B. matters to me. Gracie matters to me. Glen Sands does not. Freeda Sweeney does not."

"I don't get it."

"The only way they have any power over us," I said, "is if we enter their world."

He didn't say anything.

"Just stay here," I said. "Stay here with Gracie."

A minute later, we were in the car, pulling out of the driveway. Paer was still sitting on the stoop, puzzled, stirred up.

At the junction with the blacktop, E. B. and I switched seats. I let her drive and she was flawless with the clutch. She drove through the night and I fell asleep.

"Tell me," E. B. said. "Leo. Tell me."

I was coming out of my sleep. We were still driving home. My head was tender now, and I had a headache, whereas before it had just felt numb and warm.

"What?" I asked. "What are you asking for?"

"You slept with Jenny and you slept with this Freeda girl."

"Yes."

"Tell me that."

"This was all before you and me . . ."

"I know, but that's not the point."

"What do you want?" I asked.

"I just want you to tell me."

"Okay," I said. "I did. I slept with Jenny in June. I slept with Freeda in July."

"Okay," she said. "That's all."

"It was reckless and it was random and I regret it."

"It's okay," she said. "That's all. Go back to sleep."

The road was open before us. There was no other traffic. I prepared to deliver an explanation and an apology, but there was no energy in me. My head felt sodden, heavy. I slept again.

At home, we parked the Supra on a side street where Mom wouldn't see it. E. B. couldn't go home until morning without raising suspicion. Neither could I. We locked the car and walked down the middle of the street, beneath the streetlights. The town was as silent as the countryside had been.

We took our sleeping bags to the gazebo and spread them there, but we realized the floor was too hard to sleep on, so we relocated to the lawn. By this time it was very late, but as we lay there, I could tell that we were both wide-awake, not sleepy. Finally, E. B. reached over and touched my face.

"Right before you passed out you stood up," she said. "Do you remember that?"

"Yeah," I said.

"Do you remember what you said?"

"No," I said. I thought about it. "Wait. I said I was okay."

"You said, 'I'm okay. What's a little— What's a little—' and then that was it."

"Oh, yeah," I said, remembering. "I felt fine. I thought I was fine."

"But what were you trying to say?"

"Oh, I was trying to say, 'What's a little concussion among friends?' "

"Really?"

"I'm serious."

We laughed.

"What *is* a little concussion among friends?" E. B. asked.

"Not much, in my opinion."

We were lying on top of our sleeping bags. It was too muggy and still to get inside them. We were holding each other loosely. I could tell that E. B. was smiling, even though my eyes were against the side of her head and I couldn't see her face.

After a while, she said, "Sleep with me."

Twenty-Six

WE COULD WITHDRAW, WE COULD RETREAT, AND WE COULD hide in ourselves and in each other, but the world would reassert itself.

I woke up because my cell phone was ringing. My face had slid off my sleeping bag and my cheek was in the grass. I scrambled for a moment and reached for my phone but I had no idea where it was. E. B.'s head popped up and finally I found the phone in one of my shoes. I was instantly awake, because the only reason my phone would be ringing was that E. B.'s friend Carrie was trying to reach us because E. B.'s Mom had called her house. Our deception was in jeopardy.

"'Ello?" I answered.

"Leo!" Mom said.

"Mom?"

"Leo, where *are* you?"

My eyes were sticky. The woolly murk of dawn was approaching and I blinked my eyes. How was I supposed to evade Mom's question?

"What's going on?" I asked her. I sat up. "What time is it?"

"Were you in the house?"

"In . . . the house?"

"Why didn't you call?" she said.

"Our house?" I asked.

"Leo, wha— So you weren't there? Do you know where Paer is?"

"He's at the farm," I said.

"They don't think he is. His truck's not there."

"They who?"

"Leo, answer me: where are you?"

"I'm at Charbourg."

"Leo, stop it. Listen to me. There was a fire at the farmhouse and Gracie was hurt. Now they can't find Paer. And they couldn't find you and your car wasn't there. So tell me."

"A fire?" I said.

"About an hour ago. You don't know any of this, do you?"

"At the farm?" I said. It didn't seem real. "Is Gracie . . . ?"

"They're flying her into the burn unit right now. She'll be here any minute. I don't know any more than that. I'm in the hospital already. I was called in for a delivery."

"Oh—" I said, and my throat closed and I couldn't say anything. I made a couple of desperate gasps for air. E. B. reached for me, scared.

"Leo?" Mom asked.

"Leo?" E. B. said, slapping my back. I was still gagging a little bit.

"Who's that?" Mom asked.

"Leo!" E. B. said.

"I'm okay," I said. I felt light-headed. "I'm okay."

"Who's with you?" Mom asked.

I came clean, told her I'd taken E. B. to Charbourg with me, but that we'd left at midnight, and that we were in the backyard.

———

"I'm sorry," I told E. B., minutes later, driving her home. I looked at her in the passenger's seat of the Supra. Her hair was tangled and she was shivering. The street was wet because there had been a heavy dew in the night. "I'm so sorry. It's not always like that."

"I know," E. B. said.

"I feel responsible," I said.

"I wanted the first time to be with you," she said.

"I could have warned you."

"You did. It's not like I didn't know. It's okay."

Dawn was still on its way and there was a gloominess in the air that I couldn't tell if it was real or perceived.

"I had a dream," I said. "Or, it wasn't a dream so much as it was a vision."

"You slept? I don't think I slept any."

"No, not while I was asleep. When I was passed out at the ford. I had this vision. Of you and me. We were in the darkness. And I was lying there, facing the stars. And you were lying behind me, supporting me. And the stars shook loose and floated down. They went right through my body. But they stuck to your body. And they formed a thin layer between us. Anywhere we touched, they stuck. I don't know exactly what it meant. It was something that is starting to happen. It was right and it was real, and it represented how things actually are between us, and how they will be."

She didn't say anything, and she was looking out the window, away from me, and I began to wonder if she had heard me, or whether I had said something wrong. But when she did finally turn to look at me, she said, "Don't take me home. I want to go to the hospital with you."

"But if you get home now, your mom will never know about tonight. You won't get in trouble."

"I don't care."

"My mom won't tell your mom about tonight, you know. There's no reason you should risk getting in trouble."

"Yes there is," she said. "The reason is that I want to stay with you, and because I am a part of what happened tonight."

I pulled the car over. The streets were still empty, even though morning was near. I looked at E. B. for a moment, and she touched my hand and then kissed my cheek. I put the car back into gear, did a U-turn, and headed back the way we had come. I put the pedal down and the Supra leaped at the opportunity, moving us through the streets with purpose and surety.

As we neared the hospital there was a thumping sensation in my chest, and suddenly the air ambulance helicopter burst into view, immediately overhead.

We parked in the emergency lot—we were allowed to do *this*?—and asked for Gracie at the emergency desk. But Gracie wasn't registered yet. So we explained that she'd just come in on the helicopter and the nurse said we'd have to wait. "But we're her relatives," I said. "Are you her parents?" she asked. I told her that I was her cousin, but as I said it I realized that it probably wasn't good enough. She told us to wait. I asked if she'd seen Dr. Peery and she said "Who?" and I said, "Julia Peery," and she said she didn't know her. We took the employee elevator up to the OB clinic and there one of the nurses recognized me immediately and told us that Mom had headed down to the burn unit and he gave us instructions and we retraced our steps and went through the ER and then down the hall to the new wing and when we turned the corner we found ourselves in the internal medicine clinic and I was completely confused for a second and completely lost and turned around. We got ourselves straightened out and went up one floor and came to the front of the ICU and then, at the end of a long hallway, I saw a gurney rolling past, attended by a few people and followed by Mom. It had to be Gracie. "Mom!" I called, but she didn't hear me and she disappeared as quickly as she appeared. I took E. B.'s hand and we started to walk that way but we were stopped by a yet another nurse. We couldn't go that way. No visitors could go there.

Finally, I paged Mom on my cell phone and she called back in a couple of minutes and told us that Gracie was okay and she told us where we could wait and we had to walk almost the entire length of the hospital to get there. We crossed the skywalk and looked at the traffic below us. Finally, we got to the right place and Mom came and met us soon and we talked and then she sent us to wait at the front of the hospital for Corene, who was driving in from Charbourg by herself, knowing almost nothing about her daughter's condition, and who would be here soon. And she told us what to tell Corene and when Corene came in we gave her the update and she was relieved and we took her up to Mom.

At nine o'clock, while the doctors were still with Gracie, Paer came into the waiting room, along with Uncle Cort—who had stayed in Charbourg, looking for him. Paer had a black eye and some scratches on his face, and he walked stiffly. After sitting with his parents for a while, he and I decided to go outside. We went through the wide lobby of the hospital and out the sliding glass doors. Walking into the humidity was like hitting a wall, but it felt real and welcome after the still air of the hospital. We sat on a stretch of rock wall over by the oldest section of the hospital. From there, we had a view of the city. The day was cloudy, the clouds were close to the earth, and the city looked insignificant.

"I just got so worked up," he said. "And I was miserable after you guys left. I sat outside—I don't even know why. And I drank more. Then I remember being in the truck. I don't remember the decision to go anywhere, and I don't remember leaving the farm. But I remember driving down the road and realizing that only my parking lights were on. So I turned on my headlights and kept driving. I went up to Denise's party and I looked for Glen, but he found me first and told me to go home but I wouldn't leave and he threw a couple of punches and that's all it took. That's all I remember. I swear."

"So you didn't go back to the farm? You were never there?"

"No. I don't think I was."

"Then where did your dad find you?" I asked.

"Oh, that's the beautiful part," he said. "Dad didn't find me. The deputy did. They went out looking for me after the fire. I was parked down at Blank's Ford, asleep in the truck."

"What were you doing down there?" I said.

"I don't know," he said. "Sleeping it off. Planning an ambush. I don't know." He shrugged.

I nodded, looked up at the clouds. Then I looked at my feet. "Well . . . ," I said.

"It's like I said in June," he said. "It's a chasm."

"I don't think so," I said.

"It is," he said. "Look, it nearly took Gracie. It almost took me and you."

"There's such a thing as bad luck," I said. "That's all."

"It's more than that," he said.

"The world doesn't hate you," I said.

"What am I supposed to do? Not fight it?"

"But don't you see that if you fight it, it'll fight back?"

He shook his head, dismissing me. We sat there until it started raining.

When we were finally allowed to see Gracie, Paer and I waited outside her room while Cort and Corene were with her. He leaned against the wall and then he started crying, silently. He slid down the wall.

"It's my fault," he said. "Oh, Christ."

I knelt by him. "Take it easy," I said.

"I can't see her," he said. "I shouldn't be allowed to see her."

"It's not your fault," I said. "It was an accident."

"It's my fault I wasn't there. And it's my fault for hardwiring the circuit box. *I* did that."

I stared at him. "What?"

"The old circuit box, I hardwired it. But it couldn't handle the load with both of the air conditioners running."

"That's where the fire started? They know that?"

"Yeah. No one told you?"

"No, no one told me . . . ," I said.

"See?" Paer said, looking at me with his wet eyes. "See what I've done?"

Suddenly, my mother was there, kneeling with us. "I've seen her, Paer. I've read her chart. I've talked to the doctors. I know these guys, and they're the best in the state. They know what they're doing. Listen: she'll be okay. She's going to be fine. The burns are small. It was the smoke inhalation that was the worst. But she's through the bad part. She'll be okay, and I know that she would want to see you."

When we went into her room, she was in a sedated sleep. She had on an oxygen mask and some of her hair was singed. She had some kind of IV drip. But the only other signs of injury were the small bandages on her left forearm and left palm. She looked good. She looked healthy. She looked like Gracie. She looked like Gracie asleep. The last time I had seen her she had been asleep—when Paer had carried her from the car into the house last night. I wished out loud that she had slept the whole time—slept through the fire and the helicopter ride and any pain or fear. I wished it out loud and then I suddenly wondered if I'd actually said it or not. My mind was unclear and it had been unclear for some time and I wasn't sure if I'd said anything or not.

"Did I just say something?" I asked Paer.

He was holding her hand, the uninjured one.

"What?" he said, looking up at me.

"Did I just say anything?" I asked.

"I don't think so," he said. "No."

In the hospital cafeteria, I waited in line. I hadn't eaten anything all day and finally I had to. It was well after noon. Outside, it was still raining.

I got my food and took it to the table. E. B. and Mom and Corene were there. Cort and Paer were with Gracie, in case she woke up. I went to the salad bar and assembled a salad somewhat absentmindedly, because what had been sinking in all day was that the fire wasn't Paer's fault at all, but it was mine. Again and again, I followed the chain of events back through time. It all started with my rendezvous with Freeda. It was my fault. It was a mistake to sleep with her. And it was a mistake to cut her off abruptly and without explanation. It was my fault I hadn't asked her if she had a boyfriend. It was my fault I didn't tell her I had a girlfriend—and didn't do the right thing and stop flirting with her. It was my fault that I hadn't defused Glen Sands. And it was my fault that we had left Paer in a belligerent mood. So it was my fault that Paer wasn't there when the fire started, and it was my fault that E. B. and I weren't there. Surely we could have gotten Gracie out unhurt.

Then there was the fact that I had left Paer in July without helping him install a new circuit box or smoke alarms. And I hadn't even asked him if he'd done these things, hadn't kept after him.

I took my salad to the table and sat down to my meal. I looked at the food arrayed below me, and I heard the voices around me. And somehow, somehow I *felt* the rain, as if I were standing bare-chested within it. And then, after ignoring my excruciating headache and double vision all morning, I finally accepted them, and, surrounded by my three favorite women, and for the second time in twelve hours—the third and final time of the summer—I passed out. My face, I was later told, landed in my salad.

Twenty-Seven

I WAS FINE, OF COURSE. IT WAS NOT A DANGEROUS CONCUSSION. But they held me overnight for observation.

The next morning, I lost the battle with postbreakfast grogginess and I fell asleep. When I came to, Grandpa was sitting in the room.

"What I want to tell you," he said, "is that I'm too old to be the champion of this family anymore. Which leaves you."

As Mom drove me home, she asked me how I felt about her going ahead with her scheduled exploratory surgery, what with Gracie still in the hospital and me tired and faced with packing all my stuff for college.

"I want you to go ahead with it," I said. "I don't think there should be any delays."

"For a long time," she said, "I wouldn't face the disease, even though I knew. I didn't want to put you through the same ordeals that Corene and I went through when Anson died. And I'd given up before I'd even tried to fight. I knew the odds and I knew the disease. When your father died, see, I died, too, and that's why it didn't mean much to me to die now, let the disease take me. But that was the most selfish thing I could have done."

"I don't think so," I said. There was a calmness in me. Or maybe just a lack of energy. "I don't think so," I repeated.

"But it wasn't fair to you. Or Ruben. Or myself."

"I'm not saying it wasn't confusing and frustrating. It hurt."

"I'm sorry," she said.

"I didn't know what to do," I said. "I didn't know how to help. I didn't know what to say, or anything."

"I didn't either," she said.

"I can understand that."

"Sometimes I worry that your world is too small. That I have kept you to myself."

"My world is huge," I said. "My world is wonderful." I reached across and touched her arm. We stopped at a stoplight and she leaned over and kissed my cheek. The sunlight was powerful outside. The light turned green and we moved forward.

"Let me see if I understand something," I said. "When Dad died, you stopped driving the Supra."

"That's right."

"Because it reminded you of him?"

"And because I had a little baby. The car seat worked better in Anson's car. I drove it."

"The Supra was bought as a present for you," I said. "It was a celebratory gift."

"Right."

"And suddenly there wasn't as much to celebrate," I said.

"Except you," she said.

"But just think how cute it would have been if you and I had driven around in the Supra together. Just think of the guys we could have picked up."

She smiled. "It was tempting," she said.

We turned into our neighborhood.

"I'm like him, aren't I?"

"Yes," she said.

"Can you tell me about it sometime?" I asked.

"I'll tell you everything."

"That would mean a lot to me," I said.

"There's only one stipulation with all of this," she said.

"What's that?"

"That no matter what stage of cancer is found tomorrow, you'll still leave for college next week. I won't let this thing stand in your way as well as mine. You can't put your life on hold for me."

"But Mom," I said, "you *are* my life."

She had helped me see what I had to do, what I wanted to do, what I needed to do. The only thing I could do.

She told Corene about her cancer that afternoon. She told Cort and Paer that night. She told Corene to tell Gracie when the time was right. And she told me to tell E. B.

I did.

Twenty-Eight

PAER AND I MET IN THE KITCHEN AT THE APPOINTED HOUR—
6:00 A.M. We each ate a bagel and had some juice. Paer and Cort
and Corene were staying in the house with me until Gracie was
released. Cort and Corene were in the guest suite and Paer was
in the basement. Mom was in the hospital.

Paer and I got in the Supra and rolled out of the garage and
the sky was bright even though the sun wasn't up yet.

The drive to Charbourg was a quiet drive, and the days of
cooler temperatures had somehow made the landscape significantly more beautiful—softening it and introducing the first sug-
gestions of an autumn palate. The creeks we crossed were
mist-covered; the hayfields were shorn and smooth; the corn was
straight and pale. The road to Charbourg in many stretches
seemed organic to the landscape—tracing graceful arcs around
hills, meandering down gentle valleys. It was a road from an earlier time, and to travel it in a good car was as much an emotional
and aesthetic journey as it was a physical one.

As we drove into Charbourg we were confronted with the arrival of the morning school buses, migrating sluggishly toward
the school. It was the first day of school here—they always

started a week or more before my schools did. I was about to make the turn to Paer's house when he asked me to go up to the school instead.

We sat in the parking lot and watched the buses unload on the other side. We stayed in the car. I didn't know what Paer was thinking, and I didn't even know what I was thinking. There was nothing to say. Change, I think, was something we were just starting to accept, and, as such, words were useless as yet. We sat there and watched the kids file into the school and we watched the empty buses pull away and finally they were all gone and the front of the school was quiet and there was no one outside anymore. The school year had begun without us.

We stopped by Cort and Corene's house, partly just to poke our noses in and make sure everything was fine, but mostly because Corene had given us a short list of things to pick up for herself and for Gracie. Then we stopped by the post office and picked up Cort and Corene's accumulated mail. The old clerk, who Paer seemed to know, handed over the mail with a sympathetic smile and then he remembered something and he held up one finger and told us to wait. He walked out of sight, and we could hear him moving somewhere back in the dark part of the post office, and finally he reappeared and handed over a little letter. This letter, he explained, was addressed to Paer at the farm, but considering the circumstances, the carrier had left it here.

When we were back in the car, Paer opened the letter. It was from Gracie, and it had been mailed the day before the fire. He sat there reading it. I asked him what the letter said, and he told me that it was a list, as usual. Her Christmas list.

It was five pages long.

The farm surprised me. Not because I hadn't prepared myself for the big black hole where the farmhouse had been, but because other than that everything seemed so normal. You could

269

turn your back on the house and look out at the barn and the outbuildings and the fields and the creek bottom and you wouldn't know that anything was wrong.

We stood and looked at the burnt pit for a little while. There was really nothing recognizable in the wreckage except for little patches, here and there, of the shingles we had just put on the roof in July. Those shingles had touted their resistance to fire, and they had proven that claim.

We walked down to see the cattle—both Paer's little herd and the big contract herd. Paer's neighbor was stopping by once a day to check on the cows, and Grandpa had come every day, too, but it pleased Paer to be able to see them for himself. When he stepped into the small barnyard pasture, his cattle looked up at him. They recognized him and a couple of the calves even walked up to him. There wasn't much upkeep involved with the cattle at this time of year—they ate grass and drank from the pond and the windmill trough.

After we looked at the contract herd in the big eastern pasture, we cut north, followed the creek for a little bit, and then climbed the bluff. When we came to the spring, Paer nodded silently. He'd heard the stories about it, just as I had. And he'd looked for it unsuccessfully in the past, just as I had. Gracie had found it, and I knew she wouldn't mind that I was telling Paer about it. He, of all people, needed it. We both knelt at the spring and drank, and then I filled the thermos I had brought and we left. As we followed the creek back to the pasture, we stopped in a couple of places and looked at the water. Though the creek was still low, the recent rain and cooler temperatures had made an impact. The water was clear and inviting. The water temperature was cooler. The air was fresh. September was often the best month of fishing, and the most pleasant time to canoe the creek. September was just days away.

Then, as we were leaving, we saw something in the cellar of

the house and we were elated. It was the geode that Gracie had found at the creek in July, the giant geode. It had been sitting on the porch, and it had rolled down into the cellar when the porch burned. It seemed to be intact, though it was black now.

We stood over the burnt ruins and we hatched a plan and then put the plan into action. I volunteered to climb into the cellar. Once I got near the geode, Paer threw down a rope, which I hitched around the geode to form a secure sling. Then I attached another rope to the sling and I climbed out of the hole. We coaxed the geode out of the hole with a hand winch. When the work was done, I looked at myself and I was filthy, marred with soot and muck. The cellar, where the geode had been, was full of black water, and I had had to climb over piles of charred wood to get to the geode. It was the price I paid.

We drove back into Charbourg, where I showered at Cort and Corene's house and changed into some of Paer's clothes.

When we got to the hospital that afternoon, we walked in on Gracie in the middle of a haircut. Brian was there, working away, chatting up a storm with Gracie. They were listening to some horrible pop radio station, just like Brian always played in his salon. It had been Corene's idea to get Gracie a haircut that would get rid of the singed hair, and I had arranged for Brian to come.

"Leo Peery!" Brian exclaimed, as we entered.

"The boys are back in town," Gracie said.

I shook hands with Brian and he was eying my hair.

"When was the last time you had a snip-snip?" he asked.

"Oh, let's say it was early June."

"Okay, that's a bit too long," Brian said.

"It's just that I've been so busy at the office," I said. "Plus the damn wife and kids."

"I heard you say damn," Gracie said. "Don't think I didn't hear."

I apologized and we waited the five minutes for Brian to finish up, and he'd done a lovely job, giving Gracie a really nice look that was somewhere between a bob and a boy's haircut. She loved it. She said she felt like a new woman. She was due to be released tomorrow and would be at school the day after that. She would be the envy of Charbourg.

After Brian cleaned up and left, we gave Gracie the water from the spring and she drank it and smacked her lips and then showed us a trick with an orange. She had a whole basket of oranges by her bed and she took one of the oranges and with a knife she carefully scored a spiral in the skin from the stem end to the bloom end. She then gently peeled the skin away from the orange so that when she was done, the skin remained in one piece. When she held up the skin, it looked like an elongated S.

"Voilà!" she said.

We clapped and smiled. "I bet I know who taught you that," I said.

"E. B. did," she said.

"Exactly," I said.

"She brought me this whole basket of oranges this morning. Oh, and she also brought me these." She opened a small plastic container. There were cookies inside. "Cookies!" she said. She waved the cookies toward us in invitation. Paer and I each took one.

"Mm," Paer said, chewing.

The cookies were tender and buttery. I could taste orange and almonds and brown sugar.

"That's the best cookie I've ever had," Paer said.

"I know!" Gracie said. "Brian ate, like, *ten*. And E. B. made up the recipe!"

"She did?" I asked. It was an amazing cookie.

"She invented them," Gracie said.

"What are they called?" I asked.

"Tomorrow cookies," she said.

I smiled. "That's a good name," I said.

"Here, have more," Gracie said. Paer and I both took another cookie. "And she and I had the most *interesting* conversation about you, Leo Peery."

"Like what did you say?" I asked.

"Oh, I can't tell you," Gracie said. "Girl stuff. Secret." She zipped her lips shut.

"Can't you tell me just a tiny bit?" I asked. "A tiny smidgen? A scrap, a shred, a speck, a *morsel*?"

"No."

"Not even a morsel?"

"No morsels."

"Well, do you think she likes me?" I asked.

"What are you, slow?" Gracie asked. "*Duh* she likes you."

"That's what I thought," I said. I then asked Gracie if I could take one of her oranges and borrow her knife.

In Mom's hospital room, in the wing opposite Gracie's, I peeled the orange for her in the way Gracie had and the smell of the orange filled the room like a sunrise. Mom sat up straight when she smelled it. She looked good, I thought, but was still weak from her second surgery. We shared the orange and I was happy to be with her and when we were done eating, she said, "That was a most satisfactory orange."

Her bed was littered with bridal magazines—here she was, recovering from surgery, gaining strength for a likely third surgery, and she was planning her wedding. Corene had been helping her all morning. It was to be a late-September ceremony and she told me a few of the things she had decided and I told her that it sounded terrific.

I then remembered the springwater in my backpack and I brought it out and poured it into a glass I had brought and I told her what it was and she started crying. She held the water up in front of her and looked into the glass.

"When Anson was sick," she said, "he asked for this water. He asked us to go to the spring. But Corene didn't know where it was. I obviously didn't. Grandpa claimed the spring was dry, but that was just his way to avoid admitting that even he didn't know where it was."

"So no one knew but Dad," I said.

"No, Grandma knew."

"Of course," I said.

"And even though that was the winter she was getting over her pneumonia, she went and got the springwater for him. And brought it here."

"There's something I just remembered," I said. "In the attic of the farmhouse, I found a big box of Dad's stuff. Childhood keepsakes." I paused. "And I meant to look at it, but I didn't get a chance. And now it's gone."

Mom nodded.

"There was a hat, though."

"I know," she said. "I saw that you brought it home."

"So you remember it."

"Sure."

"Do you mind that I have it?"

"No. I'm glad you have it."

Mom drank the springwater.

"But I want to tell you that I like Ruben," I said. "I believe in him."

Mom smiled. "Thank you," she said.

We sat for a while. Then I pulled an envelope out of my back pocket.

"Gracie told me to give this to you," I said.

"Gracie, Gracie," she said, and she opened the envelope.

Inside was a piece of paper, and on the paper was an in-progress tic-tac-toe game. See, they were playing a cross-hospital game of tic-tac-toe.

"For the love of Peter," Mom said, looking at the game. "She got me again."

Twenty-Nine

THE AFTERNOON GRACIE WAS RELEASED, SHE WENT SHOPPING with Corene and E. B. Then E. B. and Gracie got manicures. That evening, we all gathered at the pool. Greg closed the pool three hours early so we could have a private party. In addition to our family—minus Mom—several of Gracie's classmates and neighbors came from Charbourg to attend. Greg, Becky, and I were the lifeguards. There was a table piled with presents and flowers, and another table where pizza, soda, and ice cream were served. Gracie wasn't allowed to swim yet, but she had a good time standing on the deck and shooting at everyone with one of those pressurized water guns. Later, I filled water balloon after water balloon for her.

Near the end of the evening, after her friends had left, Paer and I went to his truck and got the geode. We had had it professionally cut and polished, and we carted the two halves into the pool in a wheelbarrow and set them on the deck. The exterior of the geode was irrevocably blackened by the fire, but its interior was spectacular—a crowded dominion of exquisite crystals. When Gracie saw it, her eyes grew huge. We put the geode halves on the deck and Paer and Gracie and I knelt by them and then Gracie actually got down on her stomach and put her face inches away from the crystals.

"I *am*," she said quietly.

"What's that?" I asked.

"I *am*," she said. "I just am."

Thirty

ON ONE OF THE LAST DAYS OF AUGUST, I RODE MY BIKE AGAIN. I took it into the hills that follow the river north, and it rode better than I had ever remembered it riding. It rode so perfectly that it disappeared below me. In that sense, it felt like flying. I wondered if the wreck and the resulting overhaul had tweaked it somehow, made it more agreeable, shaped it toward my goals. Was the new fork really that much smoother than the old one? Were the new components better suited to my riding style? Or was the change within me?

The road unrolled in front of me, and I glided over it. On my left, vistas would frequently open up where I could see out across the river and over to the long, rising pastures on the other side. The air of the day was not the air of early summer, but the air of summer's waning—dry, calm, accepting, clear. The sunlight was soothing. The cicadas were quiet. The smells were not the grassy tones of June, but the smell of dry sycamore leaves, not yet fallen. There was a general sense of *lessening* in the air. This was not a bad thing.

Later today, I would be with Mom in the hospital, as I was

every day. But for now the day was mine, and I felt myself relaxing in a way that I had not done in a long time. I felt that I hadn't truly inhabited myself in weeks.

Of course there would be sadness.

I continued on my ride and finally I neared my destination—a certain bend in the road where there was a wide shoulder and a grassy area where people sometimes pulled off to enjoy the view. This was where I was planning to eat my sandwich before turning homeward.

As I came within sight of the place, though, I recognized a car that was parked there. It was E. B.'s car. And then I saw E. B., sitting nearby and waiting for me. This was a surprise. There was a picnic basket on the hood of the car.

She saw me and smiled.

I was in love, I realized, and not a moment too soon.

But a few hours later, when I coasted back into my driveway, there was another surprise. Jenny's van. But she wasn't in sight.

I got off my bike and I lowered it gently to the driveway. I glanced toward the front yard, then walked toward the side door. And as I came around the corner of the garage I collided with Jenny.

"Oh, jeez," I said.

"Sorry," she said, but then she headed toward her van. There was a box leaning against the side door of the house. She'd left a box there.

"What's this?" I asked. "Jenny? What's this?"

She stopped. She turned. She was standing at the front of the van.

"I'm not here to talk," she said. "I don't have anything to say to you."

I went and picked up the box. It was light. It wasn't a small box, but it was light. I opened it. There was black fabric inside. I didn't understand.

The van door closed behind me and I turned. Jenny started the van. I went over.

"Okay, I do have something to say to you," she said. "The strongest guard is placed at the gateway to nothing, because the condition of emptiness is too shameful to be divulged."

"You're quoting Fitzgerald to me? You're paraphrasing *Tender Is the Night* to me?"

"Because you're empty, Leo."

"But that quote's about actors."

"You *are* an actor."

"Jenny," I said, looking into the box again. "What is this?"

"It's my prom dress, you idiot."

I touched it. It was nice. "Prom dress," I said. "But you didn't go to prom."

"Exactly!" she said.

"Oh," I said, understanding. "Don't you think it's a little late to go over this again? I've already apologized. Come on, turn off the van so we can talk."

"It cost nine hundred dollars," she said.

"I'm sorry," I said.

"It's just my little parting gift to you," she said.

With that, she shifted into reverse. The van's tires squawked briefly and the van lurched backwards. Then there was a horrible crunching and scraping noise and the van stopped and I put the box down and both Jenny and I walked to the back of the van and there was my bike, my born-again bike, dead again. And this time it was dead for real. The frame was crushed. I looked at it, but it wasn't sinking in. It was a bike. It was just an object.

But Jenny's arms were around me and I felt moisture on her face. She was crying against my neck.

"I'm sorry," she said. "I'm so sorry. I didn't mean . . . I didn't know . . . I came over here and I didn't want to see you, I just wanted to leave the box. I didn't mean to hurt your bike."

"It's okay," I said. "It's really okay."

She was crying and clinging to me.

"Let's just say we're even," I said.

She leaned back and looked at me and smiled.

"It's a draw," I said.

She hugged me again. I hugged her back.

"I'm sorry about your mother," she said. "I wanted to tell you."

"Thank you."

"And I'm sorry about your cousin."

"Thanks."

"And I'm sorry about your bike," she said.

"If it makes you feel better, the bike cost a lot more than the dress."

She laughed. We ended our embrace and she wiped her face.

"A lot more."

"That does make me feel a little bit better."

We both looked at the bike again and I touched it with my toe. "What a fucking god damn mess," I said.

Jenny laughed.

"This whole summer kind of fell apart," I said. "And I'm mostly to blame."

"We just weren't really meant to be together. We've been at this for six years and it hasn't worked yet. So why did we think it would work this summer of all times?"

"Because we're idiots," I said.

"Doesn't matter now," she said.

"It does, though, if we can talk about it. Get it out."

She nodded.

"I'm leaving tomorrow," she said.

"I know," I said. "I remember."

"When are you leaving?"

"You haven't heard?" I asked.

"Heard what?"

"Well, I guess you wouldn't have. I'm staying here for the year. I'm deferring college."

"Oh, because of your mom," she said.

"Yeah," I said. "I'm going to take some classes at the community college. Some science so that I can get a leg up on the premed thing."

"Premed?" she asked.

"I want to be a surgeon," I said.

"Like your dad."

"Yep."

We said good-bye and promised to exchange e-mails and then just as she was leaving I asked if she could do me a favor.

"What's that?" she asked.

"Talk to E. B. sometime," I said. "Maybe not today, maybe not tomorrow. But someday."

"I will," she said. Then she thought for a second. "You guys are right together," she said. "I know that."

"That's very generous of you," I said. "I appreciate it."

She took her prom dress with her.

When she was gone, I dragged my bike out of the driveway. I would deal with it later. I went around to the sliding patio door and I unlocked it and opened it. I stepped through the doorway but I was stopped cold by the screen. The sliding screen was still in place and I had walked right into it. It was a rude surprise. It hadn't hurt, but it was humiliating and I was shaken. Then I looked into the sky and I saw a big red wasp descending steadily toward me. I was puzzled and slightly stunned. He flew directly at my forehead, stung me, and then fled. It hurt remarkably. He'd stung me right in the middle of my forehead.

"Well," I said to myself, "fair enough."

Those were the summer's parting blows.

Thirty-One

A FEW NIGHTS LATER, E. B. CALLED ME. IT WAS LATE AND I WAS in bed reading.

"Look at your watch," she said.

It was seconds before midnight.

"Almost midnight," I said.

"Yes," she said, "but also almost September."

I inhaled.